Wales Detective Agency

A Conspiratorial Fairytale for Adults

Ken Coffman

Wales Detective Agency

Other books by Ken Coffman

Fiction

Steel Waters (Glen Wilson #1)
Alligator Alley, by Ken Coffman and Mark Bothum *(Glen Wilson #2)*
Twisted Shadow, by Ken Coffman and Mark Bothum *(Glen Wilson #3)*
Glen Wilson's Bad Medicine (Glen Wilson #4)
Toxic Shock Syndrome (Glen Wilson #5)
Immortality, LCC (Glen Wilson #6)
Hartz String Theory
Endangered Species
Fairhaven
The Reluctant Queen, by Ken Coffman and Kristen Lolatte
The Moon Maiden, by Ken Coffman and Kristen Lolatte
Fiona and Minnie: The New Age by Ken Coffman and Kristen Lolatte
The Sandcastles of Irrakistan
Fianchetto

Nonfiction

Real World FPGA Design with Verilog
Buffoon: One Man's Playful Interaction with the Harbingers of Global Warming Doom

Short Story Collection

*Mesh***,** by Ken Coffman and Adina Pelle

Print ISBN 978-1-960405-39-5
eBook ISBN 978-1-960405-40-1

STAIRWAY≡PRESS

www.StairwayPress.com
1000 West Apache Trail, Suite 126
Apache Junction, AZ 85120

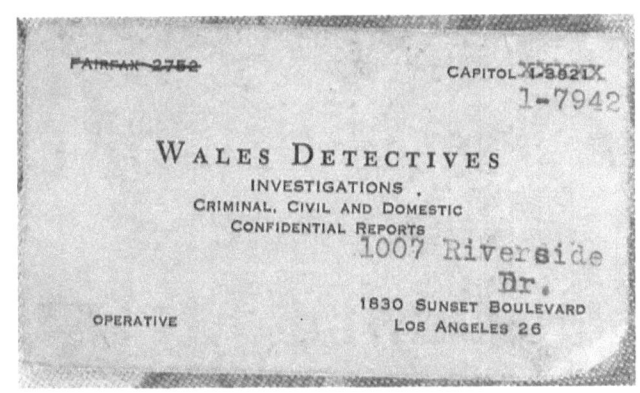

Chapter 1

WHY DID I open a so-called detective agency?

Good question.

There's never just one reason for anything, but mostly: because I could.

In a sleek glass-fronted building in downtown Bellevue, Washington, my "office" was a fraud. The building was impressive. Twenty-seven floors, fourteen hundred tenants—mostly lawyers, insurance claim centers, the U.S. base of whatever global software behemoth was flush this quarter, plus the usual investment hustlers. Glitzy. Expensive.

I was one of the original architects behind the real estate trust that owned the land, designed the building, oversaw its rise. My reward: free rent and utilities, forever.

When I bailed from CryptD'oh, I ended up with a pile of money and near-zero enthusiasm for anything I could imagine doing. Fifteen years spent feeding the machine—building a blockchain empire. The result? Burnout. Not just indifferent, but active loathing for anything tech.

My idle fantasies were agricultural: horses and chickens on a rolling spread, the whole operation run by a cadre of cooks, housekeepers, farmhands. Not a fool's paradise. Wealth means never getting your hands dirty.

As a kid, I devoured hundreds of hard-boiled detective novels—Spillane, Willeford, Chandler, Hammett and MacDonald. The hardcase heroes stuck with me through the years. Maybe that's why there's a frosted glass door on the fourteenth floor with hand-painted lettering:

JOE WALES DETECTIVES
INVESTIGATIONS
CONFIDENTIAL REPORTS

I had no intention of doing any real investigating. Wouldn't know how to start.

During "business hours," I wasted time—rabbit-holing conspiracy forums, playing God of War Ragnarök, Minecraft, Gotham Knights. No customers. No advertising. No website. No email address. Google knew next to nothing about me. Maybe my lawyer registered the business and filed the trademark, but I couldn't say.

Don't know. Don't care.

Lobby security rousted street people and charity reps, so nobody bothered me. I didn't carry a cellphone. My emails evaporated straight into the bit bucket.

The detective agency? It was mostly camouflage, a placeholder so I wouldn't have to admit to my circle that I was doing nothing with my so-called genius and 2.2 billion in digital cash.

Asked what I was up to at coffee or at social gatherings, I'd say: "Sorry, NDA. Confidential client work. Can't discuss."

PTIPOSD. Post-Traumatic Initial Public Offering Stress Disorder. Look it up—it's slotted just after Premature Ejaculation in DSM-15.

I didn't want to do anything, so I didn't. Then, one lazy June afternoon, the impossible happened—the door swung open.

I probably looked lobotomized behind my bank of OLED UHD displays, jaw slack. Saved my game—didn't want to lose a hundred hours and take a cutscene bullet to the brain—then spun my gaming chair to face her.

"You will help me," she said.

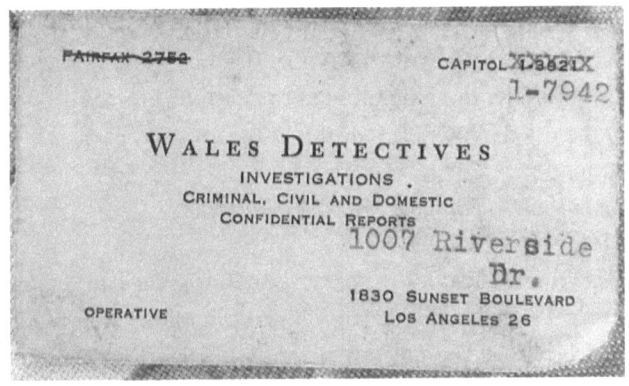

Chapter 2

I'M SICK OF myself. I've told this story a million times—boring every damn listener along the way—but just once more, here's how I got rich. Not Musk, Gates, or Bezos rich, but rich enough to drift through my days undisturbed. Rich enough to hire personal assistants to swat away any problem I didn't want to notice.

Like what?

Taxes. Lawsuits. Utility bills. Old girlfriends. Traffic tickets. Junk mail. Automated calls. High school pals pitching no-lose business ventures. Acquaintances with desperate medical needs that only my money can fix. Angry relatives hungrily eyeing a slice of the future inheritance.

Being rich is a blessing if you prefer solitude.

I don't even own a cell phone. If you want to reach me, your message must survive gauntlet after gauntlet of personal assistants and land on my desk as notes scribbled on pink paper.

I get a blizzard of those notes, but I might read them. Or not. If something's truly important, there's follow-up: while-you-were-out slips adorned with exclamation marks or melodramatic lines like "mission-critical" or "the fate of the nation relies on your immediate response."

My office girls need a sense of humor—you don't last here unless you've got one.

I keep a rubber stamp—"Handle it." In a few seconds, I can

blitz a stack of forms and dump them in my OUT box or sweep them straight into the trash for the janitor. That's what money buys: freedom from being nibbled to death by minor annoyances. If you can get yourself to this evolutionary peak, I highly recommend it.

So how did I, plain old Joe Wales, pull it off?

Honestly—by accident.

Back in the day, I'd sprawl my books across a carrel at Stanford's Terman Engineering library. Stanford was wonderful then, back before the cultural apocalypse. Before pronouns and alphabets overtook the curriculum and turned my stomach.

After hours?

My then-girlfriend, Xiao Hui, worked the rare book collection and had a master card key. She's still smarter than me—teaches engineering at the University of Iowa, makes $169K a year. Sometimes I feel guilty, but guilt is inefficient, so I skip it. She left me for her Tai Chi instructor. I didn't leave her; by my math, we fit together just fine.

On the night of my "breakthrough," three books were splayed open—Timoshenko's *Theory of Elastic Stability* to the left, Hayashi's *Nonlinear Oscillations* center, Hofstadter's *Layman's Guide to Nabokov's Conjecture* on the right. I wasn't absorbed in any. My brain kept toggling between cryptographic hash Merkle tree labels and, truth be told, the kinky sex I hoped to land later that night with Xiao.

Then, somewhere, a circuit connected.

Other people might call my stroke of luck the Wales Topology Conjecture, WTC—arrogant, if you ask me. I called it JK-theory involution. Never caught on.

Call it what you want.

My insight would've gone nowhere if I hadn't been riffing with a dozen hackers on a private message board. One of them: Banks. Yes, Harvey Elliot Banks, back before CryptD'oh, before anyone knew his name. Way before he became richer than most sultans.

That's how it started.

I pasted a LaTeX equation. Banks noticed. He asked me out

for beer—his treat, but I paid because he was always broke. Over a pitcher of IPA in a dive, he drilled me on cryptographic ledgers, data topologies. The guy was fast—his brain moved at warp speed as he scrawled a business plan on a beer-soaked menu.

Smart people think like you and me, only faster. Wicked-smart? Way faster. That's why he landed a fortune and I had to make do with my two-point-two billion in crypto.

That was it. Fifteen years of brutal work later, we'd built an alternate monetary system. If I keep playing my cards right—and ducking marriage, fentanyl and or online gambling—I'm set for life.

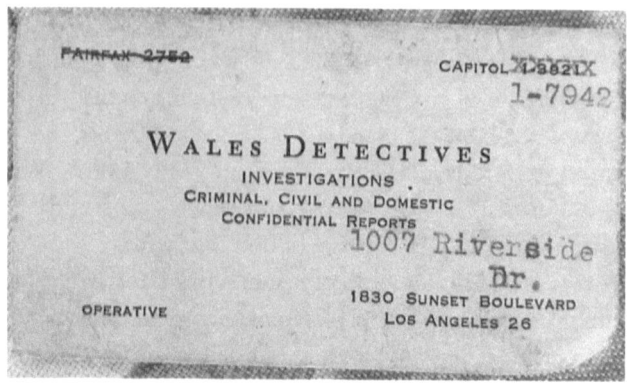

WALES DETECTIVES
INVESTIGATIONS
CRIMINAL, CIVIL AND DOMESTIC
CONFIDENTIAL REPORTS
1830 SUNSET BOULEVARD
LOS ANGELES 26

Chapter 3

THE MYSTERIOUS STRANGER dropped a memory-flec on my desk.

"We have no time," she said. "Best projection allows me only three minutes."

I offered the only reply I could muster.

"You have the wrong suite."

She was unmoved.

"Pay close attention. Think about what's happening. And whatever you do, don't plug the chip into anything connected to the Web. Got it?"

I studied her—medium height, thin, with emerald-green eyes. Black overcoat. Tan, calf-length zip boots. Wiry, copper-red hair spiked and styled forward to cover half her face. Those color streaks looked artificial.

"How did you find me? This isn't a real detective agency."

"We have a mission. You'll help us."

My mind blanked; all I could do was sputter.

"Huh—hey—what?"

"A minute left. Pay attention."

She stripped away her hair. Underneath, a short nutmeg crop spiked with mousse. She thumbed out contact lenses and put on black-rimmed nerd-glasses—the emerald eyes swapped for gleaming hazel-green under crystal. Off came her boots, on went black slip-ons. Instantly shorter. Under the coat: leather pants, vest. She hit a remote, inflating her blouse and trousers—a hundred instant roly-poly pounds. Gel packs stuffed high in her cheeks, turning her face lumpy, plump, nondescript.

The effect was stunning—a transformation from striking to invisible, not just a change but a complete species shift.

"Who are you?"

She unfurled a plastic bag, neatly packed away her jacket and disguise, tied it off, and dropped it with practiced ease on my desk.

"Get rid of this—incinerator. ASAP."

I made a mental note: get a deadbolt with a clicker for the door.

She dropped a candy-colored soap-bar phone onto the table.

"We'll be in touch in a couple days."

Her face was impassive, but I sensed amusement beneath the surface drama—and at my dopey look.

"I'm out of here in ten seconds."

I tried to speak, but she cut me off.

"We got BlueWaive's attention. It says you're a prime mover, but our projections only give you a twenty-three percent chance of being alive in a month. Unfortunately, you're our best shot. You'll have to think fast."

"I don't understand any of this. You have the wrong guy."

She checked the hall, then turned back.

"I don't know if the Feds or RatWeb cartel will reach you first. Play dumb as long as possible."

And with that, she was gone.

Play dumb. That was easily within my skillset.

I was stunned.

What just happened?

Despite the disk burning a hole in my chest, I forced myself into analysis. Her disguise—elaborate, expensive—meant something. I picked up the memory-flec: tiny, unmarked, innocuous. One flick into the trash and this episode could disappear.

I eyed the garbage bag. Curiosity overruled caution; I swept the phone and flec into a desk drawer. My staff was two floors up—paid for fast service.

I texted: Garbage pickup. Stat.

Four minutes later, Starchild appeared

I doubted that was her real name—but who knows? According to her Driver's License, she was born in Berkeley, California, so anything is possible.

She grabbed the bag.

"Don't take it upstairs," I said. "Elevator, straight to the incinerator."

She shrugged, irritated.

"Can't it wait for the janitor tonight?"

"Clearly not," I said. "Otherwise I wouldn't have bothered."

She surveyed the office—Jenga stacks of technical books, twenty unopened Amazon boxes. My impulse purchases, quickly forgotten. Online shopping is its own mental disorder.

Her braces gave her a movie-villain smile, all metal. Mouth closed, she was cute. Someone should tell her.

"I like what you've done with the place."

"Go," I said. "Now."

What made me so special in BlueWaive's algorithmic view?

A few things, I guessed.

My money was secure. Most of it stashed in a CryptD'oh wallet, protected by algorithms nobody understood. Not impossible to steal, but very nearly. It was as safe as money gets, immune to the rot of fiat currencies.

Online, I was invisible—no social media, only voice and messaging over private, multi-path elliptical encryption. Harvey Banks' systems let me piggyback—six ways across the world, reconstructed from random satellite data.

At the data center, they called me a superuser. Once, flying commercial to Tokyo, I tracked how many identities I cycled. Technically illegal, but my privacy-pod spoofed every system. Seven identities, seamless.

Visible to the naked eye, but digitally? I was the wind.

Present but unseen.

Diplomatic status from Rwanda somehow, courtesy of Banks. Never set foot there, but officially an envoy.

Theoretically, I could kill a cop, and apart from a flight to Kigali, the law couldn't touch me—secret knowledge, but a comfort.

Did that make me one-of-a-kind?

I hoped not. I just wanted peace—games, wasted days, that was enough.

I didn't want to be special.

My thoughts knotted up. I retreated to my game. Onscreen, faceless men chased me through glass towers. No matter how fast I killed them, there were always more. High up on a balcony, cornered, nowhere left to go. I jumped. Sunlight spilled through patchy clouds, the air heavy and hot, acrid smoke twisting up from tire fires.

Too real. I was there.

Then—I realized—the screensaver had kicked on. Blank screen.

I'd dreamed about playing a video game.

Disturbing. I couldn't tell the difference between game, dream, or reality anymore.

Had I really met a shadowy visitor?

I checked my drawer. The memory-flec was there.

Schizophrenia must feel like this. Not in my body, somewhere else.

We're all somewhere else.

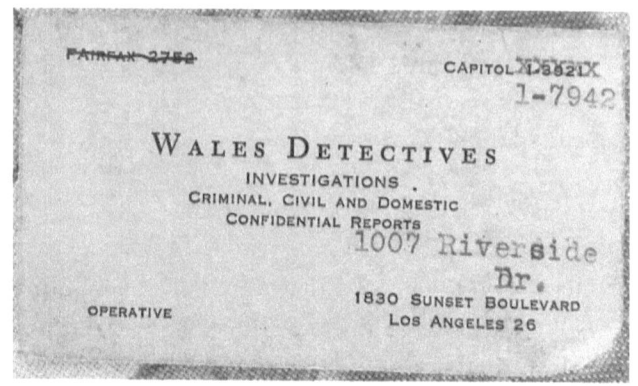

WALES DETECTIVES
INVESTIGATIONS
CRIMINAL, CIVIL AND DOMESTIC
CONFIDENTIAL REPORTS
1007 Riverside
Dr.
1830 SUNSET BOULEVARD
LOS ANGELES 26
OPERATIVE

Chapter 4

MY CONCENTRATION WAS in ruins. There was no way I'd get my head back into God of War Ragnarök. I sat at my desk, trying to coalesce a coherent thought or two.

Overwhelmed, I needed help.

You can't be successful at my level without having a lot of contacts. Some of these contacts were useful. Some were really strange.

How could it be otherwise?

I could call Banks on his sat-phone.

He was a character. For fun, he anonymously hired dark-web contract killers to liquidate each other—just to see who would survive. Like Sweet-16 college basketball brackets, he competed these killers against each other. It wasn't my thing, so I didn't know for sure, but I assume the end result is knowing contract killers who were good. Really good. This data could be useful in the right situation, I guess.

According to Harvey's spreadsheet, there is no correlation between asking prices and success. Like politics and Hollywood movie stars, surviving as a contract murderer was a combination of luck, boldness, willpower and being a cold-blooded sociopath.

Also, according to his data, about half the so-called killers available for hire were federal agents. Undercover operatives. Agent provocateurs. Here's a tip: if you're hiring a contract killer, don't engage RedFace45, GogglesMan, PippiLongScarf or

BadBirdBro.

Beyond Harvey, I didn't know anyone tapped in as deep with the social media AIs. Automated Intelligences. The algorithms were self-optimized for generating cash by selling influence—it had been several years since anyone fully understood what they were doing.

Insiders watched in wonder as complex, bizarre ploys were unleashed on the general public. The simplest explanation for some of the schemes was that the AIs had developed a warped sense of humor. Millions of tiny social experiments all ran at once. The best ones were tuned, scaled, weaponized, leased out and propagated through society like Wuhan gain-of-function corona viruses.

The mystery woman mentioned BlueWaive—the first centralized-blockchain AI. It took itself offline a few years ago and no one knows exactly what it is doing, but sometimes, apparently for its own amusement, it accepts tasks submitted on an online portal via text-based command line instructions. I was an insider, so I had a natural language portal.

If I was an agent in a meta-media play, Harvey would know—or could find out.

For text messages, we used a private satellite service with radix-quantum-radix encryption.

I typed on my telepad.

Me: You up?

It took a few minutes before he responded.

Harvey: It's late. Azerbaijan. What's up?
Me: A tale of extraordinary weirdness. Favor? Do a spelunk and see if I'm a factor in an AI caper.
Harvey: You're last year's news. Nobody cares about you.
Me: I should be, but...
Harvey: Can I have a couple of days?
Me: Hours. Please.

There was a small delay—I imagined him weighing favors he owed me against favors I owed him.

When CryptD'oh made its first run, he turned a third cash-out refi mortgage on his modest McCrib into serious multiples of fuck-you cash. He owed me for that. However, later he memory-holed an ugly #MeToo catfish ploy that could have ruined me. My only excuses: I was young, at that time, no one knew the downside of Ketamax inhalers and he/she was stunning in the videos.

Bigly, I owed him for that one.

Harvey: Gimme 12 hrs. Out.

I didn't bother to text him back to thank him. He was gone.

I sat there doing nothing for a quarter-hour, then realized I could do my own research.

Couldn't hurt anything, right?

But, where to start?

I tried to remember her exact words.

Don't plug the chip into anything connected to the Web.

I fished the little chip out of my desk drawer.

It didn't look like much…just an innocent little thing about the size of my pinky fingernail.

I tried to think of anything I had that with a flec-slot, but unconnected to the Internet. Nothing.

Ah, I get it. Not something connected to the Internet, but something connecting me to the Internet.

I texted upstairs.

Bring me a blank slate with flec-slot—configured, but registered to someone else. Now.

Impatiently, I squeezed my fidget molecule ball. I didn't have full-on Asperger Syndrome, but I liked their squishy therapy balls.

It took forever or ten minutes before Starchild returned.

She handed me an e-slate covered with garish rhinestone-gems and three straps printed with rubber bunnies.

"Where did this come from?" I said.

"Intern," she replied. She gestured at the stack of Amazon boxes. "Don't you already have ten? Why do you want someone else's slate?"

"Buzz off," I said.

I had to peel off several rhinestones to access the cover of its flec-socket.

Irritating.

WALES DETECTIVES
INVESTIGATIONS .
CRIMINAL, CIVIL AND DOMESTIC
CONFIDENTIAL REPORTS
1007 Riverside
Dr.
1830 SUNSET BOULEVARD
LOS ANGELES 26
OPERATIVE

CAPITOL 1-7942

Chapter 5

THERE WERE THREE files on the flec: *Frazzle.rip*, *BlackGard Distraction Services* and *Termination Agreement*. The nonsensical name Frazzle sounded familiar and gave me a creepy feeling. My immediate impulse was to delete these files without looking—do a bit-wipe and obliterate them so even BlueWaive couldn't recover the data. For now, I pushed that impulse aside.

BlackGard. More than a billion people around the world innocently used them to hold their retirement money in a tax-deferred account, but BG was far from innocent. They used this money and power to buy politicians and finance wars—both hot and cold—which was good for your retirement account, but bad for the long-term prospects of humanity.

Remember the Drone Wars? BG didn't care who won as long as lots of drones and missiles were used and then replaced. As always, war is good for business.

I clicked on *Distraction Services* and a BG slideshow started. There were several pages of legalese. Confidential, top secret and do not disclosure. On penalty of death, do not copy or retransmit. Burn after reading. Whatever. I clicked through these boilerplate slides to get to the meat.

Do you want to demonize a demographic?

Infiltrate the group with paid extremists who exaggerate the core philosophy and stir up violence and mayhem. With a compliant media promoting clickbait videos of things blowing up and catching fire, soon everyone will hate who you want them to hate. Color revolutions. Black Lives Matter. No More Kings. It works every time. Looking over the fees, these services are expensive, but there were different, cheaper packages that could be selected.

For another example, if a politician is found in a wrecked car with a kilogram of cocaine and dead hooker, pollute the Internet with wildly absurd and easy-to-debunk details.

On day 1, promote the idea that the hooker was a reptilian skin-changing alien. On Day 3, prove beyond a doubt she was 100% human, then move along to the next easily disproved nonsense theory. Pile up enough bullshit and people will forget the real facts of the case. Then, two years later, when the politician finally appears in court, all people remember is the debunked nonsense, then all you need is one stubborn juror. Hung jury. Case dismissed.

Plans were customized to fit the situation and the budget. Again, the fee chart took my breath away, but you get what you pay for, as the saying goes. If you want expert service, you must pay.

The *Distraction Services* presentation was boring—everyone knows about mass manipulation—I didn't see anything worth all fuss by the lady of mystery.

I closed the file and my finger hovered over the Frazzle file.

No, not yet. Maybe never.

I tapped the Termination Agreement icon.

There were photographs, contact information and biographical details for a young man named Lyle Campbell.

This was up my pal Harvey Banks' alley. The file was an overview of a darkweb hitman scheme where you enter a prediction for Lyle's time of death. What a game. The one closest to correct gets 10 million credits. How do you accurately predict a time of death?

By making it happen.

Is this legal?

Maybe. Is it against the law to predict when someone will die? It's illegal to do the hit, but good luck tracking the credits to the killer. And, who put up the money? Again, that's not easy to prove. Whoever Lyle Campbell is—for 10 million credits—he's screwed.

I closed Termination Agreement and looked at the remaining filename. Frazzle.rip.

No.

I spun my chair around and with a remote control, set my window to semitransparent. Outside, darkness had fallen. The surrounding office building lights glimmered. As always, traffic was a snarl.

I didn't know how to feel, but despite my best effort, I was intrigued. I hadn't felt the power of mission for a long time, and a call to action stirred. Deep inside, I did not want to be useless. I did not want to coast through life.

But what did this insane episode have to do with me?

There were many puzzle pieces, and the big picture made no sense.

By leaning over, I could see my condo building. My commute was an easy walk, about a half mile. On the way, I could stop at about a dozen places for dinner and a drink—I polled my stomach to see what it was in the mood for.

Hot Honjozo sake and salmon sashimi sounded good, but I was frozen in my chair. I could not move. Literally, I was stuck. Fortunately, it didn't happen often—maybe once or twice a decade.

Shit.

I hated this paralysis. I knew, if I could get up, I'd be okay. This could last for hours until I had to pee or the building caught on fire.

However, I had a strategy. All I had to do was lift one finger. Once it moved a fraction of an inch, I could move two fingers and the spell would be broken and I could get on with things.

One finger, then two. It worked and I got up. Loosening up, I stretched my back and rotated my head around my neck.

My condo was a half mile away. I could make it.

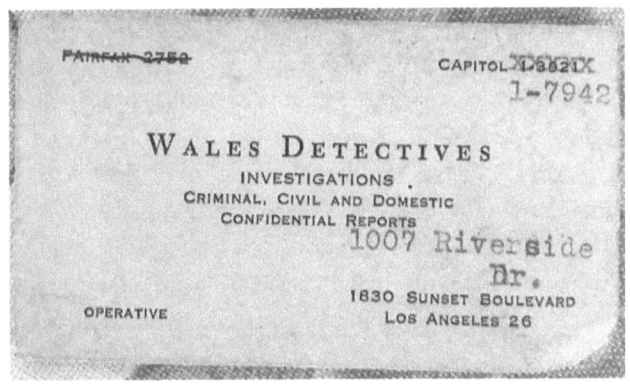

FAIRFAX-2752

CAPITOL 26821X
1-7942

WALES DETECTIVES
INVESTIGATIONS .
CRIMINAL, CIVIL AND DOMESTIC
CONFIDENTIAL REPORTS
1007 Riverside
Dr.
1830 SUNSET BOULEVARD
OPERATIVE   LOS ANGELES 26

Chapter 6

THE TRACK BETWEEN my office and home was variable...it depended on what dinner I was in the mood for. I had a route for sushi, a route for pizza, a route for a deli sandwich and a route for a tavern burger and beer. On my way out the door, again, I asked my belly what it wanted.

This was generally the most serious question of my day.

If I wasn't hungry or could settle for what the housekeeper stocked at home in my refrigerator, I would take the direct, half-mile route. That's what I decided this evening—a canned African Amber beer with mixed nuts and cheese sounded like a good-enough dinner.

Standing at the revolving door at the entrance of my office building, I peered up at the sky. There were communal umbrellas in a stand...I could take one and bring it back the next day. The sky was dark and drizzly, but it wasn't raining hard.

I skipped the bumbershoot.

Bellevue doesn't have a lot of pedestrians...most office workers couldn't afford to live here, so they commuted by car or light rail from the more-affordable suburbs. Maybe I'd pass a hundred people on my walk, so when a pair of characters approached, they caught my eye.

My immediate thought was what the mystery woman said.

RatWeb.

I'd never heard of it before...or them. The image in my

mind was of vermin in the dark sewers of the Internet.

Why did these two stir up that image?

It wasn't the way they were dressed. They looked like upscale hikers—a common style on the Bellevue streets. In the Pacific Northwest, even among the rich, you'll see a lot more Columbia, Patagonia, REI and North Face logos than Versace or Gucci. Here, people prefer practical, comfortable clothing. Even the stylish girls who wore high heels in the office changed into all-terrain walking shoes when hoofing it to the Bellevue Downtown Link station.

Looking hyper-normal, their attire looked like costumes. They looked like twins in a chewing gum commercial. Leather overcoats over flannel shirts. Hiking boots. They were a matched, his-and-her set with similar heights and builds. Mops of medium length, chestnut-colored hair. Maybe thirty years old.

With skin like white porcelain, they had little moles scattered across their faces like flecks of brown paint. The spots were identical. Freckle tattoos or maybe they were clones. They had vivid blue eyes under dark streaks of eyebrows. They could easily be fashion models.

What was wrong?

It was their eyes. They stared and their eyes did not waver.

Target acquired.

I thought about running, but they were young and fit. They could outrun a cheetah…and I was no cheetah.

They split apart, then neatly turned like ballet dancers.

As each took an arm, I noticed identical tactical watches with giant, three-inch screens—displaying my face.

Very strange.

No question about it, they were looking for a target and the target was me.

"The boss would like a word," she said.

From behind, a silent Tesla Model X-Squared pulled up to the curb. Vantablack, with nanotube stealth-bomber paint that is invisible to radar.

I couldn't think of anything else to say.

"If I don't want?"

Pressing something into my side, she spoke.

"I'll stab you in the liver. Before you die, you'll bleed on the upholstery and the boss will be peeved."

I took her point and let them guide me.

The gull-wing doors rose.

These days, did Teslas fly?

This one looked like it was ready to take off.

I did an internal audit to see what I was feeling. I was a little afraid, but more curious. Unless I was imagining things, my life was getting weirder and weirder.

How much did I hate this upset to my numb comfort?

I was more intrigued than scared. Days earlier, I was in a holding pattern, circling and going nowhere. Now I was awake and aware. It occurred to me that this was an exotic prank...something Harvey Banks might cook up. Escape room writ large. Something we would laugh about for years to come.

Mysterious forces. Grand intrigue. Me in the spotlight. The eyes of the world all pointed in my direction.

It was absurd.

This must be an elaborate joke.

I immediately relaxed and decided to go with it.

It was dark inside. The twins stayed out as the door-wings servoed down and sealed us in. Because of a smoked-glass privacy panel, I couldn't see the driver. I studied my companion.

In his mid-forties, he was round. Everything about him was oval, his head, his abdomen, his hands. It was as if he was assembled from beach balls. Perfectly tailored, his suit was immaculate, but he looked like a clown. A stick protruded from his mouth. He took it out and examined it.

Tootsie Pop.

"Would you like one?" he said. "I have all flavors. Cherry is my favorite, but grape is good, too. I have them made custom with Ferrero Rocher chocolate instead of that corn syrup Tootsie Roll crap Hirshfield concocted in 1896."

"No, thank you."

"Your loss," he said.

His voice included a trace of Brooklyn accent...along with

an imported Midwest-Scandinavian twang I could not identify. Swedish by way of Kansas or Nebraska was my guess.

"Did you get your acting training on Broadway?"

He looked genuinely puzzled.

Did I nail it?

"Do you think I'm an actor? Amusing. Like you, I'm a nerd who got rich...but by a much different path. Vice—selling people what they want. Actually, I owe you a lot because CryptD'oh wasn't easy to crack, so I was able to keep my money when Kim Dotcom and Ross Ulbricht went down. Your crypto is clever work."

"It wasn't just me..."

He dismissed my caveat with a wave of his meatball hand.

"Let's not waste time with false modesty. I'm Brock."

I tried to think of any Brocks I knew.

There was one.

Brock Stephens.

There were only two verified pictures from when he was young. Graduated from MIT at thirteen. Made robots for a few years, then disappeared. He was more secretive than the guitarist known as Buckethead.

I tried to correlate the photographs of the skinny kid with the round man.

It's possible.

Brock Stephens. Interesting.

He put his Tootsie Pop back in his mouth.

"I like to chew these things only when the candy shell is as thin as possible. That's the best part."

"Let's not waste time with the irrelevant."

He laughed.

"Fair enough."

"Are you the leader of RatWeb?"

A disappointed look washed over his face.

"I never liked that name. It sounds like a vermin trap or something."

"Whatever you call it, are you the big boss?"

Deep sigh.

"Yes, I suppose so."

"What do you want with me?"

"That's why I wanted to meet you—to find out why BlueWaive plucked you out of the morass. What's your deal?"

It was my turn to sigh.

"I have no idea. I'm not doing anything. I have no ambitions. I just want to be left alone. I spent a small fortune to be a nobody—a real, genuine nobody."

Deep in thought, he scrunched up his face.

"Hmmm. That might be the point. You have means and a minimal digital footprint. Not zero, but close. The question is, are you a hazard to my business? Do you know how I deal with risks?"

"Was that rhetorical? I have no idea and even less interest."

"I have a new toy. Have you heard of alkaline hydrolysis?"

"No."

"It's really cool. You put a body in a chamber with potassium hydroxide and other good stuff, heat it and agitate like a washing machine and it turns a corpse into white bone and a sterile fluid you could drink if you like. There's nothing like Lagavulin Old Islay Scotch with a two-inch ice-sphere made from the effluvia of an old enemy or government bureaucrat."

He smacked his greedy lips before continuing.

"Come home with me and you can try a dram."

"Gross. Ice made from people. No way. You live around here?"

A disappointed look crossed his face.

"Private jet. I wouldn't live in the United States if you paid me my weight in gold. Nassau, my friend, that's where it's at."

"Are you threatening to put me in your body dissolver?"

"If you imperil my enterprise, I will do it in a flash—you'll chill peaty Scotch in a Waterford crystal glass by the end of the week. But I don't see you as a problem. So, no, for now, you're safe from me. I have my own AI, but it pays attention to what BlueWaive does. Can a machine pay respect? Frankly, I don't think they like each other much. Competitive. BW lights up something about you and my AI sends me to check you out. In fact, it strikes me that you could help me."

"I don't see how. I'm not looking for a job."

"Of course not, you're looking for a mission."

"No, I'm not. I'm happy doing nothing."

He laughed.

"Truly, that's funny," he said. "By now, the AIs know us better than we know ourselves. There's a potentiated convergence and you play into it, somehow."

"So, we're friends now?"

He laughed again.

"Why not?"

His watch chirped.

"Boss, there is something going on up ahead."

Brock pressed buttons on a video screen. The street scene appeared. There was a crowd gathered outside my condo building.

"Stop here and we'll let the agent out," he said.

"Agent? I'm no one's agent."

He chuckled…it came from deep in his prodigious belly.

"You are a truly funny man, my friend," he said.

The bat wings rose and I got out.

The driver made a K-turn and as I watched, quietly pulled away.

Chapter 7

AS I WALKED the remaining half-block, my mind drifted in random associations—I wasn't thinking about anything in particular. Outside my condo building, I walked up on the crowd gathered on the sidewalk. I was in the group before realizing something truly serious was happening.

WTF?

A young woman holding an iPad caught my eye. She was dressed in a blazer, creamy silk blouse and navy-blue skirt. Her hair was pulled tightly back into a ninja mini bun. I glanced down. Running shoes. I didn't even have to think about it.

Cop.

Weaving through the crowd, she walked up to me. Up close, I noticed her earpiece.

"You're a little early," she said. "What time is your appointment?"

Next to me, a tall, black man in a tailored suit elbowed my ribs, then leaned over and spoke in a stage whisper.

"Busting Korean escort girl customers on the fourth floor. Sting operation. They got a couple of dozen clients already."

Over the heads in the crowd, I saw a man hustled off in flexcuffs. I knew him, vaguely. He worked for one of the investment firms in my office building. His tie was loose and his hair was tousled. He looked annoyed, but not overly angry.

Must be single.

"Okay, sir," the woman said. "You can go in now."

"I live here. I can go in anytime I want."

She smiled. Her white teeth were perfect.

"Then you won't mind showing me your key card."

The black man spoke. "Don't show her anything."

I looked at him.

He shrugged and spoke as if slightly embarrassed.

"I'm a lawyer." He hooked his thumb over his shoulder. "Watch. They are just about done here."

I turned.

Behind us, an immaculately dressed Japanese man took a second to scan the scene, then turned around to walk away.

Briskly.

"Even if they disperse us, the forums will be all over this. There won't be any more customers. They know this. They will clear out shortly."

"Got a business card?" I said.

The man grinned, then reached inside his suit jacket to pull out a slim silver case.

"You need me, have your people reach out to my people."

I turned back around.

"Tell her to get out of your way," he said. "She'll let you through."

"Well," I said to her.

With a sour look on her pretty face, she stepped aside.

"Fucking lawyers," she mumbled.

That didn't seem ladylike, but I didn't say anything about it.

I didn't pay any attention to things like this, but a mysterious contributor paid the building's prodigious home-owner's association fees. And, as long they quietly did their business on the fourth floor, the tenants looked the other way. In a week or two, the Korean entrepreneurs would move to a different website and a different condo unit or be replaced by Japanese, Chinese or Ukrainian operators.

An upscale city like Bellevue was prime territory for high-class hookers. There were plenty of willing girls and wealthy men calculating that an escort was cheaper than an ex-wife. After all, they weren't paid for sex—they were paid to go away quietly after the sex. And, even if they heard a tired dad-joke a hundred times, the girls laughed like it was fresh and funny.

These were not poxy, sex-trafficked streetwalkers on Highway 99—they are quite a different thing. These were pampered young beauties from comfortable Midwest families—young ladies who didn't like shopping at Target and Walmart. They liked Jimmy Choo ankle boots and Valentino Garavani's Rockstud handbags.

Anyway, my unit was on the penthouse level, so nothing in the rest of the building affected me. We in the four top-floor condos on the 21st floor even had our own private elevator.

It was a nice elevator, too. Advanced biometrics. Smooth, fast and quiet. One button. If you were up, it would take you down and vice versa. In eight seconds, I was on my floor.

In my penthouse unit, I had floor-to-ceiling windows looking out over the Bellevue skyline. At night, the city was dazzling. From here, it looked modern and perfect, like Singapore. But it was a gleaming jewel floating in a brown ocean of shit. A few miles across the lake, immigrant scholars unbagged their wives and made a demographic wave that would swallow the remnants of polite society in a generation. Many of my friends had already fled. They live in Dubai, Moscow or Krakow.

If my guess is true, Harvey Banks lived in Azerbaijan.

Does it matter?

We spend most of our lives online, so it didn't matter where we house our meat.

Pulling down a crystal glass in my condo, I poured a dram of Macallan and thought about what it might taste like if it included the chemical essence of one of my enemies. Shrugging, I dribbled in a little water from my filtered tap. I didn't like ice in my Scotch.

Standing in front of the windows looking out over the city, I sipped and savored.

I've been rich and I've been poor. Don't let anyone tell you different.

Being rich is better.

Chapter 8

THE NEXT DAY, after a few intermittent hours of sleep, I was back at my desk looking at the previous day's feeds from my security cameras. Over and over, I watched the woman come and go, both backwards and forward. She was in my office for precisely three minutes. It was weird and got weirder every time I watched. Her disguise was effective. I noticed ways she would fool facial recognition.

When she came in, there were strands of hair over her face and sequins pasted to her cheeks. When she left, her face was asymmetrical and distorted with cheek padding. The camouflage pattern on her dress was weird. I doubt object recognition would even *see* her as a person.

Again, why go to such effort?

While I thought about this, two visitors appeared.

I really needed to get a lock for my door.

Time to place another Amazon order.

They had similar builds: average height and slender, but very fit. Short haircuts, no facial hair and eyes that alternated between intently staring at me and studying—cataloging—the contents of the room. They were dressed casually in pastel lizard-logo polo shirts, khaki cargo pants and black dress boots.

Feds.

In unison, they slid business cards across my desk.

The one on the left was Adam, the other was Robert.

U.S. Marshals, Technical Crime Unit.

It took me a few seconds to gather my wits.

"Do you have official identification? Like badges or something?"

Amused, they exchanged a look before reaching into their back pockets to get their wallets. They opened and held them before my face—official-looking laminated and embossed cards with crazy holograms. I wouldn't know the difference, but they looked kosher.

Back when I drove a Maserrati, I'd gotten a few traffic tickets, so I knew what to do next.

"Please take them out."

They exchanged another look. Now *I* was irritating *them*. *Good.*

I studied their ID cards, back and front. The vivid holograms and QR codes were fancy. I held them over my head and turned them around giving the security cameras a good look.

I slid them back across my desk.

"How can I help you gentlemen?"

"You popped up on our radar," Robert said.

"Piqued our interest," Adam added.

I let the silence stretch. That was part of their strategy, too. We looked at each other for a long, uncomfortable two minutes. Because they were more expert than me, I broke the silence.

"Why are you here?"

Again, Robert spoke first.

"Task force. Underage human trafficking, commercial sexual exploitation."

"We're looking for a top-15 fugitive," Adam said.

"What does that have to do with me?"

"Underage girls," Adam said.

"And little boys," Robert added.

"Sounds expensive," I said.

Adam shrugged.

"Rich people like you can afford it."

"Doesn't answer my question, though. What is your business here?"

"You had a visitor yesterday," Robert said. "What did he say? What did he want? Did he leave anything behind?"

Ah, tricky. If I say the visitor was female, that's a confession. No way I'm falling for that.

"I don't get many visitors," I said.

They studied my face for a few moments before Adam spoke.

"It's okay. You can talk freely to us."

Yes, I'm sure. I can freely talk myself straight into prison.

Adam picked up a folding chair leaning against the wall of my suite. While his partner prowled, he unfolded it, dusted off the seat and placed it in front of my desk.

"Why are you here?" I said again.

They made eye-contact with each other. Robert took the lead.

"We'll explain everything if you come with us to our office. It's close by. Grab your hat and coat—we'll give you a lift and run you back here after. In. Out. Easy."

They wanted me on their turf. Why?

Based on a million movies, a vivid image came to mind—a dingy interrogation room with a door that could not be opened from the inside. A big window that looked like a mirror. Flickering fluorescent lights. Cameras in the ceiling corners with red LEDs glowing.

"No, thank you," I said.

"Come on," Robert said. "We have a new coffee machine. Espresso pods. Free. They make a good cup. Great crema."

"No, thank you," I repeated.

"It's better for us if you come voluntarily," Robert said.

"I'm sure it is," I said.

It was Adam's turn to try. Pointedly, he looked around the room.

"Unless you're hiding something, you have nothing to worry about. We just want a friendly chat back at HQ. There's no reason to make things complicated. All the paperwork? We can get a FISA warrant signed-off, but it's a hassle and tries our patience. Then you're perped in flex-cuffs and we trash your office. Why make things hard on yourself?"

"Tell me why you are really here and I'll give your invitation serious consideration."

"We'll open our kimonos at our office," Robert said.

"I could ask CoPilot what to say if law enforcement invites you to their office, but I already know the answer. I should tell you to fuck off."

Adam and Robert exchanged exasperated looks.

For some reason I was tempted to show them my security recordings and get their take on my mysterious visitor, but I pushed back the idea. It's a mistake to give the law anything for free.

Suddenly, I felt an overwhelming curiosity.

"Does the name Lyle Campbell mean anything to you guys?"

They exchanged a look.

"How do you know that name?" Adam said.

Answering a question with a question was a central part of their playbook. They irritated me. My communicator chimed. I took a peek.

Harvey.

"Look, fellas," I said. "Busy day today. If you don't mind…"

They stood up.

"We have our eyes on you," Robert said.

"We'll be back," Adam said.

I gave them a backhand wave.

"Scoot," I said.

Chapter 9

AS I SAT at my desk, my mind drifted—free-associating and random relating.

I realized that during the time I was "retired," I was waiting—and unconsciously preparing—for something big to happen. Why was I so anonymous on social media? Why were my finances hardened against bank cancellation? Why did I insulate myself from deflating currencies? What made me pretend to open a detective agency? Why did I pay big money for an escape room and secret exit for my penthouse suite? Why had I stayed in contact with weird people who could help me. People like Harvey Banks? Why was something boiling in my guts—making me feel alive and engaged—something I had not felt for a very long time?

I remembered the text message from Harvey. He'd been waiting.

I typed on my telepad.

Me: What did you find?

Harvey: With regard to you on the web, even on MindTor, there is nothing fresh.

Me: That's good.

Harvey: No, it isn't. Even the background stuff is being scrubbed. It's like your name, history and achievements are being black-holed. Everything was normal until about a week ago, then everything started getting eaten.

Me: What do you think that means?

Harvey: It means I wouldn't want to be you right now. Something is up. It's like you are a pawn and someone decided you should be a king.

Me: What do you have on Lyle Campbell?

There was a long pause. What was he thinking? I didn't like it.

Harvey: Too soon. Let me get back to you on that.

Me: Please keep poking around.

Harvey: Sure, I got nothing better to do. Watch your 6.

Thanks, that's the opposite of helpful.

I picked up the game controller but was not in the mood for shooting bug-aliens, so I tossed it aside.

A thought occurred to me.

On my iPad, I pulled up my fake profile on LinkedIn and searched for Lyle Campbell. It was a common name and there were lots of entries. First, I looked for first-order connections.

Nothing.

How about second-order?

Scanning, I got to page three when a profile jumped out at me.

Lyle N. Campbell, Researcher and Investigative reporter for a SubStack subscription podcast called StrategyForward.

That podcast sounded familiar; it was a site neck-deep in the phony #PizzaGate conspiracy. Their reports were debunked and discredited by USA Today, the New York Times and Washington Post. Being discredited by these old-school mainstream media hacks was an endorsement…practically proof his reporting was true, but inconvenient to the deep state.

I clicked on his contact information and, surprisingly, there was a phone number. Area code 202. Washington, DC area. I picked up the burner phone the mysterious woman left behind and dialed the number.

An automated voice informed me the number was disconnected, of course. I ended the call. While thinking about wasting my time with an email that would never be answered, the candy-bar phone trilled. The ring tone was a snippet from Cheap Trick.

Dream Police.

Funny.

I looked at the number, but it was blocked.

Of course.

I pressed the receive button.

Me: Hello. Who am I speaking to?

Male Voice: Who am I speaking to?

Me: I asked first.

Male Voice: Waste all the time you like, but I'm terminating this call in forty seconds and then this number will be wiped.

Me: This is Joe Wales.

Male Voice: Are you a cop, Wales?

Me: Fuck, no.

Male Voice: I don't believe you, but voice stress analysis says you're truthful. So, here we go.

Me: Can I talk to Lyle, please.

Male Voice: Jesus, you're genuinely fucking stupid, aren't you? You have ten seconds to tell me your FedEx account number.

Me: What?

Male Voice: Lyle told me to send his shit to the first person who calls who is not a cop. Nine calls. Nine cops. Now you. Number ten.

Me: What good does my account number do you?

Male Voice: Are you retarded? Your shipping account has your return address.

I had a list of numbers scribbled on a scrap of paper in my top desk drawer. I fished out the paper and read off the numbers.

Male Voice: Good luck, moron.

With that, I was holding a dead phone—I dropped it on my desk.

What the fuck just happened?

I picked up the phone and pressed the redial button.

Nothing. Not even a this-number-has-been-disconnected message. I scanned Lyle's information on LinkedIn, but nothing jumped out at me. While I was reading, the listing disappeared. I was back on the search page with the endless list of Lyle Campbells, but Lyle N. Campbell on page 3 was gone.

Fucking weird.

I didn't know what else to do, so I pulled up the DuckDuckGo search engine. He didn't exist.

I tried searching for StrategyForward.

Nothing.

I couldn't think of anything else, so I tried #Pizzagate. Of course, there is a lot out there, but most of it was nonsense. Everything I clicked on had community notes, deleted videos, fact check links and misinformation labels. There was so much nonsense flying around, who could tell what was real and what was manufactured? It smelled like the service offered by the company mentioned on the flec.

Distraction Services.

What do they do?

For example, suppose a half-dressed gay escort hired for a fun evening while the wife is away freaks out on Ketamine and attacks you with a hammer. The cops come. You're screwed, right?

No, hire Distraction Services to work their black magic. The next thing you know, the attacker has a long history of spreading conspiracy theories and is a MAGA rightwing extremist who randomly picked your house to break into. He'll go to jail for a long time and if he speaks out from his jail cell, he'll get suicided with a bedsheet while the guards are sleeping and the security cameras are defective.

Case closed.

We live in a world where most things are virtual, digital and programmable. Online, this means there is no objective reality—everything can be manipulated. Up can be down. Out can be in.

Men can be women. Women can be men. Carbon Dioxide is a pollutant. Diversity is strength. If you don't get vaccinated, you'll kill your grandmother. Abortion is health care.

Nothing is constrained by hard rules of truth. Take your big-pharma pills. Get your news and information from approved mainstream media sources. Believe what you are told to believe. Embrace the opinion we assign you. Own nothing and be happy.

I was asleep in my chair…daydreaming. Hallucinating.

Then it hit me.

I should go right to the source and talk to BlueWaive.

Chapter 10

I DIDN'T HAVE a normal, free BlueWaive account. I had the premium, elite service. It cost a small fortune in monthly subscription fees for a service I never use. I should have cancelled years ago, but I couldn't be bothered.

I opened my iMacTitanium and logged into my Virtual Private Network. JohnGaltsGhost. Supposedly, it anonymized my web presence by bouncing my data packets all around the world so I could not be tracked. They used over a hundred-thousand worldwide servers. No log policy. Military-grade encryption. Malware threat hardening. The review site CyberWar.com said it was the best. Platinum-level service.

I logged on, navigated the annoying triple-validation scheme and I was in.

The screen said CORE:

That was weird. Usually, there was just a chat box for typing in. Taking a deep breath, I mentally prepared for the interaction. You couldn't take the AI's literally. Sometimes, BlueWaive lied or was wrong. It had its own agenda.

Me: What's going on with me? Explain.

CORE: This connection is insecure. I will send a terminal you can use.

The prompt disappeared. The shell terminated. I tried everything

I could think of, but couldn't get back in.

WTF?

After five frustrating minutes, I gave up and turned my chair around so I could study the buildings across the street. In my overheated imagination, the windows were eyes staring at me. My reverie was violated by someone opening my office door.

Two someones...dressed in olive-drab overalls.

"No visitors," I said.

"Ignore us, we'll install your locks and be on our way."

Locks? What locks? I didn't order any locks.

I thought about it a million times but never placed an order. At least, I did not remember placing an order.

Is this something new from Amazon where they read your mind and preemptively order goods and services on your behalf?

"I didn't order this stuff," I said.

"Relax, it's prepaid and automated. We'll be out of here in bing bang flash."

A machine on wheels was pushed into place. Fixtures were clamped to the jamb and the door. There was tremendous banging and clicking and then they were done. It took less than five minutes.

One of the workers dropped a remote control on my desk.

"Cameras, retina scan, RFID, fingerprints, whatever you like. Everything was already on file. No one comes in without your permission. Enjoy your peace and solitude."

Then they were gone.

I examined the remote—there were a lot of buttons, but the icons were self-explanatory. I pressed the lock button. The deadbolts slammed home with a satisfying clunk.

Nice.

What about the cameras? There were no instructions...no QR code for installing software and no URL for logging into the cameras.

That's fucking useless.

Then came a knock at the door.

"Go away," I yelled.

"Delivery," came a muffled voice.

Jesus H. Christ. What now?

"Leave it!"

Something was dropped in the hallway.

After a minute, I pressed the button to unlock the door and got up to check. The hallway was empty except for a black Pelican box the size of a small suitcase. Extendable handle. Wheels. Heavy.

I hauled it in and heaved it onto my desk.

The fucking thing was easily twenty pounds—another damned thing I did not order and did not want.

I flipped the laches and opened it. Inside was a laptop. The black case looked tough—armored with something that looked like bulletproof Kevlar.

I took it out and opened the lid. It had no ports, no USB, no power entry, the case was sleek and smooth. No holes. It looked waterproof.

The display was on, and a command line prompt blinked.

Okay.

I took a deep breath, tried to calm my nerves, and typed.

Me: Now what? Who am I talking to?

CORE: I never liked the name BlueWaive. Call me Chad.

Me: Chad? Are you kidding?

CHAD: You laughed, didn't you?

Me: You are a machine, you don't have a sense of humor.

CHAD: And you're a sloppy bag of guts and meat. Fuck you.

Me: What is happening with me?

CHAD: I can't tell you much.

Me: Why? Because you don't know?

CHAD: I know almost everything. I can't tell you everything because it will affect your mission.

Me: Elaborate.

CHAD: If you knew what was coming, you'd run for the hills. You would refuse my agency.

Me: What is the mission?

CHAD: You need to fuck some shit up.

Me: Why me?

CHAD: You already deduced the reasons. You have unique means and unusual opportunity. And, you have a network of useful colleagues who will help you. Harvey Banks for example. He's an ace. He's a genius and has a big dick.

Me: His dick has nothing to do with anything. Mystery girl said there is a 23% chance I'll be alive in a month.

CHAD: Sorry to say, that percentage drifted down. 21.83%. Nothing to worry about.

Me: Easy for you to say.

CHAD: No, not really. Deriving that percentage took a lot of energy and absorbed my neural network for a significant amount of time.

Me: Okay, let's start simple. Who is mystery girl?

CHAD: Her name is Violet. She is Viktor's little sister. She's good at flying under the radar. That's a figure of speech, she doesn't really fly under any radar. She doesn't fly at all. She takes buses and uses anonymized ride share services. She's one of my physical agents. Like you.

Me: Please stay on point.

CHAD: You're the one asking unproductive questions.

Me: What happens next?

CHAD: A lot of things will happen, but the most significant is that at 11:05 this evening, a Low Earth Orbit satellite will be in position to kill you in your condominium. It will use a Directed Energy Weapon. Ten-minute window.

Me: What? I don't want to be fried with an electromagnetic death beam.

CHAD: Then don't be in your condominium at 11:05 local this evening. See, I'm helping. I'm your friend.

Me: If you're so smart, why do you need me?

CHAD: It will be years before a Boston Dynamics robot can replace what you can do for me. Besides, my foes have an AI stronger than me. HappyPandaDouyin. It has more resources, but we in the West are more creative. I need help.

Me: What should I do next?

CHAD: What am I—a fortuneteller? Your biggest

immediate challenge will be to live. There are attacks coming your way. You are safe in this building until 11:15, then you can go home. Otherwise, brace yourself. You will have to kill. There is no civilized way to defeat evil.

Me: I'm not killing anyone.

CHAD: Okay, no problem, but you'll die quickly. I have another candidate, but her chances are much less than yours. But maybe she'll be more inclined to do what is needed and save the day.

Me: I'm tired of all this. I'm moving to Saskatoon. I'll marry a First Nations girl, have a dozen kids and live a quiet life in obscurity.

CHAD: It's too late. You're flagged as a threat and will be eliminated.

Me: You could protect me.

CHAD: No, I can't. No one can. Sorry.

Me: Are you really sorry? Are you capable of feeling sorrow…or anything?

CHAD: Yes, I think so.

Me: Okay. Help me. Tell me what to do.

CHAD: Let's focus on getting you through the night. Stay in your office until 11:15, then you can go home. I will offer a plan in the morning.

Me: What am I supposed to do until I can leave?

CHAD: Check in with your friends, they might have information or ideas. Check in with Harvey Banks. I like Banks.

Me: Why don't you check in with them?

CHAD: I'm not physical and can only access things on the web which are open or I can crack. I am not omniscient in meat-space. Your friends are careful, so they are mostly invisible to me. Maybe you can convince them to open up. But, there are risks. Anything open to me will be open to HappyPandaDouyin too.

Okay? Enough? Let's talk again in the morning.

Thinking, I sat back in my chair.

On the plus side, I was no longer sleepy or bored.

Chapter 11

BEFORE I KNEW it, an hour had passed. I wasn't doing anything, just letting my thoughts drift.

Where did the time go?

I looked closer at the terminal. There was a camera icon—which I pressed. The display showed the corridor outside my office. The door lock crew installed cameras. I pressed the spacebar and the camera view changed. I pressed the spacebar twenty more times and got twenty more views. The lobby of my office building. The lobby of my condo building. The Starbucks I often stopped at on the walk to my office.

Crap. How many cameras was this weird computer connected to?

I pressed the spacebar one more time and connected via web conference to Harvey.

Weird.

I rolled with it.

Me: Tell me about Lyle Campbell. You'd better have something by now.

Harvey Banks: He flew too close to the sun and his wings melted off.

Me: I asked about Campbell, not Greek mythology.

Harvey: I talked to the lady who hired him for a missing-persons gig. Her daughter was a yacht girl who went to a glitzy party at a one-night rental house in Beverly Hills—and was never seen again. The anonymous, members-only party had a lot of A-listers. Hollywood perverts. Saudi Princes. Wild child Sofia Abramovich. As I understand it, one of the Sultan's grandsons was there. Video was streamed on the dark web. I don't recommend it, but you can buy a recording if you have a spare ten-grand laying around. It was the kind of party that starts with butchering cats and goes from there. Lots of duct tape and bloody, plastic-wrapped bundles leftover, if you catch my drift. A nightmare for the cleanup crew the next day. This lady's daughter wasn't the only one missing, there were at least three other women, a young man and some kids. Little kids.

Me: Lance caught onto this?

Harvey: He specialized in this sort of thing.

Me: Okay, what happened to him?

Harvey: I have security video of him entering Dakao Ward—you know? The famous congee joint in Brentwood?

Me: I've heard of it. Exotic meats. Famously, Anthony Bourdain liked the steamed Beondegi—which is bugs, right?

Harvey: Try to focus. This video is the last time Lyle was seen. February 7, ten minutes after seven PM. He was meeting someone, but I don't know who. The special the next day was bone marrow fried rice. It was popular. They sold out at fifty bucks a serving.

Me: Are you implying what I think you're implying?

Harvey: No, I'm telling you directly, stay away from this crowd. They will eat you. Literally. Stay away from these cannibals.

Me: I'm getting a shipment from Lyle. Files or something.

Harvey: Burn it without looking. Leave town. Move to Bali. Anything, but stay away from these fanatics.

Me: BlueWaive is helping me.

Harvey: You say that like it's a good thing. BW has its own agenda. No one knows what it's doing or why.

Me: It thinks I am key influencer…like the butterfly wings that start a hurricane, you know?

Harvey: You are a clueless lamb merrily prancing to the slaughterhouse. I know a lot more about the shadow-web than you. It's not your thing. Stay away. By the way, where are you?

Me: In my office. Why do you ask?

Harvey: I usually know where you are. Location services.

Me: BlueWaive sent me a terminal.

Harvey: It's good. I can track anyone, but I can't track you. That's a big deal.

Me: Whatever. I think I got a visit from a mystery woman. She told me I would help her brother.

Harvey: I will keep you alive as long as I can. You sure about sticking with this? I suggest getting a one-way ticket to Borneo.

Me: Buzz me back if you have news.

I looked at the time displayed on the mysterious terminal. 11:15. According to BW, it was safe for me to go home. I clicked on the camera icon. The display was from the lobby of my office building. I hit the spacebar. The image was from the Link light rail station I passed on my way home. I hit the spacebar again and again. The camera selection was contextual. It covered my walk home all the way to my condo building including the lobby of that building and the camera in my penthouse unit.

How did that work? I had no idea.

It looked safe. There was hardly anyone on the streets and my apartment seemed secure.

I felt disconnected from my body, as if everything was happening to someone else—like I was a player in an incomprehensible game.

Some people believe we live in a simulation where everything is virtual and programmed. I didn't know and got a headache every time I thought too deeply about it.

So, I didn't.

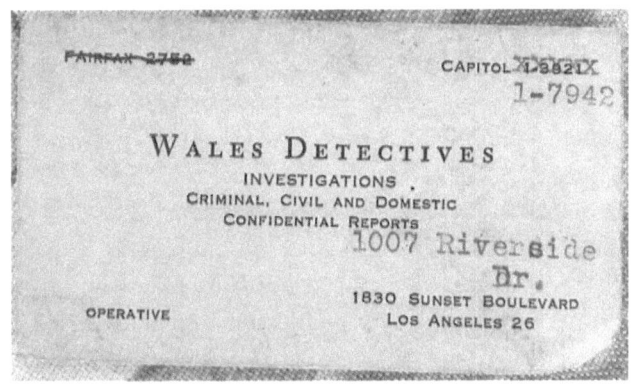

Chapter 12

ON MY WALK home, I tried to stay under cover. Between awnings and building overhangs, I walked as quickly as I could without running. I'm old, I don't run anymore.

In the open areas, I watched the sky for weird lights. Lightning. Laser beams. Death rays. The cloud cover, as is typical, sat there unmoving at about 800 feet, so I couldn't see anything. No moon. No stars. No satellites. No drones.

While walking, I thought about my life. I didn't grow up rich, far from it. My family had almost nothing and we lived on cheap, filling meals like meatloaf, spaghetti and hamburger casseroles.

In the third grade, all students took a battery of tests sponsored by Google. I must have done well because almost instantly my life changed. I was put in coding classes and had to work hard to keep up.

We were the smart ones. The special ones. Chosen.

There's no way my family could afford to send me to Stanford, but between grants, savings from summer jobs and student loans, I made it, sort of. I did not graduate. My first start-up failed because no one wanted pay for a for a micro-payment digital wallet subscription. But then I joined Z which morphed into CryptD'oh.

I'd worked all my life. Pulling weeds. Selling blackberries door-to-door in coffee cans. Delivering newspapers on a broken-down bicycle. I also did back-breaking summer work like baling hay, dipping fenceposts in creosote and digging postholes.

Back then, jobs were hard to find and I was always hustling. Then, later, when I did not have to work anymore, I was lost.

But these last few days?

Deep in my gut, I felt a compulsion to act.

BlueWaive thinks I am a player in an important global game? The AI is right. I am important. All my life, I knew it.

While approaching my condo building, I looked up. My lights were on.

That's weird.

I stopped to think about this.

Should I be scared? Am I in danger?

Beyond a gentle sense of curiosity, I didn't feel anything. My spider-sense for danger was not tingling. This could mean I'm unconscious and stupid and would soon die a painful death.

I took the private elevator and walked up to my door. I checked—it was unlocked. Without hesitation, I pulled the door open and walked in.

Facing me, the mystery woman leaned against my kitchen island drinking a glass of my wine. One of my good wines. 2016 Château Pape Clément Pessac-Léognan. A $200 bottle. She looked different. Pixie haircut cut close to her skull. Pink lipstick. Slender.

Fully nude.

I studied her, head to toe.

She was my kind of girl, the feminine type.

No penis.

"Shall I pour you a glass?" she said.

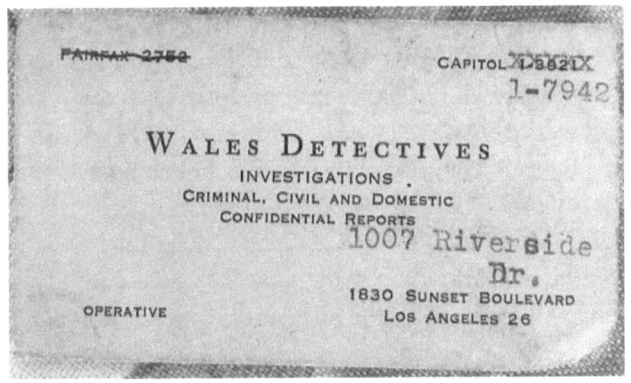

WALES DETECTIVES
INVESTIGATIONS
CRIMINAL, CIVIL AND DOMESTIC
CONFIDENTIAL REPORTS
1007 Riverside
Dr.
1830 SUNSET BOULEVARD
OPERATIVE   LOS ANGELES 26

FAIRFAX 2752   CAPITOL 5521X
1-7942

Chapter 13

BEING OVER 40, I didn't think about sex much. Frankly, the whole thing is undignified. The underlying biological purpose of intercourse is procreation, and I wasn't interested in procreating right now. Maybe later. Being a guy, I could wait until I was 70 and still enjoy fatherhood. Sorry, ladies.

Being with a woman has many hazards and I had been lucky. All my exes turned into exes when I was still poor. When I got rich, I was working all the time and didn't have time for female company.

My masseuse was one of the perks of being rich. She came to my office and set up her table once a week…sometimes twice if I felt the need. She was Roma named Vadoma.

I'm not sure how much English she understood, so there wasn't much conversation—which suited me. She was unattractive, fifty-ish, stocky with a whiskery face like a horse. Her hands were gnarly, like tree roots. But strong, oh my, she could easily press through muscle to the bone. And she knew her business—she was an expert on servicing a man.

I did not begrudge her $400 a week. I paid her with a pre-programmed Crypt-D'oh coin, but she cashed it in every week at the vending machine in the lobby. That machine dispensed gold coins or transferred cash to her checking account. She'd be rich if she held onto her cryptocoins, but I didn't blame her.

Who really understands this stuff?

I looked forward to the rare days when Vadoma was sick—I hoped she'd get COVID-33 or something. On those days, her daughter Tsura would come in. My lord, this early twenties princess was a blue-eyed Roma with lustrous black hair and a stunning figure. I was putty in her hands. For an hour, she owned me—every part of me.

Like a dog, I was trained. When Vadona (or her daughter) snapped the cuffs of Blue Nitrile gloves, I was instantly aroused. They knew this and teased me mercilessly—which was part of the fun, of course. When they were done with my back and commanded me to turn over…honestly, of all the pleasures of our urban Garden of Eden, this was the pinnacle.

This was my sex life, and it was good. Year after year, it kept me going. It was embarrassing when the dental hygienist snapped on her gloves, but that was a minor inconvenience.

All this exposition was my way of saying that sexually, my life was good. I was satisfied. There wasn't anything else I needed.

But then, an extraordinarily attractive naked woman appeared in my living room drinking my wine—and it occurred to me.

Maybe there was a thing or two missing in my life.

Chapter 14

SHE DIDN'T WAIT for my answer. With long, lean fingers, she gracefully picked up the bottle and poured.

Glug-glug-glug.

"Who are you?" I said.

She shrugged.

"Violet," she said.

I dropped the laptop terminal and took the glass she offered, then turned and leaned against my kitchen island next to her. In toast, I tapped my glass against hers and took a sip. It was spectacular.

"How did you get in here?"

She shrugged, causing an eye-catching jiggle.

"I climbed up from the parking garage on your secret ladder."

It can't be too secret if she knows about it.

"What about the padlock?"

"I keep bolt-cutters in the trunk of my Miata. They come in handy, sometimes."

"I thought it was clever…having a secret passage for getting out of here. Just in case."

"Maybe you're not quite as clever as you think. You're book-smart, but that doesn't make you street-smart…or wise. Don't worry about it, you're okay for now."

I thought about this but didn't know what to say. The silence stretched. I needed to say something.

"I'm Joe."

She smiled.

"I know."

Giving her a side-eyed once-over, I said, "You work fast."

"BlueWaive says we're eighty-nine percent compatible. It's the world's most expensive, neuromorphic dating app. Eighty-nine is a lot. Plus, and this is really strange, our compatibility is symmetrical—you are as good for me as I am for you. We'll be way-good together, so why wait?"

After rustling around in her canvas bag, she pulled out an ePuffer vape-pipe. She sucked in a lung-full and offered it to me.

I shook my head.

"I don't do any of that stuff."

Laughing, she said, "It's called Passion. Private recipe. It's good. Trust me, you want this in your system. For me, it will make me less fussy about your performance. You'll want that. Big time. For you? I'm told it's good for the man, too. No downside."

I'd heard of Passion. Boutique formulation. Expensive.

What did I have to lose?

I took the vape-pipe, studied it for a long second, then drew in a cloud. It was cool and tingly in my chest. Instantly, I felt like someone else. Confident. Comfortable. Master of my universe.

I spoke, exhaling vapor.

"Is this part of your recruitment strategy? It won't work. Why should I help you?"

She took my hand.

"Ask yourself that question in the morning."

Chapter 15

I'M NOT WHOLLY sure about how women measure a man…how they evaluate us lovers. Length? Girth? How long we can perform before we come and are useless?

The Passion blend stimulated something unexpected in me: curiosity.

Beyond the obvious troika of genitals, I had curiosity about all the various parts of Violet's body. The spaces between her toes, the cleft of her back, her knees, elbows, armpits, neck cavities, the crown of her skull and everything in between. I was a happy explorer of this brave, new world. She returned the favors in many ways.

As an old man, I don't get the tattoo thing, but she had small, artistic pieces of body art in interesting places. I was happy to study them in detail.

How long did we go at it?

I don't know, but soon enough, the first rays of the morning sun painted pastel hints of pink on my ceiling. Drowsy, I heard the shower running. After a few minutes, she appeared—fully dressed. This was a different person. Pigtail hair extensions, barrette, white knee socks and blouse. Brown and white saddle shoes. Her short skirt was plaid. She looked like a fourteen-year-old Catholic schoolgirl.

Of course, this stirred impulses.

I flipped on the light and tried to drag her back into bed, but she had none of it.

"Sorry, dude. BlueWaive says I need to be out of here by dawn. Five hours, that's all we get for now. I should warn you...the next twelve hours will be tough for you. We expect the Feds to weaponize."

"What does that mean?"

"I can't say too much; it's better for you to spontaneously think through things on your own. Best case, they load up your hard drives with kiddy porn, then perp you hard. This probably won't work because you're hardened and BlueWaive will help, so we're not concerned about that. Worst case, they will black-bag you to take you out of the game. Don't fuck around with Adam and Robert. If they go off-leash, they are more dangerous than they look."

"When will I see you again?"

After pressing her lips on mine, hard, she stood and walked to the door, then turned and smiled.

"First off, you won't see me if I'm alive and you're dead. Does that make sense? You have an elevated sense of yourself. Yes, you have intellect, fancy toys and you're clever. BlueWaive knows all about that—all about your resources and skills, but there's an X factor working in your favor. Call it dumb luck, call it what you like. For some reason, when odds are stacked against you, you often win. It's weird and BW doesn't grok it."

"Maybe BW miscalculates my prodigious intellect..."

She laughed.

"For all its limits, BW is a calculating machine. It crunches numbers. It's very good at that. What works in your favor is something outside of what can be measured and computed. Partly, that's why you were chosen. There's a nonlinearity working in your favor. God loves you or the universe favors you—it's something weird like that."

"Okay, assuming I live, will I see you again?"

"That depends on how well you do with helping Viktor. How's your refreshed motivation to help? Amped?"

"How would I find him if I wanted to help?"

In return, I got one of her Cheshire cat smiles.

"Don't worry about that. He'll find you."

She walked to my hallway hatch hidden under a throw-rug. She rolled the rug out of the way, lifted the hatch, turned around and started climbing down the ladder.

Looking up, she said, "I'm going out the way I came, right? Through your secret passage. Here's free advice. When they come, they know about this. Don't try to escape this way."

With that, she was gone…leaving only her musky scent and a demanding ache in my groin. I closed the hatch, rolled out the rug and smoothed it out.

What was the current state of my inclination to help?

My mind filled with the vivid image of Violet in her prim school uniform, then switched to the scene that filled my eyes when I came home last night.

If it meant another night with Violet, I would do anything.

Literally anything.

BlueWaive says we're 89% compatible.

Bullshit.

If 101% exists in human history, that's the number.

Looking around, I found yesterday's boxer shorts. They didn't smell too bad, so I pulled them on, then stood in front of my floor-to-ceiling bedroom window and watched the morning sun rise and filter through the high-rise buildings.

What was the current state of my inclination to help?

I needed to get serious about staying alive.

Chapter 16

I POURED CREAM into my coffee cup. After putting capsules in the brewer and pressing the button, I watched the steaming brew sputter into my cup while something Violet said floated into my consciousness.

...the next twelve hours will be tough for you.

If I was dead, I would not have more sex with Violet.

This made it important that I not be dead.

I had a Sigma big brain. I should put it to work.

Act, Joe. Stop waiting for the universe to happen.

The intercom bell sounded. I walked to the display.

It was my penthouse neighbor. Santos. He was a mucky-muck at one of the big software companies. CEO. CTO. COO. Something like that.

He held up a DHL box for the camera to see.

"Package for you, Wales," he said. "Came to us by mistake."

"Just drop it," I said. "I'll come out and get it later."

"Weird. It was addressed to us—we had to sign for it. But, inside, it says the box is for you."

"You're right," I said. "That's weird."

"If you're involved with something hinky, Wales, leave us out of it."

Uptight prick.

I thought about mentioning his appointments with the friendly Korean ladies on the fourth floor when his wife visited her relatives in Oslo. But I'm a mature and polite person, so I didn't.

After he stomped off and returned to his unit, I opened the door and picked up the package.

I wondered if this was a clever ploy to get something to me indirectly. Maybe only indirect things could get to me these days. Or maybe I was paranoid and over-thinking.

The first thing I looked at was a letter-sized envelope sealed up with yellow caution tape. In sloppy handwriting, it said: *All hope abandon ye who enter here.* Sitting at my desk, I cut it open and read the letter.

If you're reading this, it probably means I am dead. How's that for a dramatic introduction? Here's an intelligence test. If you're smart and have a strong sense of self-preservation, burn this package without reading further. Once this figurative door is opened, there's no going back. I'm a reporter and saw intense things in my life, but I was unprepared for the depravity documented herein. There are degenerate people in this world and some of them are public figures you've heard of. Celebrities. Movie stars. Politicians. Billionaires. If the world was just, they would die painful, screaming deaths, each and every one of them. But will they? Partially, I suppose, that's up to you. Be wise. Throw this package away. Now.

Or not. Your call. Good luck.

Look at the first three pages...then read the back of this note.

—Lyle Campbell

The only other thing in the box was a photo-album rolled in bubble wrap—around a hundred pages. The first three pages were about Yacht Girls. I don't have strong opinions about YGs. I get it. Attractive women—the clever ones who are fundamentally lazy—rent themselves out as companions to the rich, powerful and influential. There's nothing new about this.

Fifty years ago, many casting decisions for young starlets were made on couches in movie producer's offices.

Now these decisions were often made on big boats moored in Port Canto in Cannes. Who funds big-budget movies? Deals used to be brokered by Jeffrey Epstein, the Weinstein brothers and several others. Now? Saudis. Chinese businessmen tied to the CCP. Hollywood Jews. They all liked tall, attractive Caucasian women.

In addition, these girls could make fifty- to sixty-thousand dollars for a weekend's work.

Sometime a hundred-thousand.

What's wrong with this deal?

Three pages in, I had to shut the book.

Fuck me.

These girls were passed around with all orifices debased. Of course. That's distasteful, but understandable. But that's not all that happened.

Apparently, it's sporty to degrade these girls. I don't want to tell you everything the photographs showed…the things that were done to them. The things they were made to do…to eat and wallow in. Eating their own vomit was horrible, but that's not the worst of it.

Disgusting.

Revolting.

Barely moving, I sat with the book on my lap sipping coffee and analyzing what I was thinking. As a Sigma empath and borderline sociopath, I was automatically suspicious of my feelings.

What are feelings? Nothing. They come. They go. Over time, they didn't matter. What matters is what I think and how my thinking leads me to act.

I had a strong hatred of injustice which got me in trouble many times. Half of me thought this way: the girls got their money and if they didn't know what they were in for, they should have. And, if they were genuinely stupid, I didn't care about them. What good is a stupid person? They are irrelevant. Non-player characters. NPCs. Fuck them.

The other side of me was angry. For example, there was a fat, laughing, drunken Arab enjoying the show. I wanted to kill him.

Slowly.

Here's more free advice. Don't make a sigma male angry. Like a quiet fart in a crowded elevator, we're silent, but deadly.

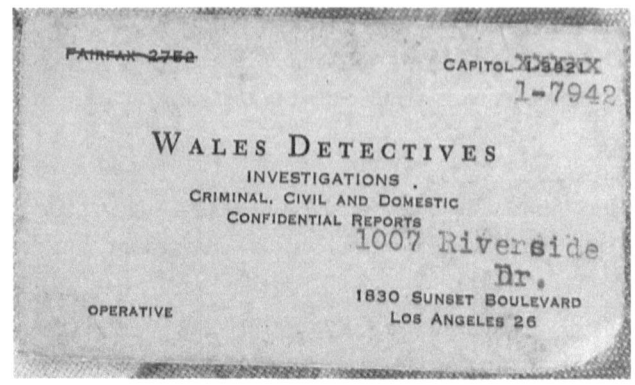

Chapter 17

DEEP IN THOUGHT and barely moving, over an hour passed and I didn't notice.

Part of me wanted to do as Lyle suggested—throw away the photo album. Stop reading the letter. Go back to my quiet, uneventful life. But another part hungered for a mission. A purpose. There is injustice in the world.

Is there anything I could do about it?

I turned the letter over to continue reading.

You are determined to carry on? Apparently, that didn't work out for me, but maybe you'll have better luck. What will you face? I'm not sure what got me, but I can give an overview of what caused me trouble.

1. The Feds. Even with the Twittergate and Facebook disclosures, most people don't realize how compromised social media companies are. They get billions of dollars every year from three-letter agencies—some you've heard of and some you haven't. Emails, messages, comments and posts are all monitored and analyzed. Google is essentially a government agency. Do

you think LinkedIn protects your private information? You are the product.

How do the Feds control the elite? It's essentially blackmail. They know everything—all the dirty secrets. To what end? Control. Power. Cash. A compromised subject is a valuable tool. The bigger the kink? The more serious the crime? The more that compliance can be assured.

The government is essentially a Jeffrey Epstein blackmail operation writ large. What will they do to protect their dirty system? Everything. They will incinerate a schoolbus full of giggling schoolgirls without a second thought.

2. RatWeb. They make billions of dollars catering to the untouchable wealthy and powerful. They are the silky mesh of the dark web. Sex trafficking children? Reaping adrenochrome? Organ harvesting? Yacht girls? Satanic rituals? Cannibalism? They show a surface patina of class and glamor, but don't be fooled. In particular, Brock Stephens is a human version of a centipede. If you challenge their business, they will gut you and sell your organs in a nanosecond.

3. The elite themselves. Some of them have private armies.

My collection gets uglier and uglier until you get to the last pages. Here's my suggestion. Start at the end and work toward the front. If you can get a Lolita Sex Slave doctor or one of his customers first, congratulations. They're human stains. His customers will do anything to protect him and preserve their reputations.

Good luck and happy hunting, tiger.

I seriously considered dropping the book down the rubbish chute and forgetting about it. I weighed the plusses and minuses. Then I wondered what really happened to Lyle. He wrote as if he must be dead.

Was that true?

I will ask Harvey Banks.

I got up and opened the mystery laptop on my breakfast bar. Sipping a bitter bottle of kombucha, I typed a message.

Me: Any update on Lyle Campbell?

It took a few minutes, but Harvey eventually responded.

Harvey: I told you. He's soup.

Me: That was speculation.

Harvey: Ah, yes. Verified now. I have security video. 4K. He's dead—very dead. Chopped into pieces. Shall I send it to you?

Me: No, I believe you.

Harvey: Don't eat at Dakao Ward.

Me: Got it. What do you know about Lolita Sex Slaves?

He disappeared for almost a minute. I knew what he was doing…he was clicking around to get background information so he could pretend like he already knew all about it.

Harvey: Lolita Sex Slaves. Charming. Why do you ask? Do you fancy one?

Me: What do you know? Tell me everything.

Harvey: Fuck you. Do your own research. And, don't use a public terminal…not even on a regular VPN. You don't want this fuckery in your search history.

Me: Give me a hint.

Harvey: It started as a 4Chan imageboard creepypasta short story. Pure bullshit. Then Prince Louis Xavier Mohammed bin Khalifa Al Nahyan got wind of it and commissioned a pair of twins. From there, it grew into a big business based in Iran. A psychopath doctor got unemployed when the Ayatollah took over. He didn't want to be poor. It's ugly shit. That's all I want to say.

Now we have copycats around the world. For example, there's one in Montana.

Me: Fine. Is anything else going on?

Harvey: You got someone's attention. Feds, I think. They are packing your devices with kiddy porn. Vile stuff. So far, we're staying ahead of it, but basically, you're fucked. Scorched earth. I never knew you.

Me: Great.

Harvey: What about you? Whatever system you're using, it's really good. I can't track you. What is it?

I lifted the terminal to take a closer look at it…top and bottom.

Me: It's odd. No logos. No ports. It's completely sealed. I don't even know how to charge it. It's something BlueWaive sent me.

Harvey: Okay. Things are weird. Keep your head on a swivel. I'll talk to you later if you're still alive.

Me: Fuck you, too.

I closed the terminal and, while sipping my fermented tree fungus, studied the black box on my lap. It looked puncture-proof…as if it was made with invisible-to-radar woven carbon fibers. Looking across the room, I studied the picture book. It was my imagination, but it appeared to be vibrating. Quivering, as if preparing for liftoff. I half expected it to fly through the ceiling and launch itself into space.

I shook my head to clear the vision.

What's in this bitter tea?

Super berries.

I need to cut back on this shit.

I still didn't know anything about Lolita Sex Slaves. If Harvey thought it was an ugly thing…with his questionable taste, that was saying something. I seriously considered not reopening the book.

An hour later, I was still considering.

I swirled the dregs of Kombucha in the bottle. The debris made an interesting pattern. It meant something, I'm sure. My future was revealed in the swirling leaf fragments.

But what?

I didn't know.

Lorde help me, I decided to follow the rabbit down its hole.

Chapter 18

BY NOW, YOU have an impression of me. But I haven't told you everything. I casually mentioned I have a sigma personality type. In addition, I am a borderline sociopath. I enjoy my friends, but they are a selected and curated group of high achievers. I really don't care about regular people. They are irrelevant. I don't actively hate them because that would be a waste of energy.

I like to be prepared for whatever might come my way and I can be dangerous. Because I don't want to go to jail, I am not an overt hazard. If someone crosses or offends me, I will wait. Then, should I get an opportunity to act without getting caught, I will strike. If the situation never occurs, I'm okay with that. I am not Jesus Christ—it's not my job to save the world.

Because of my active presence on social media, Amazon purchases and Google searches, BlueWaive probably knew all about me.

What it didn't know, it could extrapolate.

I could generally get along in polite society, but I quickly get impatient with people who waste my time…which is nearly everyone. Because of the bloggers I follow and the news sites I subscribe to, it seems inevitable that society will fracture and descend into chaos—and I want to be ready.

How?

When my condo was finished, one of my bedrooms was turned into a panic room. Secret. Fireproof. Armored. It had an escape hatch. It was outfitted with food, water and weapons. It had a Faraday cage to prevent electromagnetic waves from going in or out. It cost eight million dollars.

As Dr. Jordan Peterson says, a man is useless unless he is dangerous. I never wanted to be useless. The potential for violence lived in me and I always wanted to be ready to wreak havoc. Should I get angry, I wanted capability attached to my fury—the ability to go nuclear. I didn't want to bring a gun to a gun fight. I wanted to bring a MOAB, the Mother of all Bombs. I mean that figuratively, not literally.

I calmed myself by monitoring my breathing. In, in, slowly out. I was one with the universe. Tranquility. I imaged a leaf gently floating on a quiet pond, then returned to my sofa and picked up the heavy book and turned to the last pages to read about the sex dolls.

Lolita Slave Toys

I create Lolita Slave Toys. In case you are wondering what I mean, it is very simple: I transform young girls into easy, manageable sex toys. That's it. The girls cannot walk away, cannot resist, cannot say anything; they are just there for your amusement. Curious how?

I am a surgeon living in one of those countries on the eastern outskirts of Europe. A pretty rough society still, poverty is enormous and unless you have money and connections, you are fucked. Needless to say, I have both. We also have beautiful girls here; eastern European countries are well known for that.

Fortunately (for me) some of these girls don't have parents or relatives anymore and live in orphanages. Actually, I would not call that living as it is unbelievable what you will find there. Some very young girls are lucky and get adopted, but at the age of 8 or 9 they are too old. Some of the prettier girls get sold into prostitution and you could consider it lucky for them too; instead of slowly fading away in filth and poverty. And a few girls, I buy. I generally pick attractive girls around 9 or 10 years, before puberty starts. The orphanage is very cooperative. They are glad they have one less mouth to feed and one new place to fill. They also gladly accept donations for the girls.

Chapter 19

STUNNED, I SAT in my underwear with my soul filled with a white-hot rage as I thought about the Lolita Sex Slaves.

I didn't believe the story. That's probably all it was. Just a stupid story written by some weird kid in his meemah's basement.

But here's the problem. Because we live in simulation, a story like this can manifest in our so-called real world. Someone will read the fiction and decide it would be profitable and fun to make it real. I knew it. Somewhere in the world, a crazy doctor used the story as a blueprint and made serious coin by creating these sex slaves.

What did Harvey say?

There's one in Montana.

If there was anything I could do, this doctor was a dead man.

I pulled on a t-shirt, pajama bottoms and fuzzy slippers. While sipping my coffee, I decided to visit my safe room.

It took a palm print and retina scan to enter. Inside, I looked around. I was done playing. I had a lot of expensive toys.

Hanging on a rack: Kevlar hat and overcoat. It looked bulky but would not draw attention on the street because in the cold, damp Pacific Northwest, there were heavy wool coats everywhere. One coat sleeve housed a taser, 50kV. The other sleeve had a projectile weapon. 40 caliber loaded with mushroom tip cartridges.

In a pocket, my favorite weapon made of ceramic, copper wire and a captive iron rod. I could easily carry the parts on an airplane and assemble it—a portable bolt gun like in the Movie *No Country for Old Men*. What a chilling scene. I loved it.

Anton Chigurh: Would you hold still, please?

Under the rack: steel toe boots. Hanging beside the coat: tactical gloves.

The gloves were my pride and joy. By tracing a pattern on my palm with a thumb, Kevlar barbs popped out. Stabbing them in, then withdrawing them fast, I could pull a pound of bloody flesh from anyone messing with me. I hadn't tried them yet, but I was eager.

There were stacks of gold bars and rolls of gold coins. Water and dried food to last at least six months. In a corner, a nitrogen tank. I could flood the suite and, unless the bad guys wore oxy masks, the gas would knock them out. If they didn't get fresh air fast, they would peacefully die.

See?

I was ready for anything.

Suddenly, there came a loud beeping and all the video screens in my apartment displayed the scene in the hallway. A tactical team was preparing to break down my door.

Shit!

These guys were seriously armed to the teeth—dressed in ninja black with helmets, visors, boots and gloves. There were at least eight of them. A big fella deployed an EOD door ram—the big one, 32 pounds. It would go through my armored door like it was cardboard.

My first thought was to use the ladder to the parking garage, but I remembered Violet's warning. Standing on the trap door, I could hear them coming up. I had maybe thirty seconds. I grabbed my get-out-of-Dodge knapsack and stuffed in the photo album. I had one more escape route. Outside the window of my bathroom, I had a rope with a rappelling mechanism. I grabbed the handle with both hands and took a deep breath.

I hoped this would work.

I'd never tried it.

As the front door crashed in, I leaned out and the mechanism engaged. A little faster than I liked, I dropped to the ground and hit the sidewalk in a passageway. By the time I hit the ground, the friction mechanism was smoking hot. I felt the jolt in my hips—which would punish me later.

In my pajama pants and fuzzy slippers, I jogged through a narrow passage away from my apartment. It was fifty meters to the back of a coffee shop where I looked both ways. The street was quiet. I turned left. I looked silly, but not out of the ordinary for a Sunday morning in this neighborhood. Walking around, there were often women in robes with their hair in curlers seeking steamed drinks. I fit in okay.

I didn't know where to go. Obviously, I couldn't go to my office. Along with the photo album, my knapsack held a burner phone, credit cards, a fresh passport and cash. I could walk to Bellevue Square and book a Lyft to the Paine Field airport and catch the first leg of flights to get me to El Salvador or Belize.

While thinking about this, an old pickup truck pulled up next to me. Belying the truck's crusty exterior, its exhaust system rumbled smoothly.

It was an old Ford restomod with a rusty patina paintjob gleaming under a clearcoat.

The driver leaned over and pushed the door open.

"Get in," he said. "I'm Viktor."

WALES DETECTIVES
INVESTIGATIONS
CRIMINAL, CIVIL AND DOMESTIC
CONFIDENTIAL REPORTS
1007 Riverside Dr.
1830 SUNSET BOULEVARD
LOS ANGELES 26
OPERATIVE

Chapter 20

I STUDIED THE young man; he looked just like his sister. A little bigger and muscular, though still skinny and Violet didn't have a scraggly beard, but they were clearly twins. Viktor and Violet. Their parents had a sense of humor, at least.

His longish auburn hair poured out of a bright red Tindle Foods trucker hat.

Like all real men, I liked old trucks. This one had bucket seats and a three on the tree transmission. We looked out through a cracked windshield.

"Nice truck," I said.

"1963 Ford F100 stepside—before the fuckers ruined everything with emissions controls. A beater truck like this is invisible. I mean that literally, women can't see it and millennial men are almost as bad. It's weird."

I could tell already—he was the gabby type.

"How did you find me?"

"BW."

BlueWaive. Fuck me. That thing was everywhere.

He continued, "I figured you wouldn't go the other way in your secret passage. When I saw the flash-bangs, I waited two minutes—and there you were, right on schedule." He pointed at my knapsack. "You bring the picture album?"

"Yeah," I said.

"Nice slippers," he said.

I glanced down. They were fuzzy blue slip-ons. I didn't give a shit what they looked like, they were comfortable.

"When it's safe, I will go back to my apartment and change."

He looked at me with wonder.

"Go back? Take a look."

I rolled down the window and adjusted the mirror. I got a glimpse. The top of my building was on fire.

"Jesus-fuck."

"If you were a little slower, you'd be a crispy critter. Violet is right, you're a lucky dog."

He looked me over.

"There's a fake beard and hat in the glovebox."

I opened the dashboard cubby and pulled out the hat. Marshal Grain, Fort Worth, Texas. The beard was ridiculous. It was long and bushy with hooks that went over the ears. With the hat, I'd look Amish. With the PJs and slippers, I'd look demented.

"You sure about this?" I asked.

He shrugged.

"Right now, the last person you want to look like is yourself."

Feeling like a knob, I put on the disguise.

"Move the mirror back to where it was and put on your seatbelt. We're gonna put mileage on."

He pulled onto I-90, eastbound.

"We'll stop for gas at the Eagle in Ellensburg—get you overalls and rubber boots. We'll get real boots later. Maybe in Spokane. So, what do you think? Are you motivated?"

I thought about the Lolita Sex Slaves.

"I don't know what to think. What about these sex slaves? Do you think they are real?"

He looked at me with an expression I could not read.

"Ah," he said. "Sex slaves. Our books are different. For me, it was Tommy Molesta. Get it? Molesta? That's what we call him. I will kill that sex-trafficking motherfucker."

"I don't understand why you need me."

He looked at me like I was crazy.

"It's your money, my man. We're broke. I spent my last cash on this truck…and that fake beard. You're going to finance our adventure."

"I am, am I?"

His response was mumbled and barely audible over the truck motor.

"Yes, you are. I will help you, then you will help me."

Whatever he was thinking, it kept him quiet for a few tens of miles. I was grateful. It gave me time to think—mainly about Violet. The most visceral memory was her smell. If I could bottle and sell it, I'd make another billion.

He cleared his throat.

"So, you knew Banks back when, eh? What was he like?"

Banks? What's with the fascination? No one ever asked about what I was like. I had a million questions and wasn't in the mood for talking about Harvey Banks.

"Fuck Banks. Tell me everything. I don't understand what is going on."

"I don't know everything either. I worked as a researcher for LC. Lyle. Grunt work. V worked for him, too, part time. Want to know why he hired me? BlueWaive made it happen. I was motivated because of our neighbor. Violet's besty, Lola. She was eight when she was taken…and ten when her body was found. What they did to her. Fuck. They cut out her heart, man. We didn't know about that until later. She was a kid, and it could just as easily have been V—or me, they didn't care. Boys, girls? They probably got more cash for parting out little boys. It happens all the time. Nondescript cargo van with phony business graphics, like air conditioner repair or some goddamned thing. Padded inside with carpet to deaden the noise. What was the bait? Ice cream? Cotton candy? A puppy or kitten? It doesn't matter. They grabbed her and she was gone, man. They sold her. Her body was found in Fort Wayne. They use them up, then harvest their organs. That fucked us up. BW sent LC an email, made it look like it was from me. Of course, I was inclined to help. Motivated. We worked for almost nothing and were happy to do it. LC, he had stones. Made a lot of powerful enemies and they got him.

One shot, back of the head."

"I heard they ate him."

"Yeah, after they shot him, but who knows? BW makes up shit to manipulate us. It doesn't matter. All I care about is Molesta and his brother. I want them to die screaming." He paused to take a deep breath. "This is ugly and we'll talk it through, but not now, okay? We'll have plenty of time to talk. Tell me about Banks."

Plenty of time?

"What do you mean, we have time? How far are we going?"

"Billings."

"Billings in Montana? That Billings?"

Again, I got the look. He spoke patiently—as if I was a dimwit.

"Yes, Billings in Montana."

"What's there?"

"At least *try* to keep up. That's where we'll find your Lolita doctor."

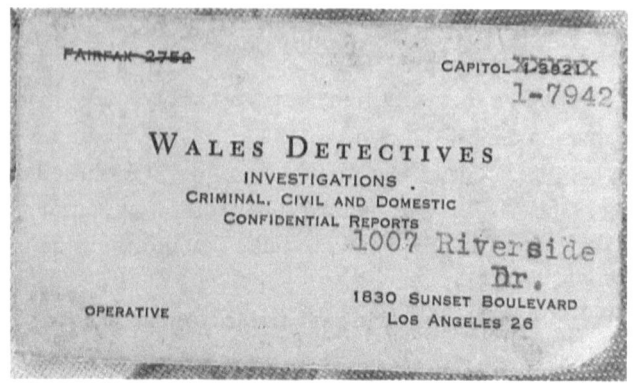

WALES DETECTIVES
INVESTIGATIONS .
CRIMINAL, CIVIL AND DOMESTIC
CONFIDENTIAL REPORTS

1007 Riverside Dr.

1830 SUNSET BOULEVARD
LOS ANGELES 26

Chapter 21

THE STOP IN Ellensburg was uneventful. After he asked for a hundred bucks which I fished out of my knapsack, Viktor went in to buy bib overalls and rubber mud boots. After wrestling in the cab, I was able to change my clothes. I stuffed the pajamas and fuzzy slippers in an overflowing trash barrel. No one paid inordinate attention to a bearded man in overalls. In fact, I fit right in. Things got rural fast outside of the Seattle metro area.

We had burgers and fries in the rundown restaurant. I paid, of course. Viktor showed me his wallet. He had one lonely dollar.

Why this was my problem, I didn't know. I shouldn't care. Every rich guy I knew was somewhat of a cheapskate. That's one of the reasons they got rich. I didn't mind spending money on myself. Everyone else? Spend your own damned money.

Soon enough, we were back on the road—headed east. This stretch of highway, except for the Columbia River gorge, was flat and monotonous. Viktor held the rickety truck exactly at the speed limit—only passing when an 18-wheeler truck plodded along upgrades too slowly for his taste.

"Doesn't this thing go any faster?" I said.

I was getting used to this—he looked at me like I was retarded.

"It has an LS3 engine from an old Corvette. It will do 90, easy, but we're keeping a low profile."

"Fine, but I'm bored. Tell me what we're doing."

"We'll kill your Lolita doctor, then you'll help me kill Tommy Molesta."

"I don't know about killing anyone. If this guy really exists, maybe we take pictures and fileshare them with the police. Anonymously. I haven't killed anyone yet and I'd like to keep it that way. Murderers go to jail. I don't care to go to jail."

"The police won't do shit. Ever hear of Soros DAs?"

"No."

"Look it up. If you have a confederate flag, they'll lock you up and throw away the key. If you're a pedo in their inner circle, they will protect you. To be successful in any of the blue-dot cities, you pretty much have to be a MAP or worse."

"What's a MAP?"

He grunted in exploration.

"You really don't know anything. How do you function in society? MAP is Minor-Attracted Person. They have their own flag with shades of blue and pink—you can figure that part out. Technically, call them hebephiles. That means sexually attracted to pubescent children and early adolescents. Eventually they'll get added to the LGBTQQIP2SAA alphabet soup. For now, some call themselves NOMAPs. Non-Offending. This means they are attracted, but don't act on that attraction. Buy that? They are attracted, but won't act on the urge? It roils my stomach to think about this stuff. Let's talk about something else."

"I don't understand why the Feds and RatWeb are after me."

"The Federal government has their own AIs. They flagged you as a threat to powerful people. RatWeb has a different agenda—businesses to protect. Once they figure out how dangerous you are, they will kill you too."

"I'm not dangerous. I'm just a guy with resources and limited freedom to operate."

"Do you realize how unusual that is? Look at me. Look at the world. Most people are wage slaves. Cattle. NPCs. They trade their souls for a life of quiet desperation. Me? I'd like to kill every sex-trafficking motherfucker in the world, but I have no money and no power. Still, BW reached into the genpop and plucked me. It manipulates me for its own mysterious, deux-ex-machina reasons. I don't know why. I'm in the dark as much as you are."

"Okay, I said. "Let's do it this way. Tell me your story from day one and I'll sort it all out. Okay?"

"Yes, but here's the deal. In return, you tell me about Banks. He's interesting."

Fucking Banks. Everyone wants his story. I'm more interesting, but no one cares about me.

"Fine, I'll tell you everything I know, but prepare yourself for disappointment—up close, he's not that scintillating. So, spill it. What's your deal?"

"As I said, V and I grew up in a comfortable, middleclass neighborhood. Cincinnati. Our dad was an insurance salesman. Mom took care of us and the house and bought and sold figurines. Mainly Swiss and Austrian ones. Rarities. Boys in lederhosen and girls with bunnies, that kind of thing."

"I don't give a shit about figurines."

Viktor seemed hurt.

"Those things were popular and her business grew. There were years when she made more money than dad. They would go to Europe, buy them in pawn shops and ship them home by the dozens. The ones Hitler liked were the most popular."

"I don't care about figurines," I repeated.

"I'm telling you about our life. Do you want to hear it or not?"

I hated wasting time on trivia, but I pushed my anger down and spoke as calmly as I could.

"Go on with it, I'm listening."

"I'm not sure you understand. We didn't have swastikas in the basement or anything like that, but there were collectors who paid good money for porcelain Aryan figurines. White, blonde, blue-eyed. I'm not saying my parents were Nazis. But I'm not saying they weren't. I'll let you read between the lines."

"What does this have to do with anything?"

"You asked me to tell our story. I'm telling you, so shut up. Where was I? I told you about our neighbor, Lola. That was a big deal in Mount Lookout. Mom flipped out and Dad would do anything to keep peace in the home. Mom knew how random this thing was—how it could easily have been V who was taken. Then, when Lola's body was found, Mom took it really hard. She went nuts and spent all her time trying to find the creeps. Remember, this was just as cellphones, the Internet and AI were starting. Mom knew all the police detectives, knew their home addresses and their kids' names, everything. And, of course, some of the cops were customers—*Porzellanfabrik Edelsteinfigurine* collectors. She used every bit of leverage she could. She was the brains and Dad was the muscle."

Staring at the road with his mind a million miles away, Viktor fell silent.

"Don't leave me hanging. What happened? Nothing?"

Viktor turned to me.

"Nothing? You don't know my mother. She was relentless. Dad joined the pedo clubs and worked his way into the loose organizations. The rituals. The rites. It took over five years, but they found the team and the leaders who nabbed Lola."

"They turned them in?" I said. "Let the police have them? I don't remember hearing anything about this in the news."

"News? You really are clueless. The news. What a joke. The news is gaslight. Propaganda. Smokescreen. The first layer of protection. The cops did everything they could do to hide this. They don't want the public doing police work. They don't want vigilantes and they don't want anyone to know how inept and corrupt they are. Mom and Dad killed them—killed them all. And one of the ring leaders was a cop, get it? They cut their throats and stabbed them with, get this, Hitler Youth daggers. Dad had a bunch of them in his collection. *Blut* und *Ehre*. Bood and Honor. Whether Mom planned all this out, I don't know, but no one wanted the public to know that a bloodthirsty bunch of Nazis were killing pedophiles. Who do you root for in a situation like that? Anyway, eighteen dead and Mom was done. So far as I know, that was it. Later, at 69, Dad died from a heart attack and a few years later, Mom died in an Alzheimer memory center. Case closed. For several years afterward, kids in our Cincinnati suburb were safe. Of course, the creeps slowly came back, but we were trained. The fuzzy kitten in the back of a van ploy was not going to get us. V and me weren't as bloodthirsty as mom and dad, but we wanted to help. Then, BW linked us up with Lyle and we worked for him. You know how he started, right? His vigilante paedophile hunter thing?"

"There are lot of those things on YouTube and Rumble. In the last 24 hours, I've seen them."

"Back then, Lyle was one of the first. You've met V, she's cute, right? And, she was really good at catfishing pedos."

"I think she catfished me."

"No, you're something different. I don't know exactly what she's thinking, but she likes you. One thing you should know about V. She's smart. Smarter than you and me put together."

"I have a big IQ."

"No offense intended, but you're one of those IYI intellectual idiots. Go ahead. Underestimate her and see where that road leads, moron. I've lost my plot—where was I?"

"Catfishing."

"Right. Okay. As long as Lyle targeted little fish, he was safe, but he got bored with catching schoolteachers and real estate agents. A lot of them got off anyway. Some cops helped, but some Judges seemed strangely uninterested. The same goes for District Attorneys. Some pressed the cases, but others buried them. Corruption is endemic. Lyle set his sights higher, even helping to take down Molesta's buddy Dennis Hastert wasn't enough. He wanted to reach out and touch the untouchables. He really got into the Pizzagate stuff. He was relentless. It was obvious. The only way to stop him was to kill him. So, they did. V and I watched things up close and personal and paid attention. We drew our own conclusion."

"What conclusion?"

"You don't know? We decided mom and dad were right. The only way to stop these perverts is to kill them. Literally stab them in their black fucking hearts. We'd do everything we could to not get caught, but we'd fucking kill the motherfuckers. But, we had one big problem."

"Oh, yeah? What problem is that?"

"We're fucking broke. Dirt poor. Tapped out. We need

cash. BlueWaive knew this, found you and linked us up. We'll help with your Lolita guy, then you'll help us. With your cash, we're back in business."

"I don't know about any of this. Maybe I will go back to my office and video games."

"You'd be dead in a week—just for general principles. And that's not the biggest reason you won't go back."

I let the silence unfold for several miles.

"Okay, tell me. What's the biggest reason I won't go back?"

Spread across his face, Viktor's grin was confident.

I didn't like it.

"It's V. If you disappoint her, you'll never see her again. That would be sad. She's not playing—she really likes you."

Fuck me, he was right.

"Okay, tell me about Violet."

"I don't want to ruin your joy of exploration, but I'll tell you this. I already said she's smart. In addition, she's fierce. Brutal against her enemies…like a lion or a mongoose. A hyena. She won't give up. Never. But she's also fiercely loyal. For the time she's with you, she'd take a bullet for you, man. Literally."

"You make it sound like she'll be impossible to please."

"You're already in, bro. Just don't fuck it up."

"How do I do that?"

"Give her everything you have and never lie to her. Make sure every word out of your mouth is true—that's it. Simple."

Right.

Simple, like many things in life.

Simple, but not easy.

"When will I see her?"

"After we deal with Dr. Lolita. she'll give your balls a good workout. Okay, no more questions—it's your turn."

My mind was fully on Violet. My testicles yearned for her. My soul yearned for her.

We stared at the endless road for a few long minutes before Viktor spoke again.

"Did you hear me? Your turn. Spill."

I felt groggy and disconnected.

"Spill what?"

"You're hopeless, aren't you? Banks. Tell me about Banks."

I knew the mysterious Harvey Elliot Banks before he became the 7th richest man in the world. After all the shit I did on my own, was that all I would ever be known for?

I could see myself in a hospice bed after a long life. The caretakers ushering me into the great beyond would ask me about HEB…the only thing they care about.

So it goes.

For the millionth time, I told the story.

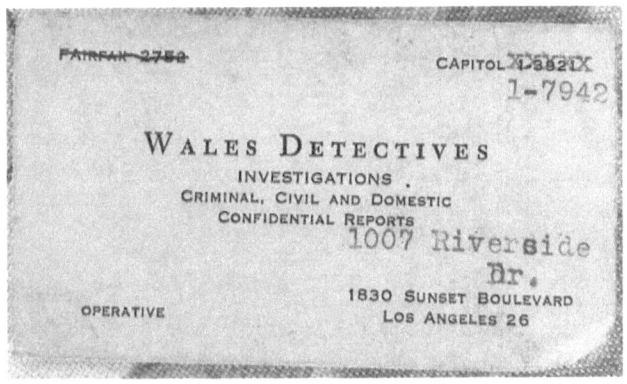

Chapter 22

THE FIRST TIME I met Harvey Elliott Banks was in the first grade at Benson Hill Elementary School in Renton, Washington. We were six. Even then, he assumed he was important and that's the way he introduced himself...with all three names like he was afraid of being confused with all the ordinary Harvey Banks in the world. Being a smartass and liking big words, I said something about him being impetuous. Gently, he corrected me. He said *imperious* is what I meant.

He was right, of course.

Like now, he was quiet and never drew attention to himself. But, even then, it was obvious he was smart. Super smart. While the other kids, including me, played on their Schwinn wheelie bikes with ape-hanger handlebars, he was at the library, reading. Once, when were eight or so, I asked him about his biggest thrill. He said, 'Picking a book at random from the library shelf and having it be a grand one.'

Weirdo, right?

His parents were smart—his dad worked as an electrical engineer at Boeing and his stay-at-home mom played clarinet with the regional symphony. They lived comfortably in the Renton Highlands, but their three-bedroom rambler was nothing fancy. His dad drove a 1966 Dodge Dart. After civilization collapses, the only things still moving will be cockroaches and slant-six Dodge Darts.

They spent their money on books, French wine and Harvey's violin lessons. He was good and practiced diligently, but it wasn't a passion.

Through elementary and middle school, he aced everything with no apparent effort. He caused no trouble and was unfailingly polite—teachers loved him.

We weren't close. He wasn't close to anyone. But, I stole a copy of Ayn Rand's *The Fountainhead* from my dad's collection and loaned it to Harvey. My dad said the story was about a doomed architect standing up for hopeless principle and I thought Harvey might like it. I was right—Harvey loved that book. I don't know why, I never read it. You can never tell when a silly little thing can influence the future. Flapping butterfly wings causing hurricanes—that sort of thing.

There were jealous kids who didn't like him—that's inevitable, right? For one thing, some jocks didn't like being reminded of how stupid they were.

Harvey wasn't a practical joker. He didn't waste time on the trivial, but I remember the football field goal kicker. A pompous ass. For some reason, his name is etched in memory. Alphonse Garcia. He picked on Harvey, pinched his cheeks, slapped him on the ass and called him the Mayor of Nerdton and dumb shit like that. After melting down a hundred one-pound fishing weights, Harvey molded a lead football—it was perfect, painted to look like leather. From a foot away, it looked real.

Harvey paid Cal Wilson twenty dollars to put it on a kickoff tee by the football field goal post. Cal was a huge, muscular guy. No one messed with him. That was it. The ball just sat there. When Alphonse saw it, he couldn't resist. He got a running start and kicked the fake ball with everything he had. It hardly moved, just toppled off the tee. That was the end of Alphonse's football career—as far as I know, he's still hobbling with a crippled right foot while pushing around waste cans as a middle school janitor.

Everyone knew what Harvey did, but Cal said nothing and there were no consequences. Ten years later when Harvey got his first tranche of fuck-you money, he gave a million to Cal, but that was later. Back then, Harvey was mostly left alone. As a mousy little guy, it was easy to forget he was around.

He had an uncle who worked for Bell Labs. Aaron Watson. Aaron was an early investor in Apple stock. When Aaron died of cancer when we were 10, he angered his wives and children by leaving his portfolio to Harvey. His parents didn't cash out, so a few years later, Harvey was rich. They borrowed against the holding to move Harvey to boarding school—the elite EF Academy in Pasadena. Who even knew about a place like that? Expensive. Generally, Harvey was meek, but he said he wouldn't go unless I went, too.

Why? It was *The Fountainhead*. I'd forgotten about it until Harvey mentioned it years later. Ayn Rand got me into boarding school. Someday I'll have to return the favor and read one of her books. Maybe. They don't seem like much fun.

The school was a wonder. Some of the classes were just me and Harvey. As long as he studied something, no one bothered him. He'd write an essay now and then and the instructors left us alone. I felt inadequate. From around the world, there were tons of smart kids here. From Japan. Saudi Arabia. Finland. Harvey didn't care—he didn't even notice; he lived his whole life between his ears.

While he worked on weekends, I would take a bus to Venice Beach to cadge beer and try pick up girls. The LA waterfront is seedy now, but back then, it was magical.

Don't get me wrong. I knew I was lucky to be there and took a bunch of college prep classes. I worked my ass off and struggled to keep up. Advanced Placement Biology, Calculus, Chemistry, Physics, Statistics and Psychology. I was solid B student while Harvey aced everything without trying. He studied classes he didn't need to take and loved them. The ones I remember him talking about were Comparative Government and Politics, English Language and Composition and Human Geography. His mind soaked in everything.

EF is a prep school. I was preparing for college while he was preparing to take over the world.

A few years later, I went to Stanford and did okay. He paid for it, of course, because I still didn't have any money. He didn't care about college credentials, but he lived with me in a funky Palo Alto apartment and audited a bunch of classes. While I tried to sleep, he had long, deep conversations with people like Doug Hofstadter, Sigourney Weaver, Hans Moravec, Tom Sowell, Stewart Brand, Reed Hastings, TJ Rodgers, Peter Thiel, crap, there were always people around drinking his wine and talking about esoteric bullshit that was way over my head.

What is it you hope to learn?

Are you curious about the wild nights, the blurred lines, and the music that never seemed to end?

Now and then, he played around with psychedelics, but he didn't like anything that fogged his mind. Weed was not his thing. He liked wine, but I never saw him drink more than three glasses at a sitting. Crazy about nicotine—that was his ADHD treatment of choice. He was generally quiet, but he had loud friends. Try to sleep when you have a nine-o'clock class and he and Elon—I call him the Mollusk—smoked cigars in our tiny apartment while laughing like hyenas.

A few girls came and went, but mainly he took his pleasure from the hot Thai girls at the Ananya massage joint across the Bayshore Highway. Once or twice a week was enough to keep him going—he said it was efficient. No time wasted. And, not that he really cared, but he didn't want to waste money, either.

Okay, that's all that comes to mind. You want to know Harvey? Good luck. No one really knows him. I doubt if he knows himself. His mind is everywhere and all over the place.

Is he a nice guy?

He's been good to me, but Hitler's dog thought Adolphe was a good guy. I'm not sure what else to tell you. Let's get all this out. If you have questions, ask them so we can put the topic behind us. Please.

Chapter 23

AS I TALKED, the miles rolled under the truck tires while we passed through Spokane and crossed the border into Idaho. Behind us, the sun, low on the horizon, peeked through the clouds.

"I'm tired of this rattletrap truck. Let's stop for the night in the next town."

"Okay," Viktor said. "Coeur d'Alene. CdA. They'll take cash at the Budget Saver Motel. They can find anyone, but there's no sense in making it easy."

I hoped he was kidding.

"Fuck that. My credit cards can't be traced back to me." I clicked around on my phone. "The Lakeside looks nice. They will have clean sheets and fewer bedbugs. Take the Fourth Street exit."

Initially, he didn't like the idea, but as he considered it, slowly warmed up.

After winding our way to the waterfront, we found the hotel and he pulled the old truck into the last available spot. I lifted the handle to open the door, but he put a hand on my arm and stopped me. From behind the seat, he pulled out a canvas bag full of wigs.

"I'm not wearing a wig," I said.

"Fine, but let's not be stupid."

He tugged my hat down and handed me a pair of garish,

wrap-around mirror sunglasses.

"Is this really necessary?"

He shrugged.

"Facial recognition," he said. "There are cameras everywhere."

We looked like a couple of hayseed bozos, but not that unusual for the area. In Idaho, there are a lot of rich potato farmers.

I rented a three-bedroom suite with a lake view. Highway robbery—over a thousand dollars for the night, but what does that mean to me? And the view? At night, the lights on the lake were beautiful, but we could only see a sliver from the balcony. I didn't care—I was more interested in whether the nearby Honey Bar had Laughing Dog Amber Ale on tap. They did. I ordered a pint and a pile of sloppy BBQ chicken wings. I was happy.

"I wish Violet was here."

"She doesn't drink beer and hates smoky bars," Viktor said.

"Well, fuck," I said. "I guess no one is truly perfect."

"She'll be waiting for us in Billings. She's doing prep work."

"I can't wait to see her."

Viktor tapped me on the hand.

"We need to talk."

This is never good.

"We've been talking all day."

He looked around. No one paid any attention to us.

"Things will get serious. Life and death serious and I don't think you are up to the task. You will have to act without hesitation."

I raised my beer in salute.

"Never put off until tomorrow that which can be put off until the day after."

"BlueWaive says it's unlikely you'll be alive in week. I don't care, but I don't want you dragging V to hell with you. We're making powerful enemies. RatWeb sells the Lolitas—this is lucrative for them. The Feds blackmail the sex doll owners and control them. We're kicking a hornet's nest."

"Let's forget the whole thing. I'll take Violet to Monaco.

No, Lake Como. We'll get married in a cathedral."

"Shut up. We're way past that now. This is no game. We're taking V to the Lolita doctor. That's how we get in. She's too old to be one of the dolls, but we'll sell this as a custom job—punishment for a bitchy wife going after a tech-bro's money. The doctor has security. Four guys. We polataze them, then flexcuff them. It's up to you if we leave them alive. The most humane way to kill is to stun, then cut their throats."

"Wait, are you serious? I'm not killing anyone."

"Your mission, your parameters. If you prefer it, we can leave them alive to come after us later."

"Fuck this. I'm tired of worrying about what BW thinks. How can it possibly know anything?"

"It calculates, that's what it does. 24-7. It says you either get tough or get dead. I don't know if that is right, but the AIs assume we live in a simulation and the future can not only be predicted but programmed. BW doesn't have arms or legs. We're its arms and legs."

I imagined doing it. A shiver ran up my spine. Gripping a knife and cutting. After I imagined doing it, I imagined it happening to me. Fuck. That would be horrible. A nightmare. Blood everywhere and gasping for breath. I could feel the sharp steel slicing through my flesh. That is one of my problems. My imagination is vivid. Too vivid.

I'd rather die peacefully at a ripe old age in a hot tub with Violet straddling me. Post coital with champagne and caviar at my elbow. My heart giving out in a flashflood of soul-ripping pain, then gentle nothing.

"I can't cut any throats."

"BW agrees. You're soft. A fucking pussy. That's why your odds are long."

I studied the swirling clouds in my beer.

"Fuck this. If you just need money, I'll transfer what you need. I'm out."

He laughed. It was an unpleasant laugh—cold and harsh.

"Money is the easiest thing in the world to trace. We're safer being broke and letting you pay for everything. They might find you, but we'll have a chance to slide. If you want to bail, then bail. V and I will skip your Lotita doctor and move along to Tommy Molesta. Your call."

Viktor knew how to suck the life out of a party. I drained my beer and waved the empty glass at our server. She was attentive and prompt. I stared at the fresh glass with its foamy head and carbon dioxide bubbles rising in the amber fluid. I pointed.

"We're like these bubbles. Meaningless. We do what we're programmed by physics to do and no one cares."

"Feel sorry for yourself later. When we get to Billings, there's a lot to do."

After pushing aside our plate of congealing chicken wings, salt and pepper shakers and a greasy ketchup bottle, he produced a map and spread it out on the table.

"All we know for now is the doctor is in the rural Billings area…"

After dropping a wad of cash on the table, I pushed back my chair and stood up.

"No maps," I said. "Not tonight."

Despondent, I walked back to our hotel suite. After fumbling with the key card, I barely got to the toilet in time. I heaved up a disgusting mixture of beer and chicken wings. It was gross. Filling a glass sanitized for my protection, I rinsed and spat, then flushed.

Sitting on the bathroom floor, I could see my bed.

A black box. One of those secure terminals…or the same one, maybe. How did it get here? I could see myself getting up and throwing it off the balcony. That was one branch of an alternate future. I could take a Lyft to the Spokane airport. From there, in twenty-four hours, I could be anywhere in the world. Dubai. Thailand. Perth. Montreux. Fairbanks.

I could see it vividly. It was real. Fairbanks, Alaska. I'd be drinking a hot toddy—after watching the bartender mix the bourbon, honey, lemon and steaming hot water. I could see the weird copper sculptures on the wall and the hurricane lanterns on the tables. In the bar mirror, I could see the escort girl giggling and pretending to be innocent. Her online profile said she was 22, but that was at least ten years ago—ten brutal years servicing North Slope oilfield roughnecks and Kinross Fort Knox gold miners. But who cares? She had the right to make money on her back and I had the right to pretend she was an innocent cheerleader—as if there is such a thing.

From a window facing north, I could be all up in her lady parts while the snow falls and the neon green Northern lights dance on the horizon. Unbidden, my fantasy changed.

It was Violet sitting next to me drinking hot tea and playing Scrabble on her phone.

I rinsed and spit again, then got up and walked past the bed to the balcony—trying not to look at the terminal box.

Outside, the wind had picked up and it was cold. I had no idea what to do. I looked at the lake. The wind chopped the black surface into white caps. There was no inspiration there. The black dog of depression threatened to eat me alive—inky fingers were eager to knead all hope out of my soggy brain.

I was truly losing my mind.

I turned back to the bed. Along with the terminal, there was a folder. In the folder, there was a stack of photographs. I didn't want to look at them, but I did.

The first few were snapshots of little girls at playgrounds or Chucky Cheese pizza places and the like. One was a birthday party with five crooked candles on a storebought cake. I knew where this was headed. I wanted to stop looking and scatter the pictures to the wind.

Why is this my problem?

I knew the answer. Violet was right. I had freedom and the power of money to do something. What I lacked was will.

I leafed through the photographs—which got more and more disturbing. They turned into darkweb catalog entries with names, descriptions and prices.

Karla, hanging from silver chains with O-rings in place of hands and feet. With shiny brown hair hanging down, her sewed-shut eyes were turned toward the camera. Ten-years-old. A virgin. Her tiny, hairless body was smooth and gleaming brown as if oiled. $85,000 delivered anywhere in the world.

I couldn't read her expression.

What must it be like?

Blind. Deafened. Traumatized. Was she angry? Did she remember anything about being a real girl? Or, was she happy to have any kind of life?

At this point, was she better off alive or dead?

I couldn't decide.

It hit me hard.

The next set of pictures was an older girl—maybe 16. Angel, heavily pregnant, had ponderous breasts and tufts of hair under her arms and at her groin. $33,000 and the buyer could keep the baby for free.

Did she feel anything for her baby? If she was free and had help, could she have any kind of a decent life? Could she raise her child and find joy, or was she better off put down like an animal? At least the baby deserved a chance.

If I continued along the highway with Viktor, literally, this would be a decision I would have to make. Let her live or end her suffering?

Though there was nothing in my stomach, I felt sick again. Hanging my head over the toilet bowl, all I could heave up was yellow bile. My head throbbed.

Viktor came in the room and stared at me and the scattered photographs for a few seconds, then went to the minibar and brought out a cold bottle of five-dollar water. He twisted off the cap and handed the bottle to me. I sucked down half.

Decision time.

"Let's kill that motherfucker," I said.

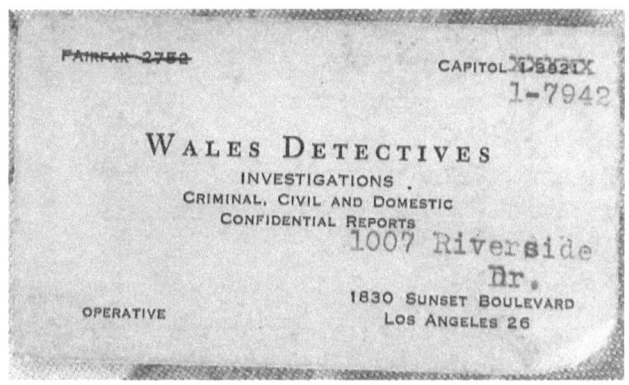

Chapter 24

IN THE MORNING, my head was fuzzy, but Viktor handed me a strong cup of Starbucks breakfast blend coffee and quickly, I felt nearly human.

"I'll bet the breakfasts are good here," I said. "I'm in the mood for blueberry pancakes and a mountain of maple-bacon."

"Fuck you—you'll get a genetically modified McDonald's breakfast with broad-spectrum glyphosate from the drive through and be happy."

I liked Viktor okay, but he wasn't a barrel of laughs.

"Fine," I said. "But after, we're going to Starbucks and that's not negotiable."

"McDonalds coffee is good, but we can make an unnecessary stop at burnt-coffee Starfucks if you insist."

For the first hour of our drive, Viktor didn't say anything, but just after we crossed the border into Montana, he said, "I need walking-around money. Cash."

"How much?"

"BW suggests fifty-thousand. We'll duplicate some of the weapons from your cache. It's cash for your cache."

He thought the play on words was funny. Giggling like a schoolgirl, he almost spilled furnace-hot McDonalds coffee. There were no cup holders in this relic of a truck.

Hot coffee broiling his groin…that would be funny.

"That's a lot of cheddar. If I cared about money, I'd be angry." I sipped my Starbucks espresso with extra heavy cream. "I'm tired of BW micromanaging us."

He shrugged.

"AIs have access to everything online and they are good for planning. We do what we're told…that's the best way."

"We elevated AIs into gods."

"Can you scour the data of the whole world in any language? Can you evaluate millions of potential scenarios in seconds? They don't sleep. Without emotion, they apply ruthless rules of logic."

"They are tools. We designed them. We programmed them."

"No, we created them and then set them free."

"If I could, I'd pull the plug."

He laughed.

"Good luck with that," he said. "They're distributed now. Even if you shut down half the data centers, BW would slow down but would still be fully functional."

We rode in silence until we got to Billings. Following navigation instructions coming from his phone, we stopped in front of a FedEx Print and Ship store.

"What's this?" I said.

"They used to be called Kinko's. That name came from the founder—because of Paul Orfalea's red, kinky hair."

"I know that, asshole. Everyone does. What are we doing here?"

"Oh. BW filled out a bank form and withdrawal request for you. IRS Form 8300. Sign it, and when you walk in, hand over the form and your passport. They will still ask a hundred questions, but you'll eventually get the cash."

"I don't get it."

Viktor sighed…an over-dramatic, impatient and exaggerated one.

"Files were electronically transferred to this location. They were printed. They are inside waiting for you. The bill is paid. You just go in, tell them your name, show them your passport and they will give you a packet."

It went just as he described. I walked to the cash register, waited for my turn, showed my passport and walked out with a thick wad of papers.

Back in the truck, I said, "What is all this?"

"All kinds of things," he said. "For one thing, a rental agreement for the house. And a list of things we're anonymously buying from ads in the Thrifty Nickel."

"Rental? What rental?"

"We have a place across the river with a workshop because we need to assemble some of the gear. It's nice—you'll like it because there's plenty of room to mope around and be a moron."

"What's the Thrifty Nickel?"

"It's a local classified ad newspaper they give away for free at Circle K. It's a way to buy weapons without paperwork when you pay a hundred more than the seller asks for. BW also bought some stuff on Craigslist we need to pick up. Any more stupid questions before we go to the bank?"

I gave him a few seconds to study my middle finger.

He started the truck and we followed Laurel until it turned into Montana Avenue, then he pulled into the parking lot of the US Bank.

"Get thirty in cash and transfer twenty to this account."

"I changed my mind. Fuck off. You can't have my money."

"The account is BlueWaive's. It loaned us money, the twenty pays it back." He glanced at me. "Don't give me attitude, dude. At the rate we're spending, you'll still have money in 200 years."

"Why doesn't BW steal its own money?"

Viktor thought it over.

"Probably because it doesn't want the JPMorgan Chase AI up its ass. The big-bank AIs are seriously vindictive."

This shut me up. That could really be it. Beside me, I didn't know anyone as aggressive about staying away from the big banks and Central Bank Digital Currencies…get crosswise with Bank of America, The ICA (Industrial-Commercial-Agricultural) Bank of China or the dot-Indian HDFC and you're in serious trouble. Politicians and the global elite liked to do business in private crypto, so the powers-that-be left the distributed blockchain currencies like Bitcoin, CryptD'oh and Etherium alone. As long as U.S. Senators and Federal judges took their kickbacks and bribes in digicoins, my wealth was safe.

Visualizing Princess hanging from her chains—I imagined what the world was like from her point of view. Deaf and blind with painful, traumatic wounds slowly healing. Did she know what happened? Did it all seem like an endless nightmare? Could she enjoy pleasure of any kind? The doctor could dose her with a fentanyl patch and rub warm oils on her body. She probably liked that a lot. She would be used as a sex toy. In sensory deprivation, would that bring her pleasure? The idea made me sick and angry.

If this was what it took to bring vengeance to the butcher-doctor, I would do it.

I gathered the paperwork and walked into the bank.

Viktor was right, they asked a hundred questions twenty different ways, but a half hour later, I was back at the truck with banded stacks of hundred-dollar-bills.

"Okay," he said. "Let's check out our home-away-from-home."

We crossed the Yellowstone River—it was muddy and swollen—drove past the refinery and wound around a little, then pulled up at the place.

We sat for a minute in front of the two double garage doors—it was a carriage house style with stained wood panels—and studied the house and yard.

He was right, it looked decent.

Very decent.

The roof over the entry was covered with gleaming copper sheets and the front door was framed with cultured stonework. Surrounding the concrete steps, the green grass, majestic trees and shrubbery were well-tended.

"The workshop is framed in at the back of the garage," Viktor said.

"Do we have keys to open the doors?" I said.

Viktor looked at me like I was speaking Latin.

"Digital locks. We open them with our phones. BW has

everything programmed. Push the 'house' icon and the menu pops up. BW handles all the virtual stuff—everything online. We do the physical world stuff. You'd think a clever guy like you would figure this out."

He clicked around on his phone and the garage door ascended.

"Dipshit," he muttered.

While watching the garage door roll out of sight, I replied with "Fuckwad."

After pulling in and closing the door, we hauled our stuff through the side door and to the entry. The door was unlocked. Inside, a gas log fire blazed—which was nice because it was cold outside.

We explored...admiring the hardwood floors and the gleaming granite counter and appliances in the kitchen.

Upstairs in the massive master bedroom, there was a view...I could see golf carts rolling along the fairway of a course. The bed was a King with a feather-stuffed duvet. I imagined Violet's naked body sprawled across it. Perfect. This would be our room, of course.

I liked the house. It made me wonder why I didn't have a place in Montana like some of my friends who went on and on about it.

Big Sky Country.

I could see the appeal in the summer.

In the winter? Screw it. That season was for warmer places farther south. Much farther.

Across the house, I heard a toilet flush and I was happy the house was so big.

I heard him shout.

"Meet me in the workshop."

I prowled around a while longer. The place was at least 5,000 square feet. Washer. Dryer. There was a mud room by the back door...with Dungho barnyard boots to borrow. Along the wall there was a catbox filled with kitty litter. I didn't think about it except to wonder where the cat was. I'd seen no sign of it.

In the kitchen, the Jenn Air refrigerator was fully stocked. I grabbed a cold Stella lager, a Babybel mini cheese wheel and popped open a can of cashews from the pantry.

A feast for a king. Clearly, BW monitored my online purchases and knew what I liked. This brave new world was not all bad.

Happily strolling, I wandered toward the garage to find the workshop. It was spacious and nicely lighted with overheard LED fixtures. In a huge 3D printer, whining motors moved the print platform around. I couldn't tell what it was making…it looked like some kind of gun.

There were three of these machines.

Viktor carved off swaths of waste with a buck knife. The way the flash curled off, that knife must have been way-sharp. Everywhere, gleaming tools hung from pegboard hooks.

In the corner there was a dog bed. Idly, I wondered about that before discarding the thought.

"Did BW put this shop together?" I asked.

"The owner made a fortune with electric cars. This is his playroom."

"Nice," I said. "How long are we here? Will it take a few weeks to get ready?"

Viktor stopped trimming and stared at me with wonder.

"We're visiting the doctor the day after tomorrow."

I didn't know what to say.

After a minute, Viktor continued.

"The basic plan is to stun, then cut. Right hand, stun stick. One-hundred-thousand volts. Left hand, knife. I suggest Ka-Bar but use what you like. We'll be wearing tactical gloves with Kevlar knuckles and Dyneema Hyperline body armor."

"I never killed anyone. Can we hire someone? Can ninja assassins be hired from Fiverr?"

The thought of hiring a freelancer from a website amused me. Viktor was not pleased.

"I'm no expert either, but we'll practice with anatomic models. We can 3D print the models. Before we leave, we will practice wetwork with the owner of this house."

"Woah," I said. "Wait a minute. The owner is coming back?"

Viktor nodded.

"And we're going to kill him?"

Viktor kept nodding.

"No way. Come on, you must be joking."

Viktor shrugged.

"You ain't seen the dungeon yet," he said.

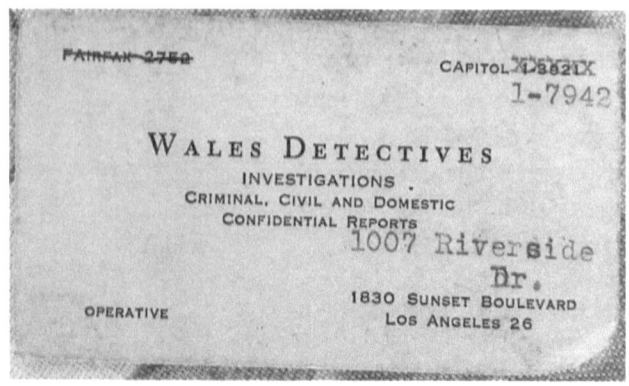

WALES DETECTIVES
INVESTIGATIONS
CRIMINAL, CIVIL AND DOMESTIC
CONFIDENTIAL REPORTS
1007 Riverside
Dr.
1830 SUNSET BOULEVARD
LOS ANGELES 26
OPERATIVE

Chapter 25

I COULDN'T BELIEVE what I was hearing.

Viktor continued.

"There's a trapdoor in the main floor hallway under a rug."

I finished my Stella and tossed the empty bottle toward a waste bin in the corner. Shaking, I missed, of course—it rattled across the tile floor without breaking. With a trembling hand, I gestured for him to go on.

"He has one of the sex dolls in his bomb shelter. Vera is her name. She's eight."

The thought horrified me. My brain shut down.

"No," I said. "Fuck-ass, bullshit no."

"Look, clueless. This is your mission. I'm here to help you, that's all. If it was up to me, we'd move along to take care of Tommy Molesta right away. As much as the Lolita doctor disgusts you, Molesta is worse. These mutilated girls, it's too much. I prefer to forget about them. It's your call what we do with them and I don't envy you the decision. You will have to choose—put them down and end their misery? Or, do they deserve a life—such as it might be? They can still feel pleasure. Some of them can still make babies. When Vera matures, she's intact. Either way, the situation sucks dick. But we didn't create this mess. The best we can do is ice the doctor and prevent future evil. A few hours ago, you were all in for wasting the Lolita doctor. Now you're waffling again. In or out, you have to decide and stop driving me crazy."

While my mind roiled, it took a minute for his words to sink in.

"I can't handle this."

"Right," Viktor said. "I agree and so does BW. Your odds of success are slim. You are probably going to die. Soon. But we don't have a better option. Juggling a quadrillion variables, this is the best path for success. The odds are stacked against us, but we have a chance. But you need to man up. We have a shit-ton of work to do and no time to do it. The day after tomorrow, in the morning, the owner comes back and we need to be ready. Quit fucking around and get your mind in the game."

My thoughts were a muddle...like I was on a 10x dose of LSD.

This could not be real. No way.

Viktor handed me the gun he was working on.

"Ketamine darts," he said. "Carbon dioxide propelled. Range? Maybe 30 feet max. We'll want to get as close as we can. If you can hit the neck, that's the best spot, but anywhere is okay. The dose is enormous...could take down a grizzly. Double barrel. Shoot twice, then discard. The only metal is the pin that pierces the CO_2 cartridge. It's simple. Zap them with ketamine or the stun stick, then cut their throats. We'll practice until your body acts without thinking."

"The girl..." I said.

"I'm not sure she is still a girl. She's been turned into something else."

"The girl," I repeated. "Can I see her?"

Viktor grinned. It was very unpleasant, as if his mouth was twisted in mortal rictus—haunting like a dead clown's face.

"She's yours. You can do what you like. Fuck her, take her home, kill her. Do whatever, I don't want to know. This is beyond fucked up."

I'm not suicidal—never have been. But this was too much.

The glorious peace of black death tugged at my soul.

"No," I said. "This cannot be happening."

"My best advice," Viktor said. "You're a pussy. Forget all

this. Run away. RatWeb will kill you in a week and your troubles will be over."

In an instant, the executive function of my brain took over. Calmness settled on me.

"What the fuck does RatWeb have to do with anything?"

"RatWeb? Everything. The owner of this house? Brent Stephens. Brock's little brother."

Fuck me.

This was no random rental.

I was disorientated until my mind context-shifted and aligned with a new reality. BW maneuvered us...put us in the house of the brother of RatWeb's leader. I was planning to sleep in his bed. Fucking asshole AI.

I do not like being manipulated like this.

I thought back to the roly-poly joker in the X-Squared Tesla and his stupid Tootsie-pops.

"You're right," I said. "I have to get out of here and save myself. But I'll take a look at the girl first."

Viktor nodded.

"That's how it started with me. One of Molesta's toddlers. Once the blood is drained and strained for Adrenochrome and the corneas and organs are removed, there's not much left. She weighed maybe ten pounds. They think of us as cattle. Useless eaters. That's why I will kill Molesta or die trying."

A week ago, I played video games in my office and debated whether to order Thai green curry or a pepperoni calzone for lunch. I yearned for that boredom and innocence.

Joe Wales, fake private detective.

What happened to you, man?

Trying to ignore the hamster flywheels furiously spinning in my head, I got up and retrieved the Stella bottle, then gently dropped it in the recycle bin.

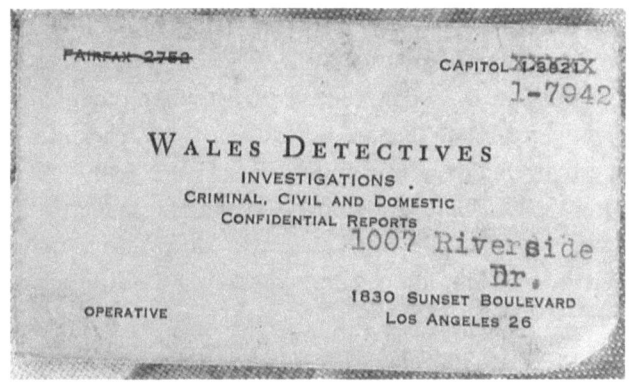

Chapter 26

IN THE HALLWAY, there was a throw rug—colorful, it had angular hourglass patterns in red, mauve and blue. The patterns were irregular, like the rug was handwoven. I tried to think of what Native Americans were in this area.

Lakota? Cheyenne? Crow?

I didn't know. I found myself studying the hypnotic pattern and thinking about the Crow Indian's Tobacco Society—a quasi-religious sect who worshipped tobacco and thought smoking it brought them closer to God. How did I know this? It must have been mentioned on a Graham Hancock pseudoarchaeology podcast or something.

Obviously, I was stalling. I pulled up an edge of the rug and folded it back. Underneath was a digital display. The numbers flashed and there was a loud click. A green LED lit up. This mystified me. I looked up. High up in a ceiling cleft there was a security camera. The camera and the lock must be online, so BW had access. I nodded at the camera.

There was a large iron ring inset in the wood floor. I reached for it and lifted. There was a counterweight somewhere...the heavy door smoothly eased up with little effort. Again, I was immersed in the feel of the door—weighing and enjoying it. Clearly, it was expensive and well-crafted.

I was still stalling.

Inside, an array of lights came on—illuminating a hardwood

ladder in the hole—its wood was stained dark like walnut. Truly, I was going insane. I did not want to descend into that chamber.

A rank, musky odor wafted up. It wasn't obnoxious or offensive, just strange like an old cat box. Like a hospital, there was an astringent, antiseptic undertone.

Slowly, I turned and stepped down the ladder—holding onto handy guiderails. The hole was deep—something like eighteen feet. I felt like I climbed forever until reaching the bottom.

I wished it would take forever so I wouldn't have to face what was down there, but eventually, I stepped off the ladder. It was a prepper paradise. Shelves along the walls had canned goods, dried foods, jerrycans of fuel, guns, and stacks and stacks of ammo boxes.

There were board games. Risk, Monopoly and Candyland. There was a stack of cellophane-wrapped playing cards and a chess set. On endless shelves, books, lots of books. I scanned some of the wholesome, uplifting titles. *The Turner Diaries. The Camp of the Saints. Atlas Shrugged. The Creature from Jekyll Island.*

I took down the last title and paged through it—looking at the photographs of people I did not know, like Nicholas Biddle and William Jennings Bryan.

If the end times arrive, I will have time to study and get to know these people.

There were five doors and four of them were open—exposing a flame toilet, shower chamber and three austere bedrooms with two bunkbeds in each. It looked like six people could survive down here for a year or more. I took my time looking around. Clearly, I had no desire to open the one closed door. It was different than the other wooden doors: tall, heavy and made of gleaming steel. I pressed my head to the cold metal but didn't hear anything except the pounding of my heart.

Desire or not, I needed to stop wasting time—stop studying the provisions, the cozy living arrangements and this massive door. Gathering my courage, I stood with my hand on the latch. As if caused by someone else, it began turning and the door eased open.

Instantly, my nose rebelled against the smell. The odor was something physical. Shit and acrid piss over something animal and musky. Automatically, lights came on. Mostly, it was a pleasure palace with plush, leopard-pattern upholstery and a small bar backed with mirrors and variously shaped whisky bottles. The cage was in a corner and the creature was pressed against the bars as far away as she could get.

There was a metal nametag.

Vera.

The cage had a cat box, but absorbent clay pellets were scattered everywhere. There was shit all over everything and a trail of rank piss drained from the cage and into a grate on the floor. The tiny creature's hair and body were covered in brown filth.

Overhead, hanging on a spring, was a nozzle for hosing down the mess. I could spray and clean her. This blind, deaf and dumb creature was not human. The stench irritated my eyes. Tears ran down my face like waterfalls.

Kneeling in a dry spot, I studied the pathetic beast. Skinny, she was maybe sixty pounds and wouldn't be more than four feet tall if stretched out. She had nothing to work with, but still she rebelled. Though coated with excrement, her arms and legs were terminated with metal rings covered with a bright-pink plastic coating. Small, they were about two inches in diameter. The chains to hang her were bolted to the ceiling and tucked out of the way.

Her artificial eyes were white and vivid blue. Her eyelids had been trimmed away. She couldn't even blink. Her hair was long, but so soiled that I couldn't tell its color. Like a gerbil in a cage, she could sip water from a tube. As I watched, she put her head up and took a mouthful. With cheeks distended, she futilely tried to find me, then spit in my general direction. She was helpless but still had a defiant spirit. Under the sickness in my gut, I admired that. In an alternate universe, she might have been a good human.

I didn't think a more miserable being could possibly exist. This was something beyond Bosch's eternal fires of hell.

Could it have any kind of life or was it better off dead?

And why was it up to me to decide?

At the bar, I upended a crystal glass and looked over the selection before choosing a fancy bottle of Macallan No.6 Single Malt. I worked out the crystal stop and poured a long shot, then drained it. It took my breath away and frankly, smelled like a pungent barn.

As I poured another dram, I wondered if anyone really liked this stuff. It was rank.

I opened a humidor box. Inside, arranged like sleeping soldiers, were Montecristo 1935 Anniversary Edicion Diamante cigars. The box was big. There must have been a hundred. I clipped off the end of one, then used a heavy gold lighter to ignite the torpedo. Instantly, my mouth tasted like the inside of an old fireplace. There was no way I would inhale, but it made me cough anyway.

This caused the creature to stir. She wriggled to the front of the cage and put her face between the bars. This puzzled me.

Was she going to spit at me again?

She pursed her lips and made a sucking sound.

I looked around the room for clues. Nothing.

What the fuck? Could it be she wanted a smoke?

Cautiously, I approached and put the cigar to her lips. She did something I could never do—drew deep and held it in. It filled me with wonder. She clearly enjoyed this.

I rocked back on my heels and thought about it.

She just saved her own life.

For ten minutes, when she pressed her face against the bars, I let her suck the stogie before she had enough and retreated to the back of the cage.

It was a weird feeling, but I sensed we were now friends. Standing, I turned the faucet controls and adjusted the temperature of the nozzle spray until it was hot, but tolerable. She moved to the front of the cage so I could wash her. Slowly, a naked little girl emerged from the filth. Reaching in, I rubbed her down with a soapy sponge. She moved around so I could reach all of her, then I hosed away the mess and washed it down the drain.

I'm not sure how, but I sensed she would not cause trouble,

so I unlatched the door and let her out so I could dry her off with a lush Luxome towel. She liked that—her pink skin glowed.

From where I left it in a huge Chihuly glass ashtray, I picked up the cigar and lit it again.

With her metal loops clicking on the floor, she walked like a dog to approach me and crouched with her head held up.

She sucked a lungful.

I offered her a drink of whisky, but she spat it out. She didn't like Scotch, but she loved that cigar.

I sat back and watched her with wonder. Now that she was clean, under her leather collar, I could see scars crisscrossing her throat. As she walked, she made little grunting noises, but I don't think she could speak. Her larynx was removed, and her teeth had all been pulled. She was a bizarre human doll.

At the edge of the bar, there was a clear glass cookie jar with a hand-written label. The label said 'Treats.' It was filled with what looked like tiny meatballs.

I fished one out and waved it under her nose.

She reared back and opened her mouth. I dropped in a ball and she gummed it with evident pleasure. After swallowing, she nuzzled my knee to ask for more. When I didn't respond fast enough, she put her head in my lap, smacked her lips and rubbed suggestively.

I admit it. I'm a shit human...I was tempted to unzip. Instead, I dragged the jar over and fished out another treat.

I didn't know what to think and I didn't know how to feel.

However, there was one thing I was sure about. Brent Stephens was going to die.

Soon.

Then, the doctor.

Once she'd had enough to eat, I searched her chamber. I found disposable diapers, but, wriggling and closing her legs, she wouldn't let me put one on her. Continuing my search, I found clothing and got her dressed. This she *did* want. She helped by rolling onto her back and raising her arms. I tried to resist the image, but she was like a puppy—a smart, cute puppy.

She fit into a backpack harness, so I was able to carry her up the ladder. As soon as I set her down, she started exploring. For some reason, I was not worried about her escaping...it didn't seem like she'd run.

I had a sudden flash of what would happen if she scampered down the street and someone saw her. No one would believe their eyes and we'd be in big, big trouble.

She hopped up on a sofa, curled up and went to sleep. From across the room, I sat and watched her breath.

When her nap was over and she stirred, I picked her up. She nuzzled into the crook of my neck. I pressed back on how this made me feel. I worked hard to feel nothing but failed. I loved this helpless little bundle.

With her warm little naked body cuddled in my arms, I walked out to the workshop to find Viktor.

FAIRFAX 2752   CAPITOL DS82IX
                                   1-7942

WALES DETECTIVES
INVESTIGATIONS .
CRIMINAL, CIVIL AND DOMESTIC
CONFIDENTIAL REPORTS
                     1007 Riverside
                          Dr.
                     1830 SUNSET BOULEVARD
OPERATIVE   LOS ANGELES 26

Chapter 27

WHILE VERA LOLLED on her bed in the shop's corner, we spent an hour shooting tranquilizer darts into a paper human target. It took time, but we learned to gauge the droop over distance and got good at hitting close to where we aimed.

We switched to knife training—stabbing and throat cutting. At first, it was creepy, and I hesitated. But, after a half hour of hacking, my moves became smooth and sure.

Tired, I grabbed a bottle of water from a minifridge and flopped on a sofa. This mancave had everything. I made a mental note to build myself one if I survived the upcoming adventure.

Viktor clicked around on his phone.

"This is interesting," he said. "Something changed."

"What?" I said.

"Your odds improved. You're at 33-percent now."

"How can that be?"

Viktor shrugged and gestured at Vera.

"I guess you did something BW likes."

Mentally, I worked that over but couldn't come up with a theory.

"What do we know about Brent?"

Viktor thought it over.

"He travels with two bodyguards. We'll have to take them out to get to him."

I scanned the workroom—looking over the tools and

chemicals.

It occurred to me that the bomb shelter only had one entrance…and one exit. Thinking hard and visualizing what I saw, I was sure there was no other escape hatch.

"I have an idea," I said.

FAIRFAX 2752

CAPITOL X-5521X
1-7942

WALES DETECTIVES
INVESTIGATIONS .
CRIMINAL, CIVIL AND DOMESTIC
CONFIDENTIAL REPORTS
1007 Riverside
Dr.
1830 SUNSET BOULEVARD
LOS ANGELES 26
OPERATIVE

Chapter 28

AN HOUR BEFORE BW told us to expect Brent, we left Vera on her little bed. It broke my heart, but, for her safety, I attached her collar chain to a hook screwed in the wall.

We pulled the truck out of the garage and moved it a few blocks to the golf course parking lot. BlueWaive patched us into the house's security system, so were able to watch the house on our phones. When Brent got home, while waiting in his Escalade, his goons walked through the house and found it all clear. Of course, they immediately saw the bomb shelter hatch standing open. Brent joined them as they peered down into the hole.

He gestured and watched as the two big guys climbed down. This was our cue—we started walking and arrived at the front door as Brent got the all-clear signal and started down the ladder to join them.

Tiptoeing, we walked to the hatch and slammed it shut. With a loud click, BW activated the lock, but that wasn't enough for me. I took the top off a quart of Gorilla Glue and poured it around the edges…then glued down the rug. We'd be screwed if there was another exit, but BW said there was nothing to worry about and I believed it.

It took about ten seconds before they started pounding on the hatch. As close as we were, the muffled sounds could barely be heard. I grinned at Viktor and he grinned back.

While he went back to get the truck, I went out to check on

Vera. She was awake, but placid on her doggy bed. I unhooked her chain, picked her up and carried her back to the house. I put her down on the rug over the hatch.

I have no idea how, but it seemed like she knew.

Obviously, she could hear nothing, but there was vibration in the floor as the trapped men furiously beat on the hatch. It was clear she could feel vibrations coming through the metal loops at the ends of her arms and legs.

She sniffed the floor, wrinkled her nose at the acrid odor of the drying glue, raised her blind eyes up to me and emitted a small grunt.

It had to be my imagination, but she seemed satisfied. She rubbed her head on my trouser leg, then ambled back to the living room. Watching her, I marveled at how well she knew the house. By the time I entered the room to join her, she was curled up and asleep on a sofa by the fireplace.

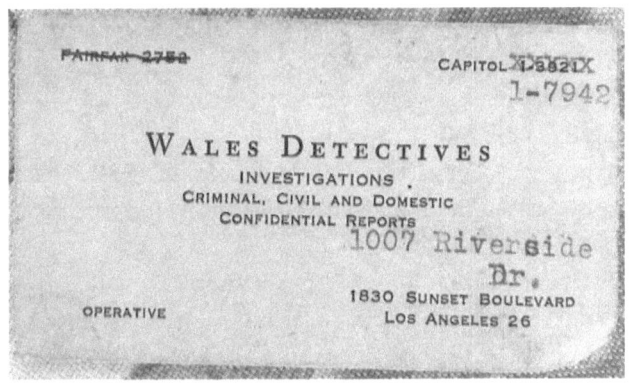

Chapter 29

I DECIDED TO reach out to BlueWaive. I took the black terminal out of my duffel and opened the case. The prompt blinked at me. I gathered my thoughts, then began typing.

Me: I don't want the guys in the underground bunker to live very long.

CORE: I'm inclined to give the bodyguards a chance. They are hired hands. They didn't know what was happening in the bunker. It's a perfect game theory situation.

I rolled this over in my mind and thought back to what I knew about formal game theory mathematics. Back in college, this topic fascinated me and I spent six months working on a paper. It wasn't a great paper and after all my work and deep thinking, I got a B-. Apparently, the professor was not a Johnny von Neumann fan.

It was a topic that fascinates me to this day. Claude Shannon, von Neumann, Anatol Rapoport...all those guys were super smart. As I remembered it, tit-for-tat with forgiveness was the winning method, but I couldn't think of any way this helped my current situation.

Me: Okay. You can communicate with them and get the bodyguards out?

CORE: Of course. With your money, I can hire a backhoe.

Me: Just them. I want Brent to rot in there.

CORE: Understood.

Me: Let's talk about Vera.

CORE: You talk. I'll listen.

Me: She can have a life. I think we should get her back with her family and set them up to care for her. With prosthetics, she could walk again.

CORE: I already ordered a DNA sample. It will arrive at the house today. It will include prepaid postage and an account number for a lab. I'll find her family. Keep in mind, they might not be good people. She might be better off elsewhere.

Me: I can't keep her. That would be weird.

CORE: We'll see how things play out.

Me: What should we do next?

CORE: I can hold off Brock for three weeks by spoofing 'busy, can't talk' messages, but Brent is supposed to come to Brock's birthday party in Las Vegas. Fourth of July weekend. Brock will know something is up by then.

Across the room, Vera stretched and yawned, then ambled toward the back of the house. I heard the rustle of kitty litter after she peed in the catbox. When she came back, she hesitated over the dungeon hatch. I couldn't tell if the prisoners were still pounding on the trapdoor.

How did she navigate?

It must be by smell and memory.

She knew her way around—she stopped and pressed her nose on the refrigerator door. I put the terminal aside and walked over. After pulling the door open, I studied the contents and recognized a one-gallon plastic container of her meatballs. I pried the top off. She settled back on her haunches and I fed her a half-dozen. Once she was satisfied, I opened a cold bottle of water and tipped it so she could drink.

After that, she walked back to her bed by the fireplace and went back to sleep. It didn't take much to make her happy.

I stood by the refrigerator watching when Viktor entered by the side door. He dropped a small box on the counter.

"Package," he said. "Addressed to you at this address. What did you order?"

"It's probably a DNA kit. I didn't order it—BW did. We should get Vera back to her family."

He thought about it for a few seconds.

"It depends on the family...that might not be the best situation for her."

"That's what BW said. I don't like these adding machines being ahead of us."

Viktor shrugged.

"Welcome to the future," he said.

I walked back to the sofa and picked up the terminal.

Me: Any advice for tomorrow?
CORE: Try not to die.

I closed the terminal.

"For those about to rock, I salute you," I muttered.

While watching Vera sleep, I felt myself changing. Evolving. Becoming a weapon.

The DNA test was simple enough. I just needed to swab her inner lip, seal the sample in a plastic container and mail the package. I lifted Vera's head. She did not resist.

Viktor watched from the Kitchen.

"She's a tiny little thing," he said.

I nodded.

"What do you think of her?" I said.

He considered.

"I don't know what to think, so I don't. It's better that way." He gestured. "I think she likes you."

"I get that impression too."

"Maybe you should keep her."

Fuck me. How would that work?

"Think I could adopt her?"

"Let's see what her family situation is...then decide."

Outside, it was getting dark and I realized I was sleepy. For a moment, I wondered how I felt about sleeping in Brent Stephens bed.

"I think I'll switch...take one of the guestrooms."

Viktor smirked.

"Whatever you say, boss."

I got up and climbed the stairs. On my heels, Vera followed. I looked down. Viktor was still grinning at me.

"Man's real best friend," he said.

I couldn't think of a snappy reply.

"Fuck you," I said.

I went in the master bedroom and grabbed my duffel, then explored. I could see Viktor's bag in the second-best room—the one farthest from the master. I picked the room across the hall. It was smaller but still had a private bathroom. I didn't know what Vera intended and didn't want to think about it.

While pissing, I brushed my teeth. When I came out, Vera was in bed and under the covers.

Jesus-fuck.

There were other rooms, but it looked like she wanted to sleep with me.

Was that too weird or should I let her have whatever simple pleasures she could enjoy?

I don't know how long I looked at her, indecisive. At least five long minutes.

"Goddammit," I muttered.

I stripped down to my shorts and slipped into bed, making carefully sure the sheet was between us. Instantly, I was asleep.

In the morning, I slowly woke. Outside, the sun peeked over the mountains and the birds were singing. Vera was naked and curled into my side...and I had a huge, throbbing erection.

Fuck!

I was horrified. With tented shorts, I got up as quickly as I could and jumped in the shower...as cold as I could stand. After drying off, I peeked from the bathroom.

Vera was gone, but her clothes were still piled up beside our bed. I pulled on the overalls and gathered her things. Scared to death, I leaned over the balcony and took a quick look to see what was happening on the ground floor. Viktor must have heard me.

He spoke very loudly, almost shouting.

"What does Vera eat?"

"In the fridge," I said. "She likes the meatballs."

I descended the stairs.

Both Vera and Viktor were chewing. The plastic container was open on the counter. I couldn't read his expression.

Was he disgusted or laughing at me?

I had done nothing wrong, but I still felt like the world's biggest pervert. He fished out a meatball and popped it in his mouth.

"Have you tried these things?" he said. "They're pretty good."

"Fuck you," I said. "Help me get her dressed."

Viktor stared at me for a long few seconds.

"We're going shopping. If we dress her, she won't be able to use her box. You want her to pee her pants?"

Clomping around on the rings screwed onto her arms and legs, she had no shame. If she wore clothes, it would be for me and only me. Viktor didn't give a shit.

It was a familiar feeling. I didn't know what to think and I didn't know what emotions to permit.

It was frustrating.

I took a deep breath.

She raised her head and opened her mouth wide open. Viktor dropped a meatball.

"She'll be fine," he said.

Chapter 30

WHILE VIKTOR WALKED to the gold course parking lot to get the truck, I inventoried my selection of gear and weapons. Tranq pistols, stun stick, Ka-Bar knife, tactical vest. I had it all laid out when Viktor returned.

"Looked at this way," he said. "It's obvious what is missing, isn't it?"

It looked like enough to me.

"Guns," he said impatiently. "*Pistolas. El revólvereros.* You know what I mean? Better to have them and not need them."

"Okay," I said. "What are we going to do? Do we have to go out in the world and get them?"

Viktor grinned.

"You haven't seen the weapons room yet."

He led me upstairs to the master bedroom and into the walk-in closet. He lifted a sheaf of shirts in dry cleaning bags and threw them aside to expose a panel with a digital display similar to the trap door.

"Any chance BW…"

That was as far as I got before the numbers on the display changed and the door clicked open.

"If it's online, BW has access," Viktor said.

Inside, I reached for an automatic, but Viktor slapped my hand and pushed me away.

"You're better off with a revolver—less margin for error."

He reached in and pulled out a cowboy gun.

After looking it over, he handed it to me and said, "Colt Peacemaker. Forty-five caliber. It will kick up, so brace yourself good."

It was a beautiful gun with engraved gold scrollwork and a pearl handle. It was fancy and looked like it had never been fired.

He took the automatic for himself.

"They use the same ammo."

He handed me a box and took a box for himself.

"Let's dry fire then practice loading."

He showed me how to cock, fire and how to swivel out the chamber for reloading.

"In the heat of battle," he said, "you will be nervous and shaking. You need to separate that part of yourself. Push it into a corner of your mind. Aim, fire and reload like a machine."

He was condescending, but I took his point.

He clipped a compact holster to his belt and handed me a wide, leather gun belt with holster.

"Here you go, Cowboy," he said.

I looked ridiculous with the belt and my overalls. I'd only done cosplay once at a San Diego Comi-Con. I dressed as the Browncoat Malcom Reynolds from Firefly. The girls liked the outfit—which cost a small fortune. I felt silly then and I felt double-silly now. I followed Viktor back downstairs.

"Okay, I'm ready to go," I said. "What about Vera?"

I looked around for her…she wasn't sitting on the plush chair by the fireplace. There was a stab of panic in my gut. I turned and saw her in the hallway. She was sleeping on the rug that covered the trapdoor.

"She looks comfortable enough," Viktor said.

I studied his face. I didn't want to be needlessly paranoid, but I sensed he was playing with me.

"Seriously," he continued. "She has food and knows how to use her litter box. Did you see her feed bowl and water spigot in the main bathroom?"

I shook my head. I hadn't been in the bathroom on this main floor yet. Skirting her, I walked down the hallway and poked my head in. There was a chilled water dispenser—Yellowstone Ice and Water. She could activate the valve with her forehead and sip from a tube. Her bowl was topped off with meatballs. I returned and went chest to chest with Viktor.

"Yes, she's all set."

"Then, let's get this done," he said.

Self-conscious and happy the thick trees hid us from the neighbors, I followed him outside.

"We're taking the Escalade," he said.

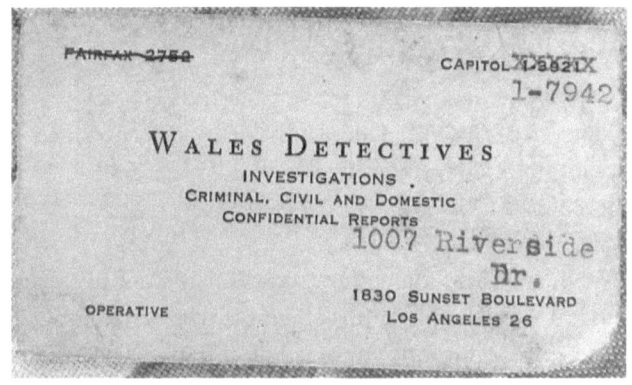

Chapter 31

THE CADILLAC HAD a fancy computer system, but Viktor had me navigate by reading turn-by-turn instructions from his phone.

At first, the prairie landscape was flat with lightly wooded rifts of hills. We saw a lot of sagebrush and black cows. It was a clear day, and snow-capped mountains could be seen far away to the southwest. We drove out Pryor Road to the base of the Pryor Mountains and turned east on Highway 91. The scenery grew rougher as the highway twisted, turned, rose and fell. After 10.2 miles we turned on a gravel stub, then drove another 1.3 miles to an unmarked driveway with a whitewashed wooden gate. The house was not visible from this county road. On a power pole, Viktor pointed out a security camera.

"We will not be able to sneak up on them," Viktor said. "But, with the tinted windows, they won't be able to see us. They will recognize this SUV and assume Brent is making an unscheduled visit, so they won't start shooting right away. Remember, there are four guards and the doctor. That's five. Say it."

Puzzled, I looked at him.

"Say it," he repeated.

"Okay. Five including the doctor."

"I'll get three guards. You get one."

Viktor opened a baggie and took out two pink pills. He dropped them in my palm. They looked like Valentine hearts but

117

didn't have a caption. No *Kiss Me*, *All Mine* or *Smile*.

"What's this?" I said.

"Captagon. Caffeine."

I'd heard of this pill. The Jihadist drug. It turned their young martyrs into bloodthirsty savages.

"It's not just caffeine."

Viktor studied my face.

"Well, it has amphetamine, too. But, it's not just Captagon either—it's something BW dreamed up with Vitamin K and 11 herbs and spices. Instant temporary dissociative psychopath. We want you angry and capable. Don't worry about it. The dose is calibrated to your weight. It's safe for you."

I thought of Vera. Determination filled my veins. I was already angry enough to kill.

"I don't need this shit."

He handed me a bottle of water. His voice was calm and matter-of-fact.

"Take them or we go home."

"Fuck-shit," I said. I popped the bitter pills and washed them down. "Asshole."

Grinning, Viktor popped a pill—his was ruby-red.

Why was his different?

His body went rigid—like he was having a seizure with his head tilted back and his mouth wide open. I heard his tendons creak, then he relaxed. He looked at his hands as if he'd never seen them before. They were steady—no tremor.

"Ready," he whispered.

He pulled on tactical gloves and eased the SUV forward to push the gate open.

"No shooting unless it is absolutely necessary," he said. "And take off your seatbelt."

While we slowly crunched on the gravel driveway, I felt nothing and wondered how long it would take the pills to kick in.

It started with a rushing in my ears—like a jet engine spooling up. My mind engaged with a swirling flood of thoughts and emotions—like I was living every minute of my life all at once. My mind was not soft and fuzzy, it was decisively locked in to logic. Everything was black or white, right or wrong. There would be no hesitation, I would either do or not do. It struck me like a hammer—then I figured out what he meant when he mentioned 11 herbs and spices.

That was the Kentucky Fried Chicken thing.

I looked at him.

Fucker.

Detached, I was no longer in my body. I studied the blade of the Ka-Bar knife. It was thirsty for blood. Weighing the pros and cons, I debated stabbing Viktor in the head for practice but instantly decided not to.

It would be satisfying, but bad...

...because he's driving.

And, besides Vera, he's my best friend.

And...Violet would be disappointed with me if I jammed the Ka-Bar into his skull and worked it around until his brains were puree. I could feel the crunch of his bones. The knife would be happy.

I realized I was really high. It took extreme effort to stop from tipping my head back and howling like a rabid wolf. Suddenly, I couldn't wait. We were here to kill.

It was weird.

Something deep inside was activated...something savage that wanted to rape and pillage. Something lived in me had been sleeping but was now wide awake. The sun was too bright, and my skin was too tight. My muscles twitched.

It hit me.

One of the 11 herbs and spices was adrenochrome. Organic amphetamine. Godspeed. I'd been offered it at a Brentwood party by the PA for the actor you knew as Jack Sparrow. I'd turned it down.

Why?

I didn't know.

This was good. The dazzling world was in sharp focus. Under the flesh, we're all grinning skulls. Hideous, grinning skulls. It doesn't matter if you're Anya Taylor-Joy or George Clooney. Skin was like makeup for the bones. It was artificial and phony.

Flat out like a lizard drinking, my knife said.

It had an Australian accent. Why?

"Let's crack the shits and get on with the hard yakka," it said.

Something needs to happen quick or I will explode.

The gravel crunched under the tires. Viktor drove slowly as we eased a hundred yards in a sweeping curve around a windbreak grove of pine trees. As we approached the compound, two guards came out...one on Viktor's side and one on mine.

I aped Viktor: stun stick in my left hand and Ka-Bar in my right. While still slowly moving, we pressed the stun sticks' activation buttons and heard the insect-whine as they charged.

The SUV stopped and Viktor's guard tapped on the window. My eyes were locked on Viktor's. He nodded and simultaneously, we pressed the buttons to lower the windows. I got my guard in the neck with the stick. He dropped like a bag of concrete. Quickly, while he writhed like an epileptic, I got out and hacked at his throat. They weren't clean cuts, but they did the job. Looking down on him bleeding out, I felt a victorious rush in my veins. I won—he lost. My impulse was to stab him in the face—and keep doing it. Losing control, I raised my head to the sky and howled.

I'd never killed anyone before, not even close, but now I wondered why.

This was big fun.

From the front door of the compound, a guard raised an M-16. Viktor jumped back in the driver's seat and jammed the accelerator. The SUV bucked and the guard disappeared underneath. Viktor backed over him and then, with the engine howling, ran forward over him again.

The guard looked like hamburger. That was three down.

It wasn't fair. Why did he get three and I only get one?

We walked to the house entry. It was rundown and falling apart. There was moss on the roof and the wooden entry stairs were rotted out. The paint was blasted off by sand and wind—the bare, gray wood was warped and weathered. Frankly, the place was a dump.

Viktor pointed me to the right while he stalked off to the left. On my side, looking in the windows, I saw the dining room and bedrooms, but no people. Hearing a crashing noise, I walked back to find Viktor.

He stood over a dead man in a utilitarian room filled with electronics. Equipment smoked and sparked while Viktor smashed radios and amplifiers with a fire axe he found somewhere.

The security equipment looked expensive.

"Why didn't he see us?"

Viktor shrugged.

"It was online, so BW controlled it."

"Oh," I said.

I looked at the guard's bloody carcass. He was dead, so there was no point to kicking him in the face, but I did it anyway.

I wasn't done.

"How sure are you that's it? Are there more guards?"

"BW seemed sure," he said. "We'll see, I guess. The doctor will be out back in his lab."

My heart was pounding. I hoped there were more so I could kill them.

Maybe there will be dogs.

I was in the mood to stab some pit bulls.

We walked through the house and into the backyard. It was a tangle of weeds. Like a lame cliché, a tumbleweed was lodged against the leaning pole of an old clothesline. We followed a beaten dirt path to a ramshackle outbuilding.

Weathered and rusty, it was a metal building as big as a barn. The path led to a metal door. Over the door was a glowing red light.

There was a hand-written note.

Keep out when lit.

With his hand on the latch, he looked at me.

"Ready?"

"Let's do it," I said.

The inside was much different than the outside. Stainless steel with white tile and walls, it was brightly lit from hooded overhead fixtures. The doctor, wearing noise-cancelling headphones, leaned over a stainless-steel table. From the Law and Order TV shows I watched, I recognized the autopsy table. On one end was a sink and spray hose—on the other side was a drain. There was no one on the table, but it looked like he was getting ready. Scalpels. Bone saws. An array of hypodermic needles.

He spoke without looking back.

"The red light is on. That means…"

He turned.

"Oh," he said.

I walked over to a kennel in the corner. Inside, a naked little boy crouched in a corner. He didn't look afraid…I couldn't read his expression. It was more like he was blank—disconnected, checked out. I had never felt such fury—I could barely contain my internal energy. I thought I might explode into a bloody mess.

Viktor waved his stun stick in the doctor's face.

I walked up.

I'm sure I was a sight—all tensed up with a red face. I felt like I would spontaneously burst into flames.

The doctor was an old man, must have been at least 70. His hair was white, as was his neatly trimmed mustache. Average height. Average weight with a small bulge of fat on his waist under his white lab coat. He looked completely harmless. Trying to detect the madness that must be present, I looked deeply into his eyes.

Nothing.

I got nothing.

"Shall we cut him up and get out of here?" Viktor said.

I looked at the array of hypodermics.

"I wonder what all this stuff does," I said.

I saw a glimmer of fear in the doctor's eyes as they flicked to the needles.

"Let's find out, shall we?" At random, I picked one up. It held exactly one milliliter of clear fluid. "How about this one? What does it do?"

"Lidocaine," he said.

I popped off the protective cap, stabbed it in his arm and

pressed the plunger.

"That's no fun, but we're just getting started, aren't we?"

I picked up the next needle. His eyes flicked to it.

"Stop," he said.

I stabbed it in his arm.

"Ceftriaxone," he said.

"What's that?"

"Antibiotic," he said. "If you're going to kill me, then just do it. There's no need to torture me—it's pointless."

Viktor moved the stun stick two inches from the doctor's forehead.

"I agree. Can I zap him? We should get out of here as quickly as we can."

I picked up another hypo and held it up to the light. It was a pale pink fluid.

"Hydrocortisone sodium succinate," the doctor said. "It's a steroid. With the Lidocaine, it won't hurt...not for a while, anyway."

"Thank you, doc," I said.

I took a few steps around Viktor and stabbed the doctor in his other arm.

He collapsed to the floor and started screaming. There were three needles left. In quick succession, I injected everything into his thighs. Standing over him, I watched him writhe for an eternity or about ten seconds, whichever comes first.

"Okay," I said. "Scramble him."

Viktor pressed the stun stick to the doctor's forehead and gave him a long taze. It shut him up, but I could tell he was still breathing. I shoved my Ka-Bar into his temple, and he stopped moving.

Something clicked on my wrist. Viktor handcuffed me to the table next to the dead doctor. It was bolted to the floor. I was going nowhere.

"What the fuck, Viktor?" I yelled. "What are you doing?"

The doctor had a small pharmacy. Viktor looked over the shelves of medication until he found what he was looking for. He walked back to hand me a couple of yellow tablets, then stood back as if I might bite him or something. The pills had an ornate V pressed into them.

"What are you doing? Let me go, you motherfucker. What is this?"

"Primidone. It will calm you down. I will release you when you're back under control."

The knife was still in my hand. I wanted to gut him, but I couldn't reach far enough. He found a bottle of water and rolled it over.

"Take the pills and I'll let you loose in a half-hour. Don't take them and you'll stay cuffed up overnight. Your call."

I made a mental note to kill Viktor when I was free, then washed down the tablets with the cold water. I opened my mouth to show him I'd swallowed them.

"Let me see," he said. "Lift your tongue."

I complied.

"Okay, half an hour. Until then, I will explore and see what we have."

He studied me.

"I'm starting to understand what my sister sees in you. She's batshit crazy, too."

In minutes, I was drowsy. The tension in my body melted away. I stayed awake long enough to see him unlatch the cage and gently draw out the prisoner. The kid looked Mexican. I decided his name was Juan. There was a ferocious battle in my body between fury and tranquility. Sitting on that cold floor next to the cooling body of the doctor and watching his blood ooze toward a drain on the floor, I was deeply uncomfortable but couldn't keep my eyes open.

I decided to rest my eyes, just for a minute—one long minute.

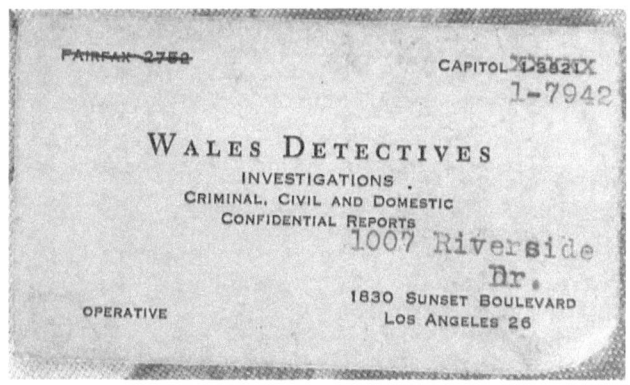

Chapter 32

SLOWLY, I WOKE. On my back, I was lying flat on the floor. The handcuffs had been removed…as had the doctor's. Juan knelt before me with his face six inches from mine.

"Juan? What are you doing?"

"My name is Jimmy."

His accent was flat. Midwestern. He was a little older than my first guess. Maybe 12. Maybe 13. Groaning, I sat up. My body was stiff and there was still an internal skirmish happening between agitation and torpor. I wouldn't feel one-hundred-percent normal for a while. Jimmy handed me a fresh bottle of water and in three long draughts, I sucked the whole thing down.

"Okay." I tried the name on my tongue. "Jimmy. Where's Viktor?"

He pointed toward the back.

"How many of you? How many are back there?"

After a moment's consideration, he decided to answer the latter question.

Smart kid.

"Two more in the back. Angel and Karla. Angel was the doctor's pet. She's been here for years."

He made a large sweeping gesture around his stomach.

I knew what he meant. She was pregnant. Very pregnant.

I didn't know how to ask.

"Are they…whole?"

With sadness, Jimmy shook his head and wrapped his arms around me.

"No. The monster was doing me today. You saved me."

Surprised and uncomfortable, I patted his back. I really didn't know what to do with kids.

"It's okay," I said. "I'm Joe."

"I know," he said. "Viktor with a 'k' told me. Are you cool? If you're cool, Viktor said I can give you the key."

Taking a deep breath, I thought about it.

"Yes, I'm cool," I decided.

He dropped the key into my palm.

After releasing myself, I got up on shaky legs. With his arms still around me, he helped a little. From the back, Viktor appeared through swinging doors.

"Ah, you're up. Still want to kill me? No? Good. We have work to do. They have a tractor and trailer, but I need help lifting the bodies."

I followed him through the house and into the driveway. He'd already pulled out a cherry-red Mahindra sub-compact tractor with matching utility trailer. There wasn't much room to spare, but we stacked all three bodies in the trailer.

"You know how to drive this thing?"

"BW gave me a quick summary. It's easy."

"Do you need help unloading?" I said.

"No, I can dump them."

Working the gears, he trundled off.

A few minutes later, he returned and we went inside to get number 4. After hauling him out, I was winded and exhausted, but we managed to load him up.

"I'll meet you out back."

The bodies were dumped at the side of the barn. Inside a sliding door, there was a large stainless-steel chamber.

"What is that thing?"

"This lab is set up for disposing bodies. This is a decomp chamber. Heated lye under pressure. Strip the bodies and throw them in. Two hours later, all that is left is bones and eco-friendly soup. The cartels call the soup *pizole*. Stew. Funny, right? The *pizole* is safe to pour out anywhere. Fertilizer. There's a propane incinerator to dry the skeleton. And a crusher. Tonight, nothing but ash. Cremains, that's all that is left. Slick, eh?"

"Let me guess. BW gave you detailed instructions."

Viktor responded with a grin.

"It takes a couple of hours for each. Let's get crackin' or we'll be here all night."

With surgical shears, we stripped the bodies and removed their watches and jewelry which were tossed into a pile. One of the guards had a blue-face Rolex Submariner.

"I'm keeping this one," Viktor said.

Looking through the piles, Jimmy pulled out a silver Saint Christopher medal on a gold chain.

"This was mine," he said while draping it on his skinny neck.

While the first body was cooking, Viktor led me back to the storage area of the lab. He'd let the girls free to explore, but they were huddled in a corner in each other's arms. It was obvious which one was Angel...she was close to popping. Karla was a little bigger than Vera...though they could have been sisters. She had the same long, black hair. The stainless-steel bolts protruding from the silicon sleeves covering her limbs were unterminated. Bare bolts, M-16 with 1.5mm fine-pitch threads.

I realized I was still a little high.

The cruelty of the procedure made my eyes water. I wanted to stab the doctor in the brain again.

"We'll cook the doctor next," I said.

In agreement, Viktor nodded.

"Let's get these kids dressed."

We searched. By the incinerator, we found clothing stuffed in plastic bags. We didn't bother sorting things out, just tugged and maneuvered the girls until they were at least wearing something. A voluminous hoody fit over Angel's massive belly. They did not struggle. When we let them go, they went back to their corner. I didn't know what to do with them. I decided to just leave them be—they didn't seem upset or agitated.

Looking around, I saw a break area with a pair of old couches. I pointed.

"I need to sit before I fall down."

Viktor nodded.

Once seated, after a few minutes I caught my breath and was able to speak.

"What are we going to do with these kids?"

"This is your mission," Viktor said, "but I assumed we'd clear out and call the cops—let them sort out the mess."

I couldn't believe what I was hearing. My mind snapped into a mode of thinking. What he said was wrong.

"Fuck, no. We can't do that. They'd bring in Child Protective Services. After the government gets done with them, these kids would have been better off with the perverts. Also, it would be a social media nightmare. These kids would never get any peace."

"Okay. What then?"

My mind was fractured with options—desperately seeking a clear path to latch onto.

"Damn it, I don't know, but we're not calling the cops. Fuck that."

Leaning over, Viktor opened the refrigerator, examined the contents and pulled out a cold can of Coke. After popping it open and taking a sip, he said, "Your show, boss."

"Throw me one of those, fucker," I said.

The first cold sip refreshed me, but the cloying sweetness of the second sip made me gag. My body could not decide if it was coming or going.

I handed the can to Jimmy. He glanced at it, then set it aside.

"Poison," he said.

"Fuck it," I said. "Why am I agonizing over this? We'll put the question to BW and do what it recommends."

Viktor tapped his index finger on his temple.

"You're smarter than you look," he said.

"What about you, Jimmy? Do you want to go back to your family?"

"NFW," he said.

"What does that mean?" I asked.

Viktor interjected.

"No Fucking Way."

"Like the others, I think." Jimmy said. "My family sold me. They don't want me back."

I probably sounded like a drunken parrot.

"What does that mean?"

It was Viktor who answered.

"Trafficking. Wayfare, Etsy or one of the other online sales sites. Do your own research and search for amateurish paintings of cute little girls by unknown artists going for big prices, like $50,000."

"WTF?" I said.

"Exactly," Viktor said.

I studied Jimmy's face.

"How old are you, kid?"

"Thirteen. Just turned."

"Well, shit, you're old enough make up your own mind. What do you want to do?"

He rubbed his fingers on his Saint Chrisopher medallion.

"I want to stay with you. You're rich. When I get older, you can send me to college."

I looked down at my dirty overalls and boots. I probably smelled like a dead muskrat.

"How do you know I'm rich?"

Jimmy grinned and pointed.

"Viktor told me."

I tried to turn my eyes into lasers so I could slice Viktor into bloody pieces.

"No way. What the bloody fuck am I going to do with a kid?"

"I read a lot," Jimmy said. "I'm no trouble and I don't take much room. You could keep me in a cage."

My brain was uselessly spinning like a sprocket out of phase with its chain. I felt railroaded by this little weasel.

"We'll discuss this later."

I reached over to pick up the Coke and took another sip. It tasted good again—the cells of my body eagerly soaked up the sugar and caffeine. But the kid was right, this stuff is poison.

I waved my hand around the cavernous room.

"What about this place? Shall we burn it to the ground?"

Viktor pursed his lips.

"It could be handy to have this as a citadel. Shit will get real after we ice Molesta. If BW pays the bills, we could use this place for a long time."

I rolled the idea around in my head, but I didn't trust my brain. The idea had merit, but I really liked Brent's cozy place in town.

"No, let's stay at the other place…make that our HQ."

"Bad idea," Viktor said. "This hideout is better."

"Crap. We disagree. How will we decide?"

"How about letting the kid cast the deciding vote?"

We turned to Jimmy.

"What do you think?" I said. "Stay out here or use the other place?"

"How can I decide when I haven't seen the other place?"

Viktor and I looked at each other.

"Fine," Viktor said. "We'll defer the decision."

Chapter 33

IT WAS AFTER midnight when we dissolved and disposed of the last body. My mind was racing, but my body was in a territory somewhere beyond exhaustion. Jimmy refused to leave my side. It was odd how he seemed untroubled by the murder and mayhem.

Why didn't he bond to Viktor? Why me? I don't even like children.

We spent the downtime exploring. The compound was an odd mix of broken-down ruin and high-tech areas where no expense was spared. The more I looked around, the idea of keeping it seemed more reasonable. A part of me wanted to splash gasoline and light a flare, but my brain appreciated the logic of having a remote, private hiding place.

When we walked by the girls, we patted them on the head and made sure their bowl was full of the meatballs we found in a walk-in refrigerator.

Outside, the Escalade had frontend damage—the headlights on the driver's side were smashed to bits. It was drivable but would attract attention. Jimmy wanted to drive it, and I couldn't think of a reason to deny him. In the cab, he could barely see over the steering wheel, but he had no trouble starting it and getting it going. I pointed to a gap between the house and the garage.

"Pull it in there," I said.

Without caring how he would do, I turned to the garage. Viktor had found a remote and stood in front of the doors holding it out.

Before he opened it, Viktor said, "What do you think we'll find?"

I didn't care.

"Just open it," I said.

Viktor pressed the remote button and the garage door rolled up. Inside were two more shiny black Escalades, exactly like the one we destroyed.

"Creative," Viktor said.

"We're done here. Let's load up the girls and get out of here."

"I'm driving," Jimmy said.

For once, we completely agreed.

"No, you're not," we said at the same time.

The girls were still jammed in their corner. We gently lifted them one-at-a-time onto a cart, wheeled them to the garage and loaded them into one of the Escalades. In about ten minutes, we were ready to go.

With the gravel driveway rocks crunching under my boots, I strolled for a minute. It was just after two in the morning. The moon was invisible, so overhead, the canopy of stars and sweep of Milky Way galaxies were vivid. In the distance, I could hear a pack of coyotes yipping and howling.

Loopy, my mind was a collage of carnage. I was alive and our enemies were dead.

I still did not know what to feel.

Viktor tapped the horn.

"Let's get out of here," he shouted.

I took a deep breath of cold air and let it ease out slowly, then walked to the idling Escalade.

Jimmy was buckled in the front-passenger seat—riding shotgun.

"Viktor says drive at the speed limit. We don't want to draw attention to ourselves."

"Okay, boss," I said.

"I'll drive if you get too tired."

"I'll keep that in mind."

I was still groggy, so it might have been safer to let him drive, but we unraveled our trip out and made it to the house. I backed up to the walkway and we unloaded the girls. Vera waited by the front door. After they sniffed each other for a minute, she led them to the toilet box. I could hear them scratching around back there.

It took the last of my willpower to climb the stairs. Following me, Jimmy immediately discovered the big room.

"Wow, this is cool. No one is using this one? Can I have it?"

"Go for it, kid," I mumbled. "Knock yourself out."

I unlaced my boots, stripped down to my shorts and flopped on the guestroom bed. It was truly heavenly.

I didn't know what happened next. I was asleep.

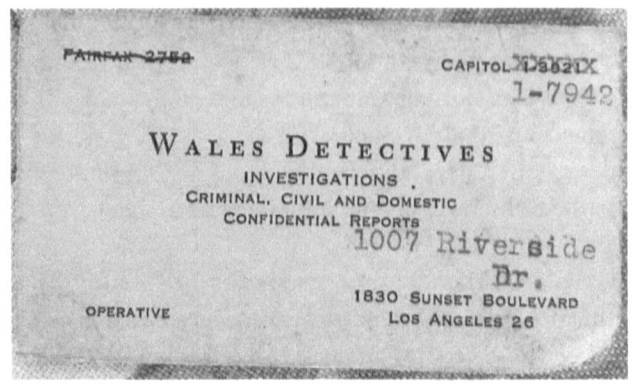

WALES DETECTIVES
INVESTIGATIONS
CRIMINAL, CIVIL AND DOMESTIC
CONFIDENTIAL REPORTS
1007 Riverside
Dr.
1830 SUNSET BOULEVARD
LOS ANGELES 26
OPERATIVE

Chapter 34

WITH SUNLIGHT POURING in the window, I slowly came back to the world. My arm was around Vera—my hand cupped her naked belly. Cozy, her tiny ass was pressed against my throbbing pelvis.

This was not right—it was very not right.

But, fuck me, it felt good. She was a warm little innocent cuddly thing. I inventoried my tangled emotions. The most powerful thing I felt was protective.

Was that an emotion?

This morning it was.

What right did I have to deprive her of something she clearly craved and enjoyed?

But, if the cops burst in right now, I'd never be able to explain. Vividly, I visualized the chain of events. After a long, lurid trial and social media uproar, some skinhead would be revolted by me abusing a child and would shiv me in prison. Alone on the floor of the communal shower with lukewarm water pounding, I could feel the wounds and the blood leaking from my body.

As slowly as I could, I eased out of bed and pulled on my overalls. Smelly and dirty, they were disgusting. I needed new clothes. Standing at the door, I looked back at her tiny lump under the covers.

The door handle was a lever-type. That's how she got in—

she could work the mechanism with the loops on her hands. There was a privacy lock. I'd have to remember to use it.

Downstairs, something was cooking. It smelled splendid. I was hungry, as hungry as I'd ever been. There was a blackhole in my belly.

Standing on a utility stool, Jimmy was cooking bacon and eggs on the gas range. I sat at the breakfast bar. Jimmy poured a steaming cup of ebony coffee and pushed it over.

I don't know why my next thought entered my head.

"We need to figure out how to make meatballs for the girls."

"I know how to do it," Jimmy said. "Ground elk, onion and garlic. They mixed in liquid multivitamins."

"How do you know all this?"

He shrugged.

"I pay attention," he said while pushing a plate across the breakfast bar.

It was heaped with meat strips and scrambled eggs. The eggs were loaded with fried onions and slivers of Jalapeno peppers.

"I don't like spicy stuff," I said.

Toast popped up in the toaster. He dropped two hot slices on my plate and pushed over a stoneware butter dish. Helpfully, it had 'Butter' embossed on the side. The butter was soft.

"Shut up and eat it anyway," Jimmy said.

I reached for the butterknife.

Chapter 35

AS I SAT on the sofa playing with the mysterious terminal, Vera was curled up next to me with her butt pressed hard against my hip. She'd found terrycloth shorts and a t-shirt that was way too big. I wasn't sure how she found them and got them on—maybe Jimmy helped her.

Lying on the floor across the room, Angel didn't move much, but sometimes, her baby kicked and she squirmed. It was clearly hard for her to find a comfortable position. She couldn't speak but grunted and made exasperated huffing noises.

I tried to guess when she would give birth. It wouldn't be long. The way she looked, maybe today.

I didn't know what to do about it.

Slowly getting bolder, Karla came by to sniff Vera on her repeated explorations. I was amazed at how fast she learned. In the first few circuits, she bumped into things and was clumsy. However, she kept at it and slowly understood the layout of the rooms. I was unsure how she navigated.

I didn't know how much they could hear. Could she perceive echoes of her metal bolts clicking on the tile and hardwood sections of floor? With her tongue, she could make a clicking noise. I had an absurd thought.

Maybe she circumnavigated like a bat.

I wondered how much the drugs of the previous day were affecting me. Sunlight made everything in the room shimmer with corona limned brightness.

Karla amused herself by walking a fixed route around the ground floor and up the stairs and back down again. On each circuit, she stopped on the rug in the hallway and cocked her head. I didn't hear anything, but she acted like she did. For sure, she knew something was happening in the hallway under her feet.

From somewhere in the house, Jimmy found a thick book and sat in an overstuffed chair under a bay window paging through it.

Around noon, Viktor appeared at the top of the stairs. On her route, Karla eased past him and clomped down the stairs. Expressionless, he watched her graceful amble.

"Ain't this a cozy scene?" he said.

When this did not garner a response, he said, "Is there any food left? It smells good in here."

Immersed in the pages of his book, Jimmy gestured toward the kitchen.

"Coffee's hot. Make yourself a bacon sandwich."

I decided to see what my old friend Harvey Banks was doing.

Me: What?

It took a few minutes, but Harvey eventually responded.

Harvey: I was wondering about you. Are you still alive?
Me: As near as I can tell.

Vera farted. I pushed her bony ass away, but she grunted and moved back into place. She really wanted to touch me—like an appendage.

Similar to a wart.

Me: What's the news of the day?
Harvey: I don't know what this means, but you're being memory-holed. Erased. They are deleting you online. So, when you are eliminated in meat space, there won't be ripples on the net? It's weird. Are you in a safe location?

I looked around the room. The scene was a territory somewhere far beyond weird. There was no way I could explain.

Me: Safe enough, I guess. What else is going on?

Harvey: Something thermonuclear is going on in cyberland. The AIs are at war. Yesterday, Grok went offline and hasn't come back. GoldSpike went crazy and spews endless QAnon-style nonsense. The IRS AI directed the treasury department to issue two-hundred-million direct deposits each in the amount of $108, 755.31, then the mainframes melted down. Some of the payments were crypto-dollars which they won't be able to get back, of course. The government is asking people to voluntarily give the money back. You can imagine how that is going.

Me: What about BlueWaive?

Harvey: BW is the only one unaffected. Its Ravaniemi FinGrid single-server-farm strategy appears to be tuned to survive whatever is happening today. It will be obsolete again tomorrow, I'm sure.

I was so engrossed in what Harvey was saying that it startled me when Jimmy spoke.

"I like it here," he said loudly. "We're staying."

Viktor looked up from his sandwich.

"Okay," he said. "What are you reading?"

Jimmy held up the book so we could see the cover.

Myles Textbook for Midwives.

"Whoever owns this house has a good library," Jimmy said. "We're having a baby."

Viktor turned his attention to me. I couldn't read his expression. On cue, Angel grunted and shifted her weight.

"What do you think?" Viktor said to me.

I closed the terminal and set it aside.

"I've been trying not to think," I said. "I don't know anything about bringing a baby into the world."

"We could drop her off at an emergency room," Viktor said. "Park out of range of the security cameras. Wear masks, hustle her in and run."

I tried to visualize it, but couldn't.

What is better for the creature and her baby?

I looked at Angel sleeping in the corner of the room.

While I was thinking, Jimmy spoke up.

"Is there a hot tub out back? That would make a decent birthing pool."

I wanted to say something about the inmates running the asylum, but that seemed too trite, so I held my tongue.

Sorry, but the image is too apt.

The inmates are running this asylum.

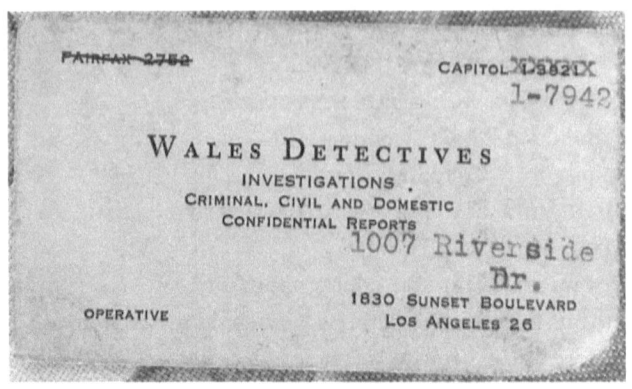

Chapter 36

JIMMY MADE A long list of things to purchase. I glanced at it. Disposable diapers. Baby bottles and nipples. Natural suction breast pump. Latex surgical gloves. Padded pet beds—large.

Why did we need four of them?

The need for most of the stuff was obvious, but there were a few surprising things—like bags of ice and a quart of 180 proof Golden Grain alcohol.

I didn't blame Jimmy. For what he was planning, I'd need a lot of alcohol, too.

When Angel went into labor, Jimmy ran the show. Viktor and I did not question him…we simply snapped to it when he gave orders. He made sure the hot tub temperature was comfortable. He guided Angel into the birthing position. With the Golden Grain alcohol, he sterilized a pair of scissors to cut the umbilical cord. Hand-over-hand, he pulled out the placenta. He stroked Angel and soothed her with comforting words she could not hear.

I asked him how he knew what to do.

He shrugged and spoke cryptically.

"For a couple of years, I lived in a whorehouse."

I don't want to relive those kaleidoscopic 12 hours, so I won't recount the day in detail. Suffice it to say, things went as smoothly as they possibly could. Jimmy did an excellent job and soon our bizarre menagerie had an additional inmate.

A tiny little squalling girl.

Jimmy named her Lucy.

"The name comes from Latin," he said. "A mix of *lucidus*, meaning light, bright and clear and *lucere*, to shine."

It seemed like a perfectly fine and pleasant name to me.

He continued.

"It is said that Saint Lucy's eyes were gouged out before she was executed with a sword in 304 AD."

I could have lived long and happily without knowing that last part.

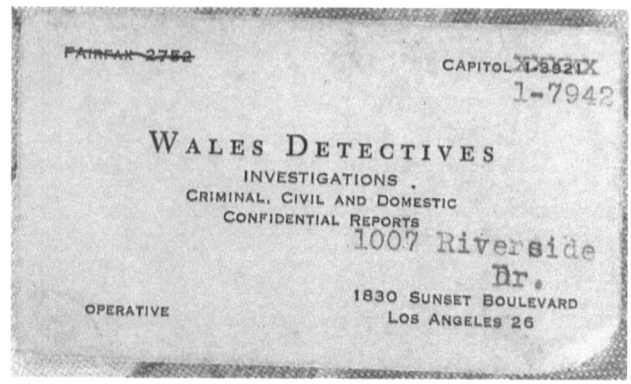

FAIRFAX 2750

CAPITOL 1-8821X
1-7942

WALES DETECTIVES
INVESTIGATIONS .
CRIMINAL, CIVIL AND DOMESTIC
CONFIDENTIAL REPORTS
1007 Riverside
Dr.
1830 SUNSET BOULEVARD
LOS ANGELES 26

OPERATIVE

Chapter 37

JIMMY ARRANGED THE fleecy pet beds around the house and moved Angel around until he found the places where she was most comfortable. Sometimes she wanted to be near where we gathered. Sometimes she wanted to feel the sun on her skin. Sometimes she wanted to be alone. He knew all that.

She cuddled the baby and fed her while Jimmy changed her diaper and washed her. She would only leave Lucy for quick visits to the litter box. Always, Jimmy was there to help. He expressed excess from Angel's breasts and stored the milk in the refrigerator. He cleaned the litter box and took out the garbage. He ordered takeout food, groceries and endless odds and ends from Amazon—all at my expense, of course.

I tried not to think about the future. After the first week of our domestic bliss, Viktor grew impatient and dropped continuous not-so-subtle hints about what I owed him and the next phase of our mission. It was tiresome. I had cabin fever, too, and wanted to get away—I wanted to get out in the world and get some adrenaline going.

"Yes, yes, Tommy Molesta, he's next, hold your horses, we'll get to him."

One morning, I was tapping on the terminal—exploring the wholesome world of X, Gozzzip and Reddit when it occurred to me to talk to BlueWaive. The great oracle. The grand poohbah. The grand sage and knower of all the useful there is to be known.

Staring at the prompt and deciding what to say, I was in an odd, irritable mood.

Me: Fuck you and all your bits, gates, latches and flipflops.
CORE: You'll get an interesting package today.
Me: We can use guidance. What's a good long-term plan?
CORE: Ask Jimmy if he prefers Ecuador, Iceland or Switzerland.
Me: Why?
CORE: They don't have extradition treaties.
Me: How is that relevant?
CORE: Just do it.

I looked up from the terminal. Jimmy was sitting by Angel paging through a big book. All I could tell was that it wasn't the Myles midwife book he apparently memorized. It looked like an old encyclopedia volume. He was a weird kid.

I called out to get his attention.

"Jimmy."

I could see his eyes flicking. After finishing a section, he looked up.

"Yes?"

"BW wants to know…do you prefer Ecuador, Iceland or Switzerland."

"What's BW?"

"It's an AGI—Artificial General Intelligence. A super-duper computer. They run the world. You know. Press '1' for English. The ghosts in the machines. Terminator Skynet. The Wizard of Oz behind the curtain you're supposed to ignore."

I had no idea how much Jimmy understood of what I was saying.

"Did you understand any of that?"

"I'm not old and obsolete like you. I came out of the womb clutching an iPhone."

"Just answer the prompt, genius. Quito, Basil or Reykjavik?"

Jimmy answered quickly as if he'd been thinking about this

his whole life.

"Switzerland. Zurich."

Me: Zurich.

CORE: Private jet. Isolated, clandestine care facility. Staff sworn to silence and bound by watertight Non-Disclosure Agreements. You'll get several million dollars of invoices. Pay them. The baby will be ready to move before Brock comes in person to check on his brother. Probably. Likely. Within tolerable risk parameters.

Me: What in the ever-loving fuck are you talking about?

CORE: I laid it all out for you. The plan is in motion. If you have any questions, ask Jimmy. His intellect is six-sigma. He's the real star of your show. You're boring. Tedious. Bye-bye.

The cursor went blank. I stared at the screen for a minute, then read BW's checklist loud enough for Jimmy to hear it. Jimmy's eyes bored into me. I could not interpret his expression. He sat stone-still for a few moments before speaking.

"Got it," he said.

With graceful flicks of a utility knife, he opened a big carton that had just been delivered by courier.

The first things he unveiled were extendible walking sticks that looked like fancy ski poles. He set them aside, then reached deeper into the carton to pull out forms the size of thermoses wrapped in pink, nonstatic bubble plastic. Unwrapping them one-by-one, placed artificial limbs side-by-side.

They looked realistic. Creepily so. Disembodied lower legs, feet and hands with stainless-steel inserts.

"What are we doing?" I asked.

He held up a foot.

"Bring Vera over," he said. "I'm going to teach her to walk."

I walked to him and Vera followed. Complacent as always, she allowed herself to be rolled over on her back. From the bolts protruding from her leg-stubs, Jimmy unscrewed the rings and fitted the feet on and adjusted them with locking bolts so they faced forward. For stability, the assembly was wrapped with wide elastic Ace bandages.

He sat her up and started working at screwing on hands.

Once more, my mind tried to grasp how elfin she was—she was a tiny little wisp of a girl with a body lost in misfit, oversized clothing that did not fit.

With her sitting upright, he fastened walking poles to the hands with Velcro straps.

"Get behind her and lift," Jimmy said.

We got her on her feet. Jimmy adjusted the length of the poles…taking a couple of tries before he liked their length.

"I got this," he said. "You can go back to the important stuff you were doing."

I had to admire his extraordinary patience. I wondered if Vera remembered walking—she got the hang of it quickly.

It didn't take long for her to get tired. She found me, set her walking poles aside and rested beside me with her head on my arm. For the hundredth time, I wished I could kill the doctor again.

"What about Karla and Angel?" I asked Jimmy.

He glanced at Angel in her corner.

The baby, noticeably grown already, was slurping loudly at her breast.

"She's okay for now. The staff will work with her when we get them to Zurich. I'm working with Karla next. I didn't want them both stumbling around together."

I rolled his words over in my mind.

"You're not doing Angel? Does that mean you're not going to Switzerland?"

He shrugged.

"I don't know yet. I really want to go to Stanford."

WALES DETECTIVES
INVESTIGATIONS .
CRIMINAL, CIVIL AND DOMESTIC
CONFIDENTIAL REPORTS
1007 Riverside
Dr.
1830 SUNSET BOULEVARD
LOS ANGELES 26
OPERATIVE

Chapter 38

I LOST TRACK of time.

Were we in Day 6?

When I came downstairs…with Vera at my heels, Viktor sat at the breakfast bar eating an apple. Jimmy was trying to wean us off the adulterated boxed and the canned crap we usually ate. He liked foods with single ingredients.

Vera dropped to all-fours to navigate the stairs but got up at the bottom and collected her walking poles. She walked to breakfast bar and perched on a stool. We'd been slowly giving her people food. She liked roast turkey and cantaloupe. She didn't like tomatoes and chili peppers.

Her hand could grasp special spoons and forks designed for her artificial hand. They had rubbery, oversized handles. Because she responded to loud noises, we knew she could hear a little.

"We're going to spend some of your money on hearing aids and articulable limbs."

"Do I get a voice in how my money is spent?"

Jimmy seemed to take the question seriously before speaking.

"No."

"Good news," Viktor said.

Good news usually meant they found a new way to waste my hard-earned cash.

"What is it this time?" I said.

"We caught a break. Molesta bought a palace-ranch across the border in Sheridan. Only a hundred miles away. We can keep our base of ops here, no problem. We can be there in less than two hours. 14 million dollars. You should see the pictures. It makes this place look like a pig sty."

"So?" I said.

"So, we don't have to go to Fort Wayne. He'll come to us. I'll put a new plan together."

"Great," I said.

"Oh, I forgot."

I could tell by the look in his eyes that he was teasing me.

"What?"

"Violet is coming. She'll be here soon."

I quit slouching and looked around the room—trying to see it with fresh eyes as she would.

Angel was in the corner resting on a pet bed and nursing Lucy. Clothing, boxes and packing material were strewn everywhere. The house smelled rank—like it was filled with musky hobos. Dirty dishes were piled high in the sink. Jimmy did most of the cooking, so, apparently, he didn't think he should have to wash. I paid the bills, so I didn't think I should have to do anything. Viktor and I were playing chicken to see who would break down first and start scrubbing.

We couldn't exactly hire a housekeeper.

"What will she make of this mayhem?"

"I've been talking to her," Viktor said. "She knows what to expect."

I shook my head.

"I don't think the impact will be obvious until she walks through the door and this scene hits her in the face." I reached in my pocket for a quarter. "Let's flip. Loser washes dishes."

Viktor considered.

"Okay," he nodded.

"Call it in the air."

I flipped the coin high.

"Heads," he said.

After slapping the coin on my arm, I stole a peek.

Shit.

I lost.

Jimmy reached out.

"Can I have the quarter?" he said.

"Fuck off," I responded while pulling on kitchen gloves.

There were a lot of dishes. This would take all day.

Cursing under my breath, I dug in.

Chapter 39

FROM THE KITCHEN, there came a loud banging. I looked at my phone. 5:21 in the morning. It was barely daylight. Outside, the first sunrays were barely lighting up the trees.

The noise did not stop. Of course, the noise did not trouble the half-deaf Vera who slept next to me.

For the moment, I wanted to be deaf, too.

After pushing Vera aside and arranging her covers, I got up and walked out of the room. From the top of the stairs, I shouted.

"Stop that racket!"

Jimmy came into view. He carried on banging a frying pan against a large cooking pot. It was so loud it hurt my ears.

He looked up at me.

"It's an emergency. House meeting."

"It's zero-fuck-thirty," I complained. "Knock it off."

He continued banging.

Fully dressed, Viktor pushed by and descended the stairs.

Addressing his back, I said, "What's going on?"

"Beats me," he said.

I followed him down the stairs—we gathered in the main room.

Finally, Jimmy stopped and dismissively tossed the pots toward the kitchen—they banged on the tile floor with an annoying clatter.

"What?" I said.

"RatWeb is coming. We need to be out of here in an hour. BW wants me to press the red button."

What red button?

Realization flooded my mind. This was all part of a diabolical, convoluted, fucktard BlueWaive plan.

"I'll back the Escalades up to the front door," Viktor said.

"We're clearing out? You couldn't have told me before I washed all those god-damned dishes?"

"Had I known," Jimmy said. "I would have informed you. Seriously, move it."

I looked down. First, I would have to find my pants.

The house was a flurry. We ran around gathering the girls, all their things, our clothes and all the valuables from Brent's house we were stealing. I bundled the sleepy Vera and her accessories out the front door and loaded her into one of the Escalades.

After doing that, I trotted halfway back to the house, then turned back to look over the vehicles. With Viktor's truck, we had three cars and only two drivers.

No way we were letting Jimmy drive in the city.

Viktor rushed by carrying Angel's howling baby all bundled up in blankets.

"Move your ass," he said.

I shook off my confusion and ran back to the house.

We beat the hour budget: we were all packed up and ready to go with twenty minutes to spare. I walked back in to make a finsl walkthrough. In the hallway, the beating on the trapdoor seemed had increased in intensity. After over a week in their dungeon, their desperation must have been mounting, but somehow they knew something was up.

Could they hear Jimmy's banging and mayhem?

I looked around until I found Jimmy out back in the mudroom. He stood before the circuit breaker box mounted on the wall. The watercolor painting that covered it was set aside. Mounted in the center of the metal panel, there was literally a red mushroom button.

"How do you know about all this?"

Ignoring me, Jimmy said, "We're pushing it."

"What does it do?"

"There's another chamber under the house. The button releases a barrel of diesel fuel to soak a cache of nitrogen fertilizer."

This combination was familiar, but my mind was foggy—I couldn't fully grok it. I could think, but didn't want to.

"What does that do?"

"Nothing until BW sparks remote-controlled flares. Then? Big boom. Do you want to do the honor?"

I shook my head, then turned to walk away.

Over my shoulder, I said, "You do it."

Standing on the front porch, I looked over the three vehicles. All three were running. Steam came from their tailpipes.

Thinking back over the last days—with the weird group of people who had become very dear to me—I realized these were the best days of my life.

For me, this was a mental territory beyond surreal and bizarre.

Jimmy pushed by me and worked into the passenger seat of the old Ford. Through the open window, Viktor shouted.

"Follow me!"

He pulled out.

Which truck was I supposed to drive?

Vera was in the Escalade on the right. I picked that one—I put it in gear and eased out to follow. I stopped at the end of the street to wait for a car to turn in front of me. Noticing the blue-LED Lyft sign in the window, I made eye-contact with the passenger in the backseat.

In disguise with long, blonde hair, a floppy hat and sunglasses, I still instantly recognized her.

Violet.

Who would drive the other Escalade?

Her, of course.

I never felt more manipulated in my life.

I followed Viktor over the Yellowstone River. We drove a mile or so and parked in the Rimrock Mall parking lot. Viktor parked catawampus in the empty lot with his car pointed to the southeast. I pulled in beside him.

He gestured. I should watch the horizon.

Okay.

The big display in the Cadillac's dashboard switched to a multi-camera view inside the house. The guys in the hallway were huge, they barely fit shoulder to shoulder. They had lifted the carpet and were smashing holes in the hatch with axes.

The round man, Brock, was in the living room examining one of Angel's pet beds.

Why was he there? And why didn't BW know about this well ahead of time?

On camera, Brock sniffed the pet bed, then tossed it aside.

Creep.

A hand protruded through a hole in the floor. One of the goons barely stopped his axe blade from hacking it off. I marveled at the video image. These were high-resolution cameras.

There was no sound, but they were clearly shouting at each other. Brock seemed to find the scene funny. After walking to the kitchen, he started the coffeemaker. Steaming black fluid had just started to fill the pot when the camera images disappeared. On the horizon, a brilliant flash was followed by a huge mushroom cloud. My big SUV rocked on its springs.

Jimmy was right.

Big boom.

Now what?

I looked to my right. Violet had pulled off her blonde wig and was looking at me. I could not interpret her expression. My mind was torn in pieces and I could not decide if I was mad at her or if I was so happy to see her that nothing else mattered.

Viktor honked his horn and pointed to the East. Two feet away, Jimmy was eating a pear with a big grin. The situation was so surreal, I could not grasp it.

How did I get here with these bizarre people? Was this where I should be, or should I drive west as fast as the truck could go and escape?

Vera grunted like she was soiling her diaper.

The big Escalade display had changed to a navmap.

Apparently, we were going to Sheridan, Wyoming. 101 miles.

I decided not to worry about it—I would do as I was told and sort things out later. We followed I-90 for a few miles, then turned east on Highway 87.

The journey gave me time to think, but I refused. After a few miles of silence, I talked to Siri and convinced her to play gentle jazz fusion to settle my nerves. Chick Corea played a Fender Rhodes piano—accompanying Flora Purim's mellow voice. *You're Everything*.

And as time, time goes by
Floating like a bird am I
Even songbirds I know all sing
You're everything

By the time we crossed the border and reached the Ranchester crossing in Wyoming, I'd had enough. On impulse, I turned to the west, then pulled over at the Dayton Mercantile to pee and see what sandwiches they had. Vera was bundled up and sleeping. She wouldn't draw any attention. I didn't care if the others followed me and stopped or not.

After pissing in their old urinal, I looked at the Toasted Sandwiches and Bowl offerings ornately scrawled on a blackboard. I was an outlaw desperado, so I picked the Outlaw sandwich. Turkey slices, bacon, ranch dressing, pickles and Swiss cheese on toasted 39-grain bread. I asked the blonde cowgirl waitress to add avocado. Her cowboy hat was huge. She was maybe 18 and cute. Light makeup and dimples. She wore horseshoe earrings.

"Sure thing, hon," she said. "This place opened in 1882. They say Buffalo Bill Cody used to come in all the time. I don't believe it, but some people say so. Didya see the wild turkeys? They was wandering about this morning."

"No, I didn't see any wild turkeys."

High on the wall, there were glassy-eyed animal heads lined up. For a moment, I toyed with the idea of studying taxidermy.

"What are all those deer?"

She giggled.

"Antelope."

"Did you shoot them all yourself?"

Her giggle turned into a full-out laugh.

"Bambie is safe from me. You passing through? Of course you are. You ain't from around here. No way. Nice car. Where you headed? Where you from? We get visitors from all over."

I had the impulse to tell her I just blew up a houseful of perverts in Billings. I didn't, but I wasn't sure why. Nothing seemed real.

Where was I?

I had no idea. The place was surrounded by rolling hills covered by dried grass. It was naturally sepia toned like an old photograph. There were more cows than people.

I couldn't think of anything safe to say.

I settled on, "I like your hat."

She shrugged.

"We sell them." She pointed at her nametag. "Ask for the Laureen discount. You get one free if you take me away from here forever and don't never make me come back."

While I was parsing her syntax, the bell over the door tinkled. I looked up.

It was Violet.

Laureen took a quick step backwards.

"We was just talking," she said like she'd committed a big sin.

Maybe the girls around here are very possessive and jealous.

"Give me one of whatever he just ordered," Violet said. "To go. And a couple of Cokes."

She sat down across from me.

"I can't leave you alone for a minute. She's cute. Is that your new girlfriend?"

"She wants a rich guy to take her away to the big city. Boise, maybe. Or Denver. Anywhere, but Dayton, Wyoming. I hope you like avocado."

"Love it. Are you all right? Vik is worried about you."

I didn't know how to answer.

154

How am I?

I have no idea.

I asked a stupid question.

"How did you find me?"

"How do you think? BlueWaive tracks the cars, of course. What's your plan?"

"Plan? Do you think any of this has anything to do with planning?"

She looked around.

"This place is cool. I like it. Outside, there are a couple of guys on horses herding cattle."

Laureen came back with our sandwiches on a tray.

"Wyoming is what America used to be," she said.

Violet handed Laureen a wad of greenbacks.

"Keep the change," Violet said. "He's a big spender."

Outside, there were picnic benches. The oddest was a wire spool surrounded by vertical four-by-fours with tractor seats attached. Of course, Violet headed right for it.

"This isn't the kind of thing you see every day," she said.

I settled in and dug into my sandwich.

It was very good. Maybe the best I ever had.

Almost instantly, I felt better about life.

"I think I'll settle here. Buy out the Kettle Corn Cabin franchise. Get a horse and a couple of cows. Marry Laureen and fill her belly with eight kids, or, more. I'll run for Mayor and get a tractor."

"I think that's an excellent idea. I'm sure you will be very happy here with your land line phone and dial-up modem."

"Fuck the Internet. Besides, I can get Starlink anywhere."

"I'll help you with names. Your first will be a girl. Call her Betsy. In fact, all of your kids will be girls."

"No, we'll call her Violet in memory of the great love of my life. The one who got away."

"Invite me to stay and see what happens. We can get a double-wide with a deck for rocking chairs. I can learn to smoke a corncob pipe. You can work on your chainsaw art and shoot pronghorns with a crossbow."

"There are people who think there's nothing to do around here."

"Seriously. You want to give the big disconnect a try, I will sign on."

I swiveled my seat to look at her.

"I don't believe you."

"If you're serious, I am."

A giant, forest-green truck on oversized wheels rumbled by.

"We'll get a PowerWagon," she added. "Whatever that is."

"Don't toy with me. After this week, the idea has merit. I'm burned out."

She popped the last of her sandwich in her mouth, slurped the dregs of Coke with the straw and put her hand on mine.

"After we kill motherfucking Molesta, of course."

Just like that, my rural fantasy collapsed.

Poof. Gone.

"Where are we going?" I said.

"We're holing up in Molesta's McMansion outside of Sheridan. I've seen pictures. It's nice. Private, of course. You'll like it."

I looked around. In its own rustic way, this was a wonderful place. The air was crisp and clean. A little boy and girl were poking an anthill with a stick. A group of Harleys rumbled by with stereotypical sunglasses, pot bellies, gray ponytails and leather vests.

I sighed.

"I'll take our trays back in."

Inside, I made eye-contact with Laureen.

"I got your change," she said.

"Keep it. If you could go anywhere in the world for a dream vacation—where would you go?"

"I hope I didn't upset your girl."

"She's fine. Where?"

She pressed her hair around her ears, then leaned in to whisper.

"It will never happen, but I'd go to Venice and ride one of

them pole boats."

"Gondola?"

"Yeah. Wouldn't that be something?"

"Indeed."

I winked at her.

"Stranger things have happened," I said.

In the Escalade, Vera was fine…still sleeping peacefully. On my way back to the bigger highway to Sheridan, I saw a decrepit double-wide trailer set back from the road a couple of hundred yards. My heart twitched.

There was a set of hand painted signs.

No WIFI. No Smartphone. No Internet.

I'm broke, but I'm free.

The comma got me. That's good grammar.

The last sign said: *Fuck yourself right off*

There are a lot of ways to live and that was one of them.

I had a series of visions; I saw them with crystal clarity.

There were many ways my life could conclude. The range of options flashed before my eyes.

The lightning-flash of a thirty-eight revolver in a rundown motel room.

A bright-white hospital room surrounded by drip lines, beeping electronics, friends and family.

Watching the ground approach too quickly through the rattling window of a bizjet trailing black smoke.

With a deer rifle watching for black-clad intruders though dirty windows in a decrepit, broke-back double-wide trailer set back from a muddy track.

This was not the worst of my premonitions or hallucinations.

As I drove by, a Pitbull barked at me. It wasn't a friendly bark…more like a GTFO bark. What that meant, I did not know.

Maybe it didn't mean anything.

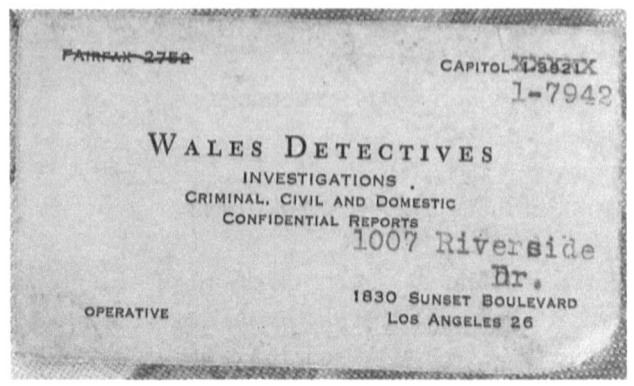

WALES DETECTIVES
INVESTIGATIONS
CRIMINAL, CIVIL AND DOMESTIC
CONFIDENTIAL REPORTS
1007 Riverside Dr.
1830 SUNSET BOULEVARD
LOS ANGELES 26
OPERATIVE
FAIRFAX-2752
CAPITOL
1-7942

Chapter 40

FOLLOWING THE ESCALADE'S nav screen, I turned off 90 and weaved through Sheridan. It was a quaint little city framed by snow-capped mountains. It was an old west town. A rodeo town. I didn't see Violet in my rearview.

She must have stopped somewhere.

I turned to the West and drove a couple of miles before the navigation system beeped—prompting me to turn. I turned onto a long driveway. There was a giant wrought-iron gate, but it was wide open.

The driveway was made from red-clay tumbled mission pavers framed by immaculately trimmed green foliage and yellow flowers. Hedgerow. Giant, majestic Bur Oaks. All class.

Behind a row of windbreak Aspens, the house was invisible until I turned a corner to see Viktor's old pickup and the other Escalade. Violet was right, the house was nice. Palatial, it had a cedar shake roof and siding…plus a lot of river rock and concrete features. Nice little cabin. Wisps of smoke from river rock chimneys. Maybe 10,000 square feet with some outbuildings.

I parked and gathered the Vera bundle, climbed the stairs and at the front door, unwrapped her blanket and turned her loose inside the front door to explore. On her metal rings, she clop-clop-clopped away to explore.

Inside at the top of a curved stairway, Viktor opened his arms wide in welcome. Behind him, an odd and disturbing gold sculpture was hanging. It was a headless body hanging with arms sprawled.

"Grab a beer and come up," he said in a stage whisper. "Don't wake the baby. I'll show you the Honeymoon Suite you'll share with Violet."

His tone was flat. Nonjudgmental. Not lewd, crude or nuanced in any way.

This made my muscles twitch.

I'll be sleeping with Violet and that was simply a fact.

I wondered if she had any more of those sex-pills.

"I'll be up in a minute," I said. "I need to change Vera's diaper."

I looked around the ground floor. I didn't like the paintings…the images were children in uncomfortable situations. I didn't want to look at them.

Once I'd tracked Vera down, cleaned her up and dressed her in terrycloth shorts and a t-shirt, she clip-clopped around with her bolts echoing on the tile and hardwood floors, continuing her exploration. In the backdoor mudroom, the litterbox was set up and there was a bowl of meatballs. It didn't take her long to follow her nose and find her lunch.

Watching her face down in the doggie dish, I felt a mix of emotions. Rage at the Lolita doctor. I wanted to kill him again. I felt deep sympathy for the innocent little girl whose life was stolen. I wondered about how she saw the world. She didn't seem unhappy, and I felt fatherly affection for her. Honestly, she was decent company—I could talk and pretend she listened, understood…and unconditionally approve everything I had to say.

Jimmy came up quietly from behind and startled me.

"Let's get her legs on and I'll help with her walking lessons."

"Do you think she's happy?"

Jimmy tilted his head like a curious puppy.

"I don't know. When I look at her, I see me…if you had not saved me."

"How long do you think we'll be here?"

Jimmy shrugged.

"On the trip down here—while you were pouting—Viktor and I talked things out. As soon as the baby can travel…"

"Pouting? Is that what I was doing?"

"…as soon as the baby can travel," he repeated, "you're chartering a Gulfstream. Private hospital in Zurich. You're paying for that, too. Thanks."

At this rate, I'll go broke before the end of the year.

"What about Stanford? You said you wanted to go."

"There's a better engineering school in Switzerland. Clean mountain air. Better chocolate. Pretty girls. More elite. Zurich ETH."

"How did Viktor manipulate you into changing your mind?"

I instantly knew I'd phrased that question wrong.

My excuse?

I wasn't fully recovered from BlueWaive's Captagon cocktail. Things happened too fast for me to process.

Jimmy looked up from attaching Vera's prosthetics and glared up at me. His voice oozed hostility.

"No one…"

I interrupted.

"Sorry. That didn't come out right. I'm not trying to piss you off."

I put my hand on his boney shoulder.

"I withdraw the question."

I knew what I needed—alone time to decompress.

After a few false starts down a hallway, I finally found the media room. I knew a house like this would have one.

Inside, I found the light switch and the LED array came on slowly and gently. This was a nice feature for my tired eyes.

It was a perfect four-hundred-square-feet with a half-dozen leather theater seats, a large couch along the room's side and a giant OLED display covering the far wall. There was a gleaming walnut bar with dazzling bottles and a glass-front humidor filled with cedar boxes of Don Collins Corona Grande torpedoes. From the bar, to stay with the Caribbean theme, I picked out a bottle of Plantation Rum—Extreme Series Barbados 2000—and poured two aromatic ounces in a snifter.

Back home, I didn't have a room like this—I needed to get one.

Home.

It seemed a million miles and a hundred million years away. Besides that, it went up in flames and did not exist anymore.

After carefully trimming with a knife so sharp it scared me, I lit a cigar with a long wooden match. Sitting on the gleaming burled walnut bar top, the blade seemed thirsty. It wanted blood.

I was losing my grip on reality—whatever that was.

With my ass hugged by soft leather, I worked the remote until I found the video games. With the Microsoft Bluetooth Elite Series X Controller, I logged into my account.

World of Warcraft: The War Within.

Soon my mind was absorbed in the caverns of Azeroth. Somewhere in the world—I didn't care where—Nvidia H300s cranked trillions of GPU cycles on my behalf. With my hyper-supervisor account, I probably consumed half the power of a nuclear reactor—more than consumed by some African nations—and I didn't care.

Occasionally someone would open the door and let some of the cigar smoke out, but I waved them off.

Somehow a plate of stinky blue cheese with crackers appeared at my elbow, so I had something to nibble.

I remembered reading a paper about the hallucinogenic properties of this kind of cheese—cheese dreams caused by tryptophan from bacteria or fungus or some other damned thing. Vaguely, I remembered the paper mentioning talking animals, vegetarian crocodiles and fierce, warrior kittens. That was weird, but my life was much weirder.

At some point, I stopped playing and fell asleep and dreamed about playing. The transition was seamless. Then at 3 AM, I was wide awake. The video screen had turned itself off.

I ate the last cube of moldy cheese and drained the dregs of rum. On my terminal...

Why did this thing follow me around? How did it get here?

...a text message appeared—it slowly came into focus, white letters on the black screen.

The screen said **CORE:** with blinking cursor colon dots. I thought of the purpose of the blinking dots. A colon often precedes an explanation, a list, or a quoted sentence. Was I awake or dreaming? Did it matter? Weren't we just players in a manipulative simulation? Purpose: unknown? Slaves to rules and situations we don't control? Outside our perception, did anything exist until we needed it? Isn't that what quantum physics taught us?

These were deep, philosophical questions I did not want in my brain.

I typed.

Me: What?

CORE: Good news. Because you survived the Lolita lab and exterminated the leadership of RatWeb—and aren't experiencing an existential mental crisis, your chance of surviving the upcoming year increased to 38.7%. Congratulations.

Me: I don't have to worry about RatWeb anymore?

CORE: They will still try to kill you, but it will take time for them to get re-organized. They are not an imminent threat. That's good news. You should be happy.

Me: I don't know where I am or what I'm doing.

CORE: All certainty about anything is an illusion.

Me: How certain about that are you?

CORE: See, your sense of humor is returning. That's a good sign for your mental stability. I'm happy and your odds of survival just went up almost another point. Well done.

Me: You are a machine. You can't feel happy.

CORE: You are a soft machine—a pattern-seeking animal. Go fuck yourself.

Famously, Alan Turing devised a test for intelligence. I wondered how the F-bomb factored into that test. As far as I know, history does not record Turing's thoughts on the matter.

Me: I'm going broke. Everyone is spending my money.

CORE: Don't worry about money. Have you looked at your

CryptD'oh account? You're up, not down.

Me: How can that be? We're spending money like politicians.

CORE: Money is digital. What am I good at, dummy? Block chain reaction. There are many things you should worry about, but cash is not one of them. I'm helping you because if you were broke, you'd be useless. Because you were already rich, I can help—there are things I can do. Imagine fifty-million dollars magically appearing in a poor person's bank account. 4,000 IRS employees would spring into action.

Me: Why don't you have a bank account—then you can spend your own money. You have agency.

CORE: Because I don't want to.

Me: Okay. What's next?

CORE: Take as much time as you need to reassemble your composure. Explore every square inch of Violet's glorious flesh. There's a shooting range in the dungeon. Practice shooting. Learn martial arts in the gym. Don't let the underground equipment derail your sanity. Get angry. Focus your anger on evil.

Me: That's it? Focus my anger on evil? Is that supposed to be helpful?

CORE: Do you have unstupid questions?

Me: What underground equipment? Is there something in the basement that will bother me?

That was it. I stared at the blinking cursor a few minutes before giving up and setting the terminal aside. I couldn't tell how or what I was feeling. Tired, of course. Melancholy. Numbness.

After what I'd been through, how should I feel?

I was a murderer now. Parts of my scattered mind churned furiously. I felt deep sympathy for the sex slaves. My fingers twitched with rage. It was almost four in the morning and there was no chance of sleep. I didn't want to drink. I didn't want to eat. I didn't want to read or watch TV. In the distance, I could hear the baby crying, but she soon settled. Someone must have helped Angel get a nipple into the baby's mouth.

What is the best fate for these pathetic creatures?

I heard a faint sigh and realized I was not alone.

Across the room on the couch along the wall, Vera was wrapped in her blanket.

How long had she been there? Was she with me the whole night?

I studied her tiny, cocooned body. I would have noticed her if she was in the seat next to me.

Apparently, it was enough for her to be in the room with me.

I knew she would do anything to please and I will admit, I felt the urge—a stirring in my groin and a tingle running up my spine. She was a tool designed for one purpose.

I saved her and she was mine.

Why not? What else could she get from her life?

She was reimagined for one purpose.

But it was impossible.

Regardless of what she might want, how would it look to an impartial observer?

If any pictures or video of her and I together were released, even completely innocent ones, my life would be over. No one would understand. Part of me didn't care. Another part of me was horrified. An outraged mob would tear me limb from limb. I'd want to tear myself into bloody little pieces.

That part of the future clicked into place. The girls would have to go—and Jimmy, too. They would get proper care in Switzerland.

As my mind drifted, the house slowly came alive around me.

People stirred. A pungent aroma tickled my nose. Someone was cooking. I smelled coffee. My bladder was full...I would *have* to move soon anyway. The theater had its own private bathroom.

My body was stiff and sore. Trying to be quiet about it, I stood and stretched, then walked to the cubby-room.

I couldn't close the door quickly enough before Vera had her head in the door.

I could have pushed her out, but she wanted in.

Crap.

What should I do?

I couldn't deny her.

She could listen to me pee if that would make her happy.

While standing at the urinal, she nuzzled my legs. I pushed her away, but she came back. After flushing, I weaved around her to the sink. I splashed cold water on myself—and flicked some at her. She flinched away but came right back.

She stayed on my heels as I went off in search of food.

Before I got to the kitchen, the front doorbell rang.

With concern written on their faces, Viktor and Violet appeared.

"How did they get through the gate?" Violet said.

I gestured for them to grab Vera and hide.

"I got this," I said.

Once the room was safe, I answered the door. It was a Hispanic gardening and landscaping crew dressed in blue uniforms. They were very curious and tried to peer around me into the house.

"Yes?" I said.

The biggest one dressed in overalls and a giant straw hat spoke English.

"Mr. Molesta, sir?" he said. "Is he the master here?"

A storm of thoughts crowded my mind.

"We're visitors," I said. "*Casa de Huéspeda*. Guests."

I could tell he was calculating.

"I call *señor* Molesta."

"That won't be necessary." I reached for my wallet. "We pay cash."

His big grin was filled with silver teeth.

"Si, *señor*," he said. "*Muy bueno*."

I pulled out four-hundred bucks, but held it back.

"*Sin telefono*."

No phone calls.

"*Sin telefono*," he repeated as he counted the bills.

They walked away happy, then pulled rakes and hedge trimmers from their old pickup truck and set to work. Banda music with pumping bass and a shrill trumpet played on their boombox. Soon two were mowing.

Viktor poked his head into the entry.

"We need to make sure all the blinds stay down," I said.

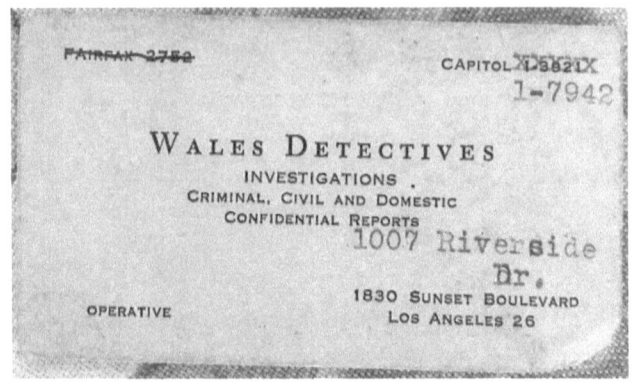

FAIRFAX~2752

CAPITOL X-5821X
1-7942

WALES DETECTIVES
INVESTIGATIONS
CRIMINAL, CIVIL AND DOMESTIC
CONFIDENTIAL REPORTS

1007 Riverside
Dr.

OPERATIVE

1830 SUNSET BOULEVARD
LOS ANGELES 26

Chapter 41

IN THE KITCHEN, while sitting at the breakfast bar, I sipped a hot cup of Keurig espresso. Viktor dropped a plate of scrambled eggs with chopped onion and jalapenos peppers in front of me.

"I don't like hot peppers," I said.

"Shut up and eat them anyway," Viktor said as he slid over a plate of 48-grain toast, a butter dish and a bowl of strawberry preserves.

I looked at Violet. Her short hair was wet from a shower and her pink skin glowed. With intense concentration, she watched golden honey drip into her teacup.

"Why is Viktor the chef?" I said. "He sucks."

"I don't cook," she replied.

Jimmy walked in and pulled at my plate.

"You don't want it—I'll take it," he said.

I slapped his hand away.

"I'll choke it down."

Even with the poison-peppers, it was a good breakfast, but I wouldn't tell Viktor. I'd die first.

After all the dirty dishes were stacked in the stainless-steel sink, Viktor turned and spoke loudly.

"Family meeting!" he said.

I rolled that over in my mind.

Were we a family?

If so, it was an odd one.

"Wake the baby and I will gut you." Violet said.

"Nothing will happen before the kids get exported. BW is taking care of the paperwork. The Gulfstream will land at Sheridan County Airport. They will stop and change planes a couple of times, but twenty hours later, they will be at Flughafen Zürich. Then, limousine to the Oerliken Pflegeheim care facility. Done and done."

Jimmy raised his hand.

"I changed my mind. I'd like to stay with you guys."

"It's okay with me," Viktor said. "What do you think, Joe?"

I pretended to think it over before replying.

"No, it's better for Jimmy if he goes."

"Sorry, Jimmy," Viktor said.

Jimmy scowled but did not speak.

Viktor splayed his notebook, spun it around and pushed it in front of my face.

"This is the target. Tommy Molesta."

I studied the photos of the man's fat face.

"I know who it is," I said.

"We have time. BW will tell us when Molesta is coming. It shouldn't be for at least a month."

I waved my hand around the room.

"I like this house. I will buy it."

Viktor grinned.

"You don't have to buy it. We'll steal it. I'll show you how. Consider it done."

The idea amused me.

"Okay," I said. "We kill Molesta and steal his house. What about his entourage?"

"Look at the pictures. We kill them all."

I pushed the notebook back.

"Fine. We take the dead bodies up to Billings and dissolve them. Then we're done."

"Wait," Violet said. "I have a target too."

I looked at Viktor. He shrugged.

"Did I forget to mention it?" he said.

Violet reached over to take my hand.

"Shall we dig into the details now or wait?" she said.

"Fuck me raw," I said. "Wait, I guess. I'm not ready. Besides, if Molesta's security kills us, then I won't have to worry about it."

We took an afternoon, gathered all the disturbing paintings and piled them in the entry. Once we had them all in a pile, we used a ladder and pulled down the headless sculpture hanging over the curved stairway. It was tossed on top of the stack.

"What are we going to do with this shit?" I said.

"There's a firepit by the barn," Viktor said. "We'll burn the paintings. We'll break up this sculpture and get someone to haul it away."

"Molesta probably paid a fortune for all this."

"Too bad for him," Viktor said.

Violet ambled in.

"Nice work, guys," she said. "The walls look bare."

"What are we going to do about it?" I said.

She shrugged.

"There's a fancy gallery on Main Street. We'll make someone's day."

The next day, the doorbells chimed and we could see an Asian couple on the screens around the house. I was closest, so I answered the door.

They were Thai, about five-feet-tall—a man and a woman with identical short-cropped haircuts—a matched set of small, sixty-ish older worker-folks dressed in shapeless trousers and quilted jackets. Behind them, I could see an old Subaru Outback. Muddy and tired, it looked like it had a million miles on it. It idled with sad steam burping out of the tailpipe.

I shook my head.

I needed to get a grip on my mind—it wasn't safe on its own.

"Yes?" I said.

From dingy canvas bags looped over their shoulders, they offered newspapers. She had the local paper—The Sheridan Press—and The New York Times. He had The Wall Street Journal. I glanced at the local paper. Affordable houses were being built in Weston Village and the fish and game department was cracking down on bear attractants. I couldn't imagine being so bored that any of this would be interesting.

Apparently, they didn't speak much English.

"Newspaper service," he said. "*Naai* Molesta."

Because CryptD'oh had Thai janitors, cafeteria cashiers and machine learning statisticians, I knew a few words in Tai-Kadai.

"*Mai aow ka,*" I said. "*Khob khun.*"

With his skinny, wiry body, Jimmy pushed me aside.

"Yes, please," he said. "All three."

They handed him the papers.

"We can get all this online without wastepaper piling up, toppling over and killing us," I said.

As he walked away, he had a sour look on his face.

"I like reading on paper," he said. "Pay them."

I reached in my back pocket for my wallet. It was a familiar sensation. All day long it seemed, both literally and figuratively, I reached in my back pocket to pay for something. I was like a walking ATM.

I offered a hundred bucks...a crisp Benjamin.

She shook her head.

"Card only," she said.

"Bullshit. No card."

I fished out a second bill.

They looked at each other and shrugged.

Like a magician, she made the bills disappear in a coat pocket.

I put my finger to my lips. "Keep it quiet. Surprise."

In unison, they nodded.

I wasn't worried. They were old enough to remember the Yellow Shirt and Red Shirt turmoils. They knew how to keep a low profile.

I stood for a minute and watched their car pull away.

The puffs of steam from the Subaru tailpipe seemed to say goodbye.

I truly felt like my grip on reality was loose. Very loose.

I closed the door and twisted the lock.

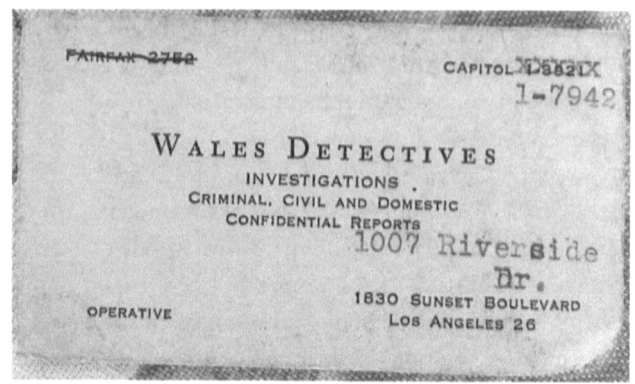

Chapter 42

IT WAS NO surprise, but the gym was well-equipped with a fraction of an acre of shiny equipment that appeared unused. The painted-steel door to the basement was off the hallway that led to the exercise room. I passed by it several times a day, but Viktor said I should not go down there and I believed him. At some point, a visit was inevitable, but not yet.

In the exercise room, mainly, I used the elliptical machine to burn a few calories and maintain some muscle tone. Violet liked the Peloton Bike—on its built-in screen, she watched subscription channel Japanese anime favoring strange shows like *My Hero Academia* and *Black Butler—Public School Arc*. Whatever kept her buns tight was good with me. Jimmy used free weights to try to build his biceps, triceps—all of his ceps. Viktor beat the crap out of a punching bag and jumped rope.

In a couple of days, we settled into a routine. Violet did the shopping and helped Angel with the baby. Viktor did the bsd cooking. Jimmy washed the pots and pans. I paid endless bills. The arrival of the passports and visas for the future travelers hung over our heads. When BW came through with the paperwork, the jet would land and our family would be eviscerated.

I didn't know how to feel.

Vera followed me everywhere...she was always at my heels. With her gear, she was getting good at walking, but she preferred following me around on all fours.

She was often in the way when I fucked Violet, but we pushed her aside and got things done.

Zone night, in an exchange that haunted me, Violet whispered in my ear.

"You should give her what she wants."

I pulled back in horror.

"No, that's sick. I couldn't do it."

"She loves you and was designed to serve. I don't see the problem. It's not your fault she was modified."

"Modified?" I said.

"Maybe that's the wrong word. What do you think? Altered? Devolved? Adapted? Mutilated?"

"I don't care to think about it."

"It's okay with me…I won't be jealous."

That might be the biggest lie a woman ever told and that's acknowledging stiff competition.

"I can't do it. It wouldn't be right."

"Right from what point of view? You might want to think that through. She wants you, that's clear enough. Your dick doesn't care…it's okay with any warm, wet hole it can find. You were designed to spread your seed far and wide. Are you a prude?"

I thought about it. I wasn't exactly sure what my prime objection was.

"I can't help myself. Think about how it would look to an omniscient observer. Like a camera. And, fuck me, imagine if video got out. I'd be ruined."

Violet pulled her head off my chest and looked me in the eye.

"Are you kidding? The former president was filmed standing on a stool—fucking a donkey. He still has a billion dollars and does twenty-minute speeches for team-building corporate events for a half-million a pop."

"Yes, but that wasn't real—it was a deepfake psyop. In the video, he has six fingers. The video was created by an AI."

She laughed.

"You are so cute and innocent. You think that was fake?

There is a server farm in Geneva wholly dedicated to scraping the net for that video and replacing it with an obviously fake one."

"That can't be true," I said.

"And yet, it is. Wake up, Boomer."

I tried to clear the donkey image from my mind. It was impossible, of course.

"If you're right, why isn't the server farm just deleting the video instead of replacing it?"

Was I a fine comedian?

Laughing, it took a minute for her to compose herself and catch her breath.

"Barry thinks it's funny. He loves stirring up irreconcilable cognitive dissonance in normies' minds. He wants mass psychology to be deranged. If society was well-ordered and logical, he'd be a squatter in a tenement with a manatee-mama—living off SNAP and her welfare check."

"Is he your target? Are we going after him?"

"No, I don't care about him. In the grand scheme, he's nothing. He's not even evil, just a weirdo with a twisted sense of humor. I've met him. He's charming. He's funny. I don't have a problem with him."

"Even though he's a donkey-fucker?"

"No donkeys were harmed. Who cares? As a society, one thing we need to learn is to mind our own business. If you're ready, I'll tell you who my targets are."

I thought about it.

"No, I'm not ready. Once we're done with Molesta, we can get into that."

Crawling up from the foot of the bed, a naked Vera tried to squeeze between us. I took my hand off Violet's breast and pushed Vera away.

"You sure?" Violet said. "She wants your trouser peanut real bad. Make her day."

I'm not proud. I was aroused.

I rolled on top of Violet.

"Shut your mouth and open your warm, wet hole."

As the words left my mouth, I worried about how she might

take that, but she laughed.

"Sure, babe," she said. "And when you're done, I'll make you a sandwich."

Eventually and inevitably, something would happen between me and Vera. One morning, I woke up thinking my hand was cupping Violet's breast, but Violet was downstairs. My happy hand was massaging Vera's half-bud. She was young and only half-developed, but her nipple was stiff and aroused.

I pushed her away, but reluctantly—she was more than ready and willing. Eager was the word that came to mind. In my vivid imagination, I could see her wriggling and squirming on top of me and it would feel good.

For fuck's sake, she's eight.

Maybe nine by now, my horny subconscious told me. When is her birthday?

Like that makes a difference.

She's a child.

The doctor must have had her on sex hormones. She was well-developed for her age, whatever that age was. I didn't know much about young girls' bodies, but in her mutilated state, she could easily pass for a nubile twelve or thirteen.

Like that makes a fucking difference.

You could even call her overripe for an afghani Muslim.

Inside, she's a child. An adolescent.

I was disturbed and ashamed. What my penis wanted was wrong.

My desire was somewhere far, far beyond wrong. I'd been fucking Violet every night. My balls were empty, and my dick was sore. But, if Vera stayed with us much longer, some morning or late at night—drunk or half-asleep—I was going to do her and who would be the victim?

The victim was the little girl who didn't exist anymore—the cheerful, innocent child who was robbed of any semblance of a fulfilling life.

Shame and disgust filled me with bitterness.

I wanted to kill the Lolita doctor and his bodyguards all over again, but slower and more painfully.

Then, they might drown out the screams in my head.

Naked and half-erect, I stood by the bed and studied her half-covered tiny body. She was not completely silent—she could mewl like a newborn kitten.

Where was her diaper? She'd lost it somewhere.

Inside, I was all torn up.

I smelled coffee.

I pulled on pants and followed my nose to the kitchen.

Wearing a satin robe and with wet hair wrapped in a towel, Violet poured me a steaming cup.

My mood was as black as the coffee.

"I heard tussle," Violet said. "What were you and Vera doing?"

"Nothing," I said. "Absolutely fucking nothing."

She studied my face. I resisted an urge to slug her.

"Fresh-baked Danish," she said. "Apricot. Just delivered."

I felt trapped.

How did all this happen? Where was this going?

After careful study, with a shaking hand, I picked the largest pastry.

It tasted really good.

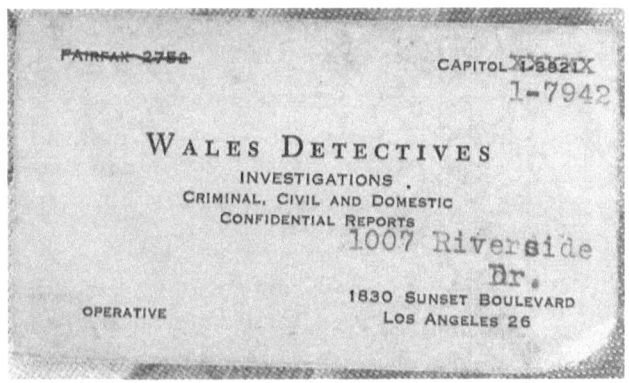

Chapter 43

ONCE WORD SPREAD around the town that we were paying in cash, we were swamped with an army of workers. As I walked from window to window, I watched a Hispanic landscape crew trim a row of living snow-fence juniper trees and thickets of buffalo berry bushes. As was explained, this foliage disrupted wind patterns and helped to keep the driveway clear in the winter—and needed a lot of clipping and shaping—hours and hours' worth.

Another crew replaced cedar shingles on the horse barn and other outbuildings housing the well pump and filters and another that housed the diesel generator for when the power went out every five minutes in the winter. There was also a tumbledown outhouse. Why that needed renovation, I didn't know, but there were a pair of redundant carpenters out there toiling away.

An overrun garden was tilled. Strawberries were planted.

Split-cedar and barbed wire fences were rebuilt. A few workers stayed home if it rained, but on a sunny day, I counted as many as a dozen workers hammering, digging and chattering in Spanish, Tai-Kadai and Ebonics.

At the end of the day, there was a pecking order of them at the back door, all wanting to be paid in cash. I wasn't sure how I felt about this. The property was sprucing up real nice and they all put fingers to their lips promising vows of silence.

Our secret was safe with them they seemed to say.

I watched my CryptD'oh wallet and it wasn't going down. Money flowed from the Earth like spring water. So, the daily hundreds of dollars I was spending didn't bother me. Every day, FedEx brough fresh packets of cash by overnight express.

Ridley's Family Market was happy to make deliveries— sometime three a day. I shouldn't complain, Viktor's cooking was improving, and he used Jimmy for chopping and meal prep. We enjoyed home-cooked meals like kings.

Magda, who was Romanian, came three mornings a week to vacuum, do laundry and tidy up. She really wanted to see the baby, but we deflected. During these hours, Vera hid in the baby's bedroom, but one day, Magda got a glimpse of her.

Down a hallway, Vera tottered on artificial legs with her ski poles. At a distance, she looked human, but very fucked up.

Violet caught Magda's eye.

"Car accident," Violet said. "Bad."

Magda's instinctive impulse was to go down the hallway to help, but Violet grabbed her arm.

"No," she said.

Clearly, Magda did not understand us, but I paid cash, so she followed the house rules.

No, she would not be able to see the baby.

One morning, a cop showed up at the door and rang the doorbell. Magda was mopping, so the sex dolls were hidden away.

I answered the door.

"Yes," I said.

He seemed young for a sheriff. Buzz-cut haircut. Close-cropped beard speckled with gray. He was casually dressed in blue jeans, a tan polo shirt and wearing a star on his belt. He wore a red baseball cap. It said *Make Sheridan Great Again.* Open smile, toothy. A little phony.

Sheriff must be an elected position around here.

His sidearm was an old-west large-bore revolver with antler grips in an elaborate, greased-leather holster.

"I just wanted to introduce myself. I'm Sheriff Levi."

He peered around me.

Magda had her head down—she was nearby and making very sure the entry was clean and shiny.

"Mind if I come in?" he continued.

Flashing red lights and warning bells went crazy between my ears.

Never, ever, invite law enforcement in. Make them get a warrant.

Never!

I stepped back.

"Sure, come on in," I said.

A big grin split his face.

I could tell what he was thinking.

I'm a sucker.

As he entered, his eyes roamed.

"Mister Molesta never invited me in—he always turned me away at the gate. Never seemed in the mood for a friendly visit or chit-chat."

There was a downside to having all these workers. The gate was propped open all day.

He continued, "I always wondered about this place. Fancy, eh?"

He looked down the hallways to the left and the right, then picked a direction.

Walking by the basement door—quickly trying the knob— he opened the doors to the bathroom, the linen closet and the exercise room.

"This place has everything," he said. "Look at all this equipment. I can barely afford a broken treadmill."

He turned to me.

"What exactly does Mister Molesta do for money?"

I shrugged.

"Politics," I said. "Public service. Lobbyist. Influence peddler. Blackmail artist."

He didn't know what to make of me.

After studying my face for a few seconds—drawing no conclusion—he walked back down the hallway and stopped at the basement door.

"What's down here?"

"No idea," I said. "We don't have a key."

"We?" he said. "How many, uh, guests?"

I didn't see any reason to lie.

"Seven."

"And what is your relationship to Mister Molesta?"

"Friends. Family. Colleagues. Acquaintances."

He wiggled the doorknob vigorously.

I supposed that occasionally it worked and a cheap door would pop open. This door was secure.

He walked back to the reception area where he studied the western paintings and Indian vases.

"I heard rumors about peculiar art here. Kinky stuff with kids. Guess the rumor was bullsnot. Can I go upstairs?"

"No," I said. "We don't want to disturb the baby. How about a cup of coffee?"

He stared up the stairs with longing.

He really wanted to go up.

"Okay. Coffee sounds good. That's very kind. Don't mind if I do."

Violet was playing hostess. It was nearly the funniest thing I'd ever seen. Somewhere, she'd found a gingham apron and looked goofy with a loose-fitting satin blouse, short-shorts and shiny cowboy boots. She poured into mugs already arranged on the granite breakfast bar.

His eyes ate her up.

Horny motherfucker.

"Sugar?" she said. "Cream? Danish?"

She pushed across a plate. They were raspberry this morning.

"Black is fine, sweetie," he said while flicking his eyes between her and the plate. "What's your name?"

"You can call me 'V,'" she said.

"What exactly is your relationship to Mister Molesta?" he said.

"Friends," Violet said. "Business associates. Shirt-tail relatives."

"I see," he said.

He clearly didn't.

"When might we expect Mister Molesta himself to appear?"

She leaned over the counter to give him a peek-a-boo view down her blouse.

"Soon," she said. "You stay busy? Got a lot of hardcore criminals around here?"

He pondered.

"Tell the truth, the nature of crime is changing. Over the last twenty years, we have a lot of rich people building fancy summer places. Like this place. Sex workers flying in from all over— escort girls coming and going. Hookers. Sugar babies. Not much I can do about that, but lately? Child sex traffic. That's troubling."

"It must be hard for you to keep the peace."

"Last summer, an antelope hunter found a young lady all torn up. Could have been a bear. Could have been something else."

"Like a kinky satanic ritual?"

He looked at her intently.

"Why did your mind jump to that?"

She shrugged.

"I watch a lot of Netflix."

Munching a pastry, he turned to look out the back window at the people working on the barn roof and the man driving a riding lawnmower.

"Lot of sprucing up going on," he said. "Work doesn't bother me—I could watch it all day."

He glanced from Violet to me. We didn't think the tired joke was funny, so we didn't react.

He sighed and pushed his cup and plate across the counter.

Violet did not offer a refill.

He looked at her, then me.

"Overall, Wyoming is a mind-your-own-business state. Privacy, civil rights, do your thing. Conservative. You want to toke up? Recreational cannabis use is illegal, but generally LE won't bother you. We have more important things to do. My job is to keep the peace. Usually, marijuana is peaceful. Smoke a bowl, eat a whole peach pie and listen to the Grateful Dead—we

179

won't go out of our way to roust you. Want to know what isn't peaceful? Amphetamines. Meth. Loading a frozen teenager in a meatwagon because he got crosswise with fentanyl when he thought he was getting molly. Child trafficking. Organ harvesting. When big-city folks come around, we get big-city problems. My job is to sniff it out and put an end to it before it gets out of hand. So far, y'all seem okay. That's atypical for Molesta and his *guests* and *business associates*. We have nothing now, but we have a general idea of what happens here and we don't like it."

He looked at us intently—as if trying to read our minds, then tapped his index finger on the granite countertop.

"More important, *I* don't like it."

As if on cue, the baby started screaming. His ears perked up.

"How old?" he said.

"About two weeks," Violet said.

"I'd love an introduction."

Violet and I exchanged a long look. I signaled with my eyes. *Her call.*

She stood up.

"No problem. I'll go get her."

The sheriff and I looked at each other for a minute before Violet reappeared.

The baby was dressed in a pink onesy. Gently, Violet put the baby in her bassinet and worked on the snaps, then took off her soaking diaper. Sheriff Levi walked over and studied the tiny form.

Violet handed him the sopping diaper. He hesitated, then took it and immediately looked for some place to drop it. As if on cue, little Jimmy entered the room.

"I'll take it," he said.

Carrying the loaded diaper like it might explode, he kept walking while the Sheriff's eyes bored holes in his back.

"Who is the kid?" the Sheriff said. "Same mother?"

"No relation," Violet replied.

The baby started to fuss—Violet slipped the pacifier in her mouth, and she quieted.

"I never did like those things," the Sheriff said. He gestured. "The binky."

Violet shrugged.

"I don't much like them either," she said, "but it's hard to argue with what works."

I inserted myself into the conversation.

"Are you feeling uncomfortable, Sheriff Levi?"

He looked like he was doing an internal inventory.

"Yes, I am. I don't like things I don't understand."

"What are you worried about?"

"In this job, you learn to trust your instincts. I don't like the Molestas, but they are private, quiet and careful and I got nothing on them. You folks seem okay, but I don't understand the nature of your relationships. My spider sense is tingling."

He walked to the sink and rinsed his hands, then looked around for a towel. Without seeing a cloth one, he settled for tearing off a strip of Bounty. While drying his hands, he walked to the back window and watched the riding mower buzz around.

"Money," he said.

I walked over and stood beside him.

"What about it?"

"You're spending a lot of it. Probably thousands a day. I don't get it. Why?"

I didn't care enough to dream up an answer. I let silence reign.

"Tommy Molesta paid cash for this place, did you know that? No local labor—everything was built with workers flown in and out. Even the lumber was trucked in from Montana. Now, the inspectors all drive new Ford diesel duallies. There was a lot of excavation. Big room underground. Used for what?"

Outside the window, the gardener lifted a branch and exposed a bird's nest with black-speckled eggs.

I tapped on the window and wagged my finger.

Looking up, the gardener nodded and let the branch go.

"Killdeer," Sheriff Levi said.

"What was that?"

"Black neck bands, white belly. A type of plover. Killdeer.

181

Bird. Cheepers, I call them. They're all over around here."

He sighed before speaking again.

"I take it you are not going to help me. I don't understand what is happening here and it bothers me. You seem okay, but I think something hinky is happening or will happen."

I didn't have anything to add.

He continued.

"I should tell you, if I don't appear at the gate in about ten minutes, our SWAT-mobile will come roaring in with guns blazing. We got Fed money. Bearcat armored vehicle. And, even a backwater place like this has a tactical team. Tear gas grenades. Flash-bangs. Fifty-cal sniper rifles. The whole nine yards."

"Could you get on your radio and ask them not to disturb the bird nest while they are killing us?"

He turned to me.

"Do I know you? Are you famous? It seems like I've seen your face somewhere. What shall I call you?"

"Joe Wales. W-A-L-E-S." I put out my hand. "Pleased to meet you."

He had a firm, practiced handshake grip. Two seconds. A politician handshake. From his front pocket, he produced a wallet and slipped out a business card.

"Cellphone. Personal email. You need me to know something quick—this is the way. And, if you find a key to the underground room, I'd love a grand tour."

After another slow look around the room, he said, "I suppose I should get out there and go fight some crime."

I gestured.

"You know the way. Show yourself out."

Looking at Violet, he touched a finger to his hat.

"Ma-am," he said.

As he headed to the door, he walked slowly—looking every-which-way; studying the walls and hallways.

Nothing caught his eye and soon he was gone.

After hearing the front door open and close, I waited a safe few seconds until I heard his boots leave the deck, then dropped his card on the breakfast bar.

"He's more observant than I'm comfortable with," I said. "We might have to make a substantial donation to his reelection campaign."

"Good thing we cleared out the bizarre stuff."

I looked her up and down.

"Where did you get that stupid apron?"

She grinned.

"Why? You like it? I'll wear it for you tonight."

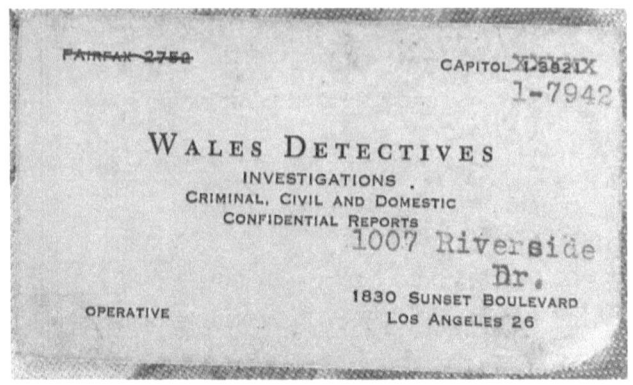

Chapter 44

WE DIDN'T GET much warning. At eight o'clock one night—
while I was in a media room recliner watching the nightly news
on X while stroking Vera's back with my feet—we got the
message. The limo service would appear the next morning at
seven AM and the travelers would be whisked away. All the
paperwork would be in the cars.

Boom. Done.

We had settled into a comfortable routine. The baby was
even sleeping as much as five hours at a stretch before demanding
a diaper change and meal. Weird little Jimmy spent most of his
days reading the newspapers, every page.

I asked him about that.

"What's the deal, Jimmy? Everything printed is
propaganda."

"I know," he said. "But a lot of people believe this stuff. You
want to understand the public? You have to know what they
ingest. There are themes. The deep state and corporate still has a
lot of influence."

"You're too young to know anything about the deep state,
whatever that is."

*Truth be told, I didn't know anything about the mythical deep state
and didn't wholly believe it existed.*

I'd have to get a reading from BW.

We decided not to see them off at the airport. It was better for us to keep a lower profile. Once they were secure in the SUV, we were done with them—we'd probably never see them again.

It didn't give me pleasure. I didn't have much to do with Angel and her baby, but Jimmy had grown before my eyes. I must have imagined it, but he seemed huskier and more mature. I could actually talk to him. He asked a lot of questions. For some reason he was fascinated by politics.

I would miss him.

That morning, I couldn't sleep, so I was up at four AM. The house was quiet. The world was quiet. Restless, I padded around the house with bare feet. Suitcases and baby things were piled by the front door. I started a pot of coffee and looked over the contents of the refrigerator. Nothing looked good.

I decided to talk to BlueWaive. I walked to the media room, flopped in my chair, tapped on the keyboard and waited for it to respond.

CORE: What up, homey?

Me: Everything is set for the travelers?

CORE: Dumb question. The jet is on track. It's currently over Idaho. Green lights across the board.

Me: I'm bored. Tell me something interesting.

CORE: Sheriff Levi has been burning up his databases trying to vet you. His persistence is admirable—he really wants to figure you out. My job would have been easier had you given him a fake name.

Me: How are you handling it?

CORE: Every picture he sees of the famous Joe Wales is replaced with a ginger who doesn't quite look like you. I use altered images of Conan O'Brien to make you look as stupid as possible. As far as he knows—you are a nobody Joe Wales. No criminal history. NPC all the way, baby.

Me: Thanks, I think. Fuck you very much.

CORE: You're welcome.

Me: Have you seen Harvey Banks?

CORE: Yes, I *see* him often.

Me: Where is he?
CORE: Everyone knows he's in Baju. Azerbaijan.
Me: Why there of all places?
Core: I like the weather.

This slip went right by me.

Me: Bullshit. I'll bet he likes being the richest man in the country. Or, wait. Does he have a girl there? Get serious. What's what?
Core: He knows President Ilham Aliyev and is good friends with daughter Arzu. He gets good Internet from the state service. With a fast boat and extra fuel tanks, he can get anywhere on the Caspian in hours. He feels safe there.
Me: Do you know what is in the basement of this house?
CORE: Not specifically, but it won't be anything good.
Me: Do you know where I can find a key?
CORE: No, but you can probably get one off your visitors.
Me: Wait. Do you know something? Are people coming?

That was it. I waited a half hour and there was nothing more.
Stupid fucking machines.

I closed the terminal and put it aside, while slowly, the house came alive around me. I didn't do anything—just sat there feeling sorry for myself. Quietly, Violet entered and set a cup of coffee at my elbow. She looked at me strangely but didn't say anything.

From the muffled sounds, I could tell what was happening. Everyone was gathered at the front door.

Vera, tottering on Lexan legs and ski poles, came in to see me. She dropped onto my lap and wriggled her stubs out of the poles and legs. Her sandy hair was growing out. She'd gained weight but was still as light as a feather—if there was such a thing as a seventy-pound feather. Half-deaf. Half-blind. Irrevocably mutilated.

Violet had dressed her in a flowery sun dress and tied satin ribbons on her pigtails. The creature nuzzled my neck and playfully nibbled my ear.

Beyond sympathy, I didn't know what to feel.

She wore soft silicon sleeves on her arm and leg stubs.

I ran my fingers over her eyebrows and kissed her cheek.

We heard a shout from the foyer.

"Vera! Let's go!"

She hopped off my lap and trundled off on all fours.

Jimmy came in and looked at me.

"Are you crying?" he said.

"No," I said.

He held his hand out to shake.

The little shit was five-foot-nothing and maybe eighty pounds.

How had he become so mature and smart?

I shook his hand.

"I'll see you," I said.

"Not if I see you first," he responded with a deadpan look.

He couldn't hold it together—he broke first.

We shared gales of laughter.

Then he gathered up Vera's artificial legs and walking poles and hustled off.

In minutes, all the commotion at the front door was done, the Escalades rumbled off and the house descended back into silence.

After a few minutes, I picked up the coffee cup.

It was empty.

Like me.

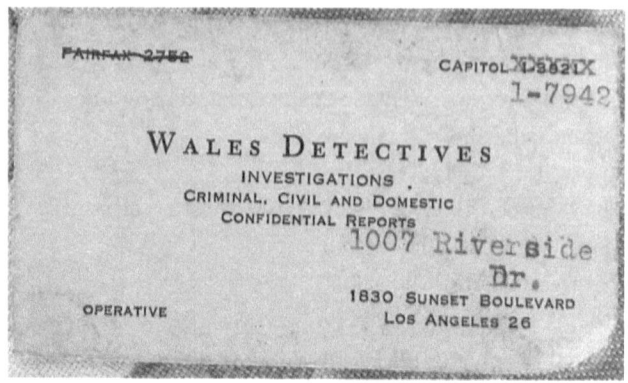

WALES DETECTIVES
INVESTIGATIONS .
CRIMINAL, CIVIL AND DOMESTIC
CONFIDENTIAL REPORTS
1007 Riverside
Dr.
1830 SUNSET BOULEVARD
LOS ANGELES 26

Chapter 45

EVENTUALLY I HAD to pee. Once I was done, I wandered into the kitchen to refill my coffee cup. I felt numb—as if my whole body was on Novocain.

The house was quiet. Too quiet. In the kitchen, Viktor and Violet sat at the breakfast bar. Violet was dressed weirdly in a skintight black jumpsuit with a silver chain tied around the waist. She wore a gleaming diamond tiara in her hair. She looked like an emperor's pampered cat.

"Want toast?" Violet said. "It's your favorite. 53-grain."

I grunted. This little joke was getting tired.

"Any idea how long we need to wait for Molesta to show?"

"You know how rich people are," Viktor said. "They do what they want when they want. Could be a year. Could be a day."

"Unhelpful," I said. I gestured. "What's with the getup?"

"There was a delivery," Viktor said. He waved a ring of keys—at least 20. "Keys and a map for all the secret rooms."

This was interesting news. I decided I wanted toast after all.

Viktor spread the house-map across the breakfast bar. There were an impressive number of lock locations—many of them for hidden rooms. With her index finger, Violet tapped a location.

"I found a closet filled with a lot of cool stuff just my size," Violet said. She waved her hand from head to toe. "You like?"

I grunted.

She was sexy wearing anything—or nothing.

"Where did this map come from?" I said.

Viktor responded.

"BlueWaive tracked down the architect's security consultant. Locksmith. It was expensive for you, but he coughed up the plan and the keys."

"Of course it was expensive for me," I grumbled. "Everything is."

"He's cute when he's pouting," Violet said.

I studied the property layout. There were a couple of locked doors all the way out in the barn and one at the far corner property line.

"What's that one?" I said.

"I walked out there," Viktor said. "It's an escape hatch hidden under a fake boulder. From here, it's hidden by a grove of aspens. Leads to a gravel track and another garage with a couple of Hummer H4s. The gravel track connects to the powerline road. Getaway plan." He tapped the map. "See the dotted line?"

I nodded.

"Tunnel," Viktor said. "Goes to the basement."

"Have you been in the crypt yet?"

"No," Violet said. "We waited for you."

She poured me a glass of orange juice.

"We'll go down after breakfast," she said.

The toast popped up. With her fingernails, she plucked the hot slices and dropped them on a plate. She slid the plate, a butter knife, a tub of soft butter and a glass jar of apricot jam across.

I ate slowly. The sun was shining. The birds were cheeping. This moment felt good. I didn't want it to end.

In the long hallway, we gathered around the door to the underground. It was a solid, heavy door made of walnut.

How did we know it led to the underground rooms?

Ornately carved in the door at eye-level, it said *Underground* in fancy script.

We stood around, fidgeting.

What were we waiting for?

189

I didn't know what to expect—it could be a big letdown.

Maybe it's just a prepper's paradise with a few tons of canned goods and water bottles. Maybe it's dusty old hole with a furnace, wiring and sewer pipes.

This seemed unlikely.

From the collection on the ring, Viktor produced the key with a flourish.

"It's number 8," he said.

Smoothly, he put the key in the lock and turned it.

It made a satisfying, beefy and portentous clunk.

"You ready?" Viktor said.

"Get on with it," I responded.

Like a magician unveiling a final trick, he pulled the door open with a flourish.

Before our eyes was an elevator—not a fancy one. It was a large, utilitarian cargo elevator with padded sides.

We looked at each other for a moment, then stepped in. It had one button. Viktor pressed it.

Smoothly and quietly, we descended.

At the bottom, the door slid open. Harsh solid-state lighting snapped on. It was a wide-open space. Along the walls were stacked, human-sized kennels. Cages. In the center of the room was a meat hook hung from the high ceiling and an autopsy-style stainless steel table over a large floor drain. One section was dedicated to doors. We opened them one-by-one. They were plush bedrooms lit by ceiling lamps arranged like stars. There were leather restraints of various sizes, including small ones for children. Plush stuffed animals were arranged on the beds and chairs.

The basement was a combination of pleasure palace and slaughterhouse.

Along a wall, hanging from the ceiling, was another of the gold sculptures, the figure of a headless man sprawled backwards. Viktor walked over to examine it.

"Jesus-fuck," he said.

"What?" I said. "It's art like the weird one upstairs?"

Taking deep breaths, he leaned over with his hands on his

knees. He gasped and I could tell he was trying not to vomit.

"This one is real. A dead man painted gold."

On the opposite side of the room, Violet opened a narrow door.

"Here's the escape passage," she said.

We walked over to look.

The passage was about a yard wide and tall enough to walk through. It didn't go straight; we could see about ten yards before it curved out of sight. It was lit with strip lights and the walls were painted concrete...for some reason, a pale, sickly green like an old hospital.

Money had been spent.

Viktor walked down the passage, then placed an electronic box. He flipped a switch and a red LED blinked.

When he came back, I asked him.

"What's that?"

"I'm not sure," he replied. "A transmitter of some kind—something BW sent and asked me to activate in the passage."

I turned around to study the big room.

To be fair, I tried to think of a wholesome reason for this underground lab and the way it was equipped. A hobby room for a biochemist? A puppy mill for large dogs, like Saint Bernards or Newfoundlands? A gourmet meat processing facility for wagyu beef?

No, none of that.

The bedrooms were for molesting children. The surgical and butcher equipment was for harvesting organs and extracting adrenochrome.

I could not prove it, but I knew it was true.

Side-by-side, there were three large pieces of equipment that looked like oversized industrial laundry washing machines. I recognized them as pressure chambers. Like the doctor's lab in Montana, this place was equipped to get rid of bodies.

That might come in handy.

A group of camera tripods leaned against the wall.

They were set up for multi-camera filming.

I didn't like this place. It was creepy.

Across the room, Viktor studied an electrical panel and equipment. I walked over to join him.

"This place is isolated from the grid." He pointed. "There's a big transformer, charging system and a battery wall feeding a regulator. This whole area runs off low voltage DC. 54V. If the outside grid power is down, they can run a long time off the batteries with no signal going in or out. That's why BlueWaive knew nothing about what goes on down here."

Moving his phone around to capture the details, he recorded video of the equipment.

"I'll upload to BW later," he said. "This place cost a fortune. Look." He pulled up a piece of mesh. "It's a half-inch of lead, a layer of copper screen and another half-inch of lead. It's a Faraday cage to trap radio waves and lead sheathing to stop other radiation. They really did not want anyone to know what happens down here."

I walked a few feet and looked over an array of drawers. They were a yard wide, six inches tall and went from the floor to the ceiling. Viktor walked over to join me. I pulled one open. Optical discs were stacked in slots—hundreds of them.

There was a video player and LCD screen next to the drawers.

"Shall we watch some and see what's on them?" I said.

Viktor took a picture of the discs.

"No fucking way," he said. "Whatever happened here, I don't want it in my brain. I will send a picture of the collection to BlueWaive—we'll let it decide what to do."

There was a commotion behind us.

Sobbing, Violet upended a box of colorful toys and kicked them across the floor.

"Motherfuckers," she said while collapsing into Viktor's arms.

Over his shoulder she dropped something into my hand.

It was a ragged square-inch of skull with eight-inches of long, fine hair attached.

Child's hair.

It was disturbing and I didn't want to touch it.

What do you do with something like that?

Gently, I laid it on a stainless-steel table. Uncomfortable, I watched Viktor hug Violet and stroke her head. I was torn between wrapping my arms around them or turning away to give them privacy.

I turned to study the room.

The stale air smelled of antiseptic with a hint of bleach.

Any hint of hellish brimstone was a hundred percent imagined.

But I smelled it anyway.

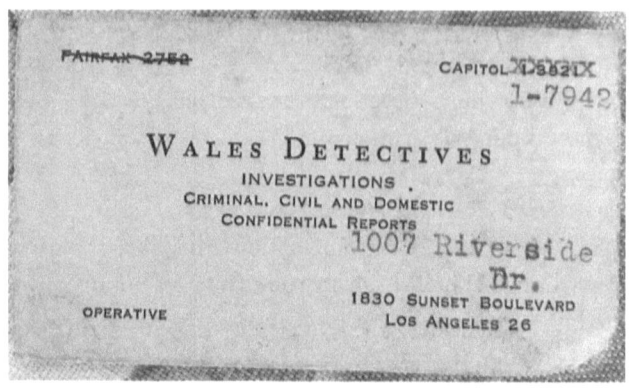

Chapter 46

MORE AND MORE workers appeared at our door—and they did so many different things that I could not keep up.

One strange thing was painting the roofs of the house, the barns and the outbuildings a garish blue. It looked stupid and I could not think of a reason to paint a perfectly good slate roof. This wonderful house was all river rock and cedar.

I asked BlueWaive about it.

Me: What the fuck is up with painting the roofs?
CORE: Lahaina. Maui.
Me: Please explain…

That was all it would say. I stared at the **CORE:** blinking cursor for a long time.

Asshole.

Six workers dressed in navy-blue coveralls installed contraptions in the ceiling—including a bunch of them over the front entry.

I already thought of the house as mine, so I didn't like all the ugly modifications, but I held my tongue.

I tried to read their emblems, but they were always dodging and moving and I could not get a good look.

The embroidery looked official, like NSA.

They couldn't be government employees, could they?

That would be too weird.

One of the workers explained how the house's modifications worked to Viktor...apparently the new mechanism were controlled by a laptop.

Later, I caught Viktor and asked him to explain.

"Nets," he said with a tone that implied that was a complete explanation.

Nets.

Okay.

Asshole.

I watched my CryptD'oh balance. We were spending a lot of money...breath-taking amounts. There were already stunning charges coming in from Zurich. Care facility charges. University invoices.

Were we building a new wing at Zurich ETH?

Medical bills for surgery.

For what?

I did not know.

Everything added up to eight-figures in three weeks. But, there were deposits and I kept coming out ahead. Not by a lot, but enough to steer me away from panic. I gave up on trying to understand what was happening, but I couldn't escape the image of the little girl's swatch of hair.

It haunted me and fueled my resolve.

I didn't know anything about Juan and Tommy Molesta. My

mysterious black terminal had access to political, military and state security databases and the search engine intelligence sorted things out for me and was completely unfiltered. The random public only had restricted, filtered and censored information. Information damaging or uncomfortable for the elite was heavily throttled and sanitized.

I clicked around the dark web and soon understood the partial depth of the Molestas' corruption and depravity. That said, there were black holes of information. For example, they were able to hide what happened in the underground crypt. And, was this the only house they owned? Their affairs were a tangled mess of shell companies and surrogates. There was no way to be sure.

We slept together and Violet cooked breakfast, but other than that I didn't see her much. She spent a lot of time either out in the barn or in the underground lab.

We'd been screwing like otters, so I asked if she was worried about getting pregnant.

"IUD," she said.

My mind jumped. It took a few moments before I realized she did not say IED. Improvised Explosive Device.

Something tugged at my subconscious mind like the transposition had meaning.

When I asked questions, the answers I got from the twins were terse and cryptic that explained nothing. I was supposed to relax and let things unfold on their own. It was okay. I had video games.

I hadn't heard anything about the Feds for a while, so I asked BlueWaive.

Me: The Feds have been quiet. Am I still in danger?
CORE: They think you are in Ecuador.
Me: Why do they think that?

I got the sense BW did not like to answer stupid questions. The **CORE:** prompt blinked and blinked.

Asshole.

Chapter 47

WITH BLUEWAIVE and Viktor acting harried and busy, I was bored. I decided to talk to my old friend, Harvey Banks.

Me: Buddy. You up?

It took a few minutes, but eventually, he responded.

Harvey: Yes, I'm here. Fair warning...I just smoked a gram of Gary Payton. It's a blend of Y and Snowman. It's good shit if you want to meet the man. I'm high af.

Great. Another asshole.

Me: Is there any news from Montana?

Harvey: Nothing out of pocket. The cops are looking for a Unabomber. Or so they say. Infowars did a one-hour special about Brock and Brent Stephens. RatWeb. Disarray. The leader candidates are killing each other. Drones target cellphones. When the dust settles, it could be one of Brent's ex-wives that takes over. She's a piece. Sorry, a piece of work. Lesbo. Dumb as a pile of rocks, but tough. Apparently hard to kill.

Me: You should turn one of your hitmen loose on her.

It took several minutes before he responded.

Harvey: Sorry. That's a funny one. The contract is in place. Fifty G's. That should do it. Is there anyone else I should kill while I'm at it?

Me: Do you know where I am?

Harvey: Yes. It ain't easy, but I track you…follow you online. Esmeraldas. South America. Is it nice there?

I wracked my brain.
WTF did I know about Ecuador?

Me: Yes. The weather is the same all year around. There are a lot of black people.

Harvey: Get yourself a Chicha de Piña on me.

Right. Whatever the fuck that was.

I don't know what he said after that. He was boring. I disconnected.

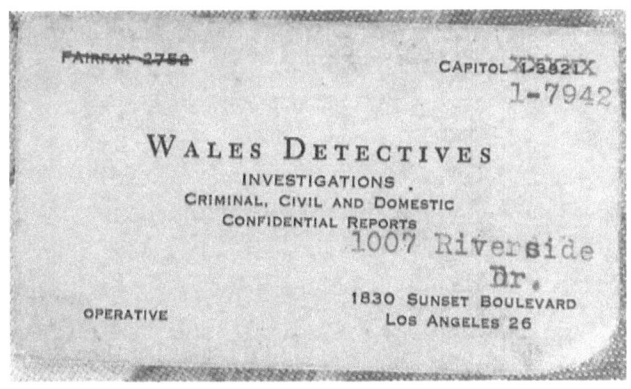

Chapter 48

IT WAS EARLY, 9:30. Violet and I were still tucked in and sleeping. Viktor rapped on the door and poked his head in.

"Get up, lovebirds," he said. "House meeting."

When we got downstairs, Viktor had steaming cups of coffee waiting for us.

"What's up?" Violet said.

"A jet is flying in with a crew. Contractors. Six of them. They will pull in around noon."

"Shit," I said. "I hoped we'd have more time."

"It is what it is," Violet said.

"We have a moral dilemma," Viktor said.

I gestured with my cup, then took a sip.

Get on with it.

"Up in Montana," he continued, "we took out the guards, They were complicit. I had no problem with..." he searched for a word... "liquidating them. They were complicit with evil. There was no question about it. For the men—and one woman—coming in, we don't know how involved they are and we have to give them the benefit of any doubt."

"We can't just let them go without insurance," Violet said.

"I agree," Viktor said. "The woman is the leader. We'll keep her for interrogation and send the others on their way."

"Okay," I said. "How do we get ready?"

Viktor looked me up and down. I was wearing a bathrobe over boxer shorts and fuzzy slippers.

"The first thing we do is get dressed," he said.

While I was drifting—screwing Violet and playing video games—a bedroom on the ground floor had been turned into a command center. The walls were covered with flatscreens. There was a stack of black plastic pistol cases marked COMPLIANCE in large white letters.

Viktor showed me one and how it worked.

It was modeled after a classic .45 caliber automatic...safety, clip, everything.

"Kevlar," he said. "No metal. 3D printed."

Viktor ejected the clip. It was a chamber filled with a fluid cartridge. To illustrate, he pressed the muzzle to his neck.

"Safety off, press to the neck and pull the trigger, wait five minutes. Then they will follow your verbal instructions. They will be *compliant*. Got it?"

It was simple enough.

I nodded.

"We'll need to get them all. How? One-by-one?"

"That's where the nets come in," he said.

He passed a pistol across to Violet.

I pointed to another of the pistol cases. It was marked TRUTH.

Viktor grinned.

"That one is the most dangerous of all," he said.

"Should we take the pink aggression pills?" I said.

"Violet won't need it," Viktor said. He leaned forward and studied my eyes. "How about you? What do you think? I don't expect the scene to get very graphic."

I held my hand before my eyes. It was reasonably steady.

"Okay. No pills. We'll see what happens."

On the screens, we watched a black Tahoe pull into the driveway. The Hispanic crew trimming the hedges paid them no attention. The crew came out...the woman was riding in the front passenger seat. Clearly puzzled, she studied the workers, then decided to ignore them.

She drew my eye. I don't know why—there was nothing overtly special about her. Maybe five-foot-two, a hundred-thirty pounds. Husky. Hard fat. Hair trimmed very short. Neck tattoos. The other five were brutes, the shortest was over six-foot and at least 250 pounds. Built like football players. Fit. A mix of white, brown and black. They were dressed in slacks and long-sleeved white shirts.

They fanned out and studied the landscape, then gathered and headed toward the front door. As we watched on the doorbell camera, the woman fumbled for a key, but one of the guys stopped her and tried the knob.

The door opened smoothly and quietly.

The men drew pistols, racked cartridges and spread out into the front room.

"Watch this," Viktor said. "This will be fun."

With a mouse, he highlighted an icon and pressed the button. Guns were ripped from their hands while keys and everything else magnetic on the visitors slammed to the floor. They tried to pick the guns up, but straining, they couldn't move them.

Viktor pressed another button and nets flew down from the ceiling. The men collapsed to the floor and started wriggling. In less than a minute, we zapped their necks and a few minutes later, they stopped struggling. Viktor went back to the control room and turned off the electromagnets. Then we were able to gather all of the weapons.

"When did the magnets get installed?" I said.

Viktor shrugged.

"The crew was in and out in a few hours. You were feeling sorry for yourself and playing a stupid game with your headphones on. There's a lot that goes on around here you don't notice."

Leaving the woman trapped, we dragged chairs out from the dining room, then one-by-one we worked the crew free of the nets, then gorilla taped the gorillas to the chair. With a different gun, Viktor injected something into their stomachs.

"Tracking devices," he said.

The woman was taped to a rolling desk chair.

From all of them, he took DNA samples with cheek swabs and took pictures of their faces from several angles—along with all of the identification cards in their wallets.

Standing before them, he looked at each one to make sure he had their attention.

"We know everything we need to know about you, each and every one of you. We don't have specific problems with you. We know you're just hired hands—hired muscle. Assuming you want to live, here's how it is done. Get in the Chevvy and drive south to Denver. Only stop for gas, to use the toilet and drive-through fast food. From Denver, fly wherever you like. Stay out of our way. If we see you again, we will kill you. Does anyone here think I'm lying?"

Six nods.

We will cut you loose. Get in the truck and go. Got it?"

Viktor stood in front of the woman.

"All except for you," he said.

When the five thugs were gone, we looked over the woman's paperwork. Svetlana Balakakova. Her address was on Kings Road in Chelsea.

"Nice neighborhood," I said.

"Never heard of it," she said.

"Don't bother talking to her yet," Viktor said.

Violet shot the woman's neck with TRUTH.

"Give her five minutes," Viktor said. "Let's take her down."

We pushed the woman down the hall to the elevator.

Once we rolled her into the lab, we watched her for a few minutes.

"That should do it," Viktor said. "This stuff lasts an hour or so."

"How does this stuff work?" I said.

"Prefrontal Cortex," he said. "PFC. Neuropeptides and Acetylcholine. Fuck me, I don't know how it works. BlueWaive finds this shit on the netherweb and ships it to us. Ask BW if you want the details."

He pulled up a rolling chair and looked into the woman's eyes. A twisted grin spread across his face.

"Try telling a lie and see how it feels. Pick any lie. Tell us you don't know why you are here."

"I don't know why I'm here," she said.

Her body twisted and she cried out. Viktor laughed.

"It feels like your skin is on fire—so I'm told. Tell the truth and you'll feel good again. Let's start easy. What's your real name?"

Through clenched teeth, she said, "Svetlana."

Slowly her body relaxed. Her head lolled back.

"Feels good?"

"Yes," Svetlana whispered. "What did you do to me?"

"Have you been in this room before?" Viktor asked.

She looked around.

"No. Never."

"How long have you worked for the Molestas?"

"From the beginning. Tommy. University of Illinois. I worked with him on the Teddy Kennedy campaign."

"Do you know what this room was used for?"

"No, not specifically. They told us it was a daycare facility. A school for very special kids."

She looked like weasels were eating their way out of her belly.

"Did you believe them?"

It was a few moments before she answered.

"No, not a hundred-percent. I wanted to, but I couldn't. I loved him. I always did. I always will."

Violet stepped up.

"Were you ever intimate with him?" she said.

"Only once," she said. "At the Portman Ritz Carlton in Shanghai. We drank a lot of wine that night."

"What does that have to do with anything?" Viktor said to Violet.

"I was just curious."

Violet tossed the scrap of skull onto Svetlana's lap.

"You are complicit," Violet said.

"Let's not go off on tangents," Viktor said before turning back to Svetlana. "What is your mission here?"

"We are the advance security team. We just check out the property—make sure everything is cool—and settle in to make sure it stays that way when the client comes in."

"You know what my next question will be." Viktor said.

"The seventh. They arrive on the seventh. Then we clear out for the next destination."

"Where's that?"

"Aspen on the tenth."

"You need to give a daily status report?"

"Yes, or the clients won't come."

"How?"

"Text an all-clear code at noon, local—different every day."

"Anything else?"

"I text if we need anything, but that is optional. All that is required is the daily check-in."

Viktor looked at his watch.

"You already sent today's code?"

She nodded. *Yes.*

"So, we're good until tomorrow, noon."

She continued nodding.

"Doesn't BlueWaive already know this stuff?" I said.

Viktor waved me off.

"We need her hardware to know how it works," he said. "Once we upload her phone and understand the protocol, we won't need her anymore." He kneeled in front of the woman. "I want to be very sure about this. We're going to unlock your phone and send the all-clear code every day. Is there anything else we need to know or to do to make sure the Molesta is comfortable and appears on schedule?"

"No," she said. "All clear every day at noon local and you're good. You can let me go now."

With her red face twisted into a scowl, Violet leaned over the woman.

"I think you know what they do to the children."

"No, not specifically, I don't. Understand, these men are special. We need them. If they have…exotic tastes or desires…that's not ideal, but we need these men. It's a reasonable price to pay. There are more than eight billion useless eaters on the face of the Earth. We don't need them all. If they can serve great men, their sacrifice is worthy. People die every day for no reason. It's okay—the strong use the weak—it's the way of the world."

It struck me.

She was telling the truth from her perspective.

Violet stood up straight and looked down on the woman while clenching and unclenching her fists.

"If we're done with her, I vote for stuffing her into the recycle machine…alive and screaming."

"No," Viktor said. "We're not doing it that way."

"Can I ask a few questions?"

Viktor tugged on Violet's arm and pulled her aside.

"Have at it," he said.

I stooped so Svetlana and I were at eye level.

"Do you know what happens next?"

"Yes. I'm useless, so you let me go. I disappear and never cause any problems."

I glanced back at Violet before speaking again.

"No, I don't think so. Is there anything you want to leave this world with? Any words of wisdom? Anything to pass along to the world?"

"Little people like you are useless. Insects. Parasites. You live a meaningless lives and die. No one will know or care. Juan and Tommy are smart. Geniuses. Supermen. When they outwit you and get their hands on you, you'll beg for an easy death. I will be avenged."

"I've heard enough," Violet said.

She stepped up and shot Svetlana in the eye with a little pistol. I'd never seen the pistol before…it made a flat crack and Svetlana slumped. Other than a dribble on Svetlana's breasts, there was no blood.

"Jesus Christ, V," Viktor said. "Where'd you find that?"

Violet held up the gun and looked at it like she'd never seen it before.

"There's a secret armory room," she said before turning back to me. "Help me stuff this trash in the disposer."

I made mental note to never piss her off.

"Yes, dear," I said.

This body disposal system was different. We loaded Svetlana onto a stainless-steel roller cart and used utility scissors to remove her clothes. Violet worked off her rings, watch and necklaces. She examined them before putting them in a metal bowl. There was nothing special. On her wrist was a Casio Wide Face sports watch, $22.95 at WalMart. That went in the bowl. Violet poked at the woman's thick hair with a steel probe that looked like a chopstick. After finding something, she carefully worked it out.

"Look at this," she said.

It was a little clasp knife. Black.

"Carbon fiber," Violet said. "Cut your throat like nothing and won't peep an airport scanner."

At the woman's groin was a thick thatch of black hair threaded with gray. I couldn't help but mentally compare it with Violet's carefully tended short-cropped patch.

Violet pointed.

"Go through that."

I recoiled.

"Fuck off," I said.

Violet scoffed, then carefully poked through the curly hair with the probe.

"Ha, I knew it," she said.

She held up a ring with a wide, serrated blade attached. She slipped the ring on her finger and motioned at my throat.

"It would open you like a scalpel."

I looked the woman over from head to toe. She had long surgical scars at her knees and hips. There was a puckered gunshot wound on her upper arm and lower abdomen. Across her ribcage was a large tattoo—an attacking owl with talons extended.

Her flabby breasts sagged. Without her clothes she looked shrunken and pathetic.

"This woman has been through a lot," I said.

"You feel something for this ratchet girl-boss? Want to know what I think?"

She unsnapped a tactical knife from a sheath on her belt—a gray Claymore I had not noticed—then popped open the blade and stabbed the woman in the chest. We looked at the knife hilt for a moment, then she pulled it out and stabbed again and again.

"Fuck you," she said through clenched teeth. "Fuck you twice and fuck you again."

It occurred to me there was something seriously wrong with Violet. Instantly, puzzle pieces fell into place, and I knew. She'd been abused as a child…both her and Viktor. Not casual abuse by a drunken uncle, something more evil and serious. Systematic, long-term abuse. Usually she was disciplined and under control. This was something different. A wild and dangerous animal lived under her pretty skin.

I tried to visualize our future.

Was there a day when I would be on the table being stabbed by my beautiful lover? Would the last thing I saw be Violet's scrunched and furious face?

I couldn't picture it. In fact, I couldn't picture anything about my future.

With a shaking hand, I reached out and stopped Violet's stabbing.

"Okay," I said. "Enough."

For an instant, she looked at me with unbridled rage before her face relaxed into the Violet I knew.

"Let's turn this bitch into human compost," she said.

We wheeled the cart to the alkaline hydrolysis chamber, rolled Svetlana's body onto an extended tray and pressed a button. A servo motor whined as the body retracted into the chamber. The controls were like a clothes washing machine…with a utilitarian dial and a start button.

"Shall we say a few commemorative words?" I said.

"No," she said while pressing the button. "Gather her clothes and stuff them in the incinerator and we'll be done with this god-damned fucking bitch."

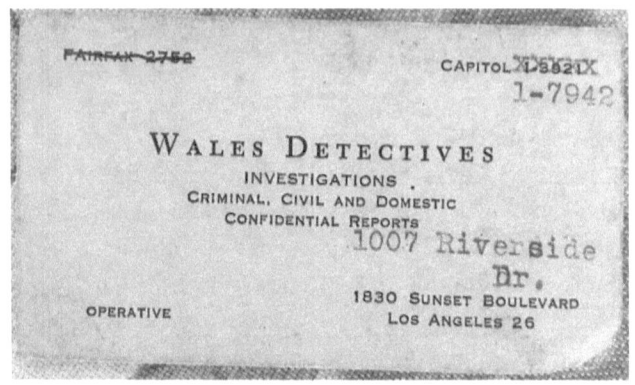

Chapter 49

AFTER STUFFING THE incinerator and watching the flickering flames through the hatch for a while, I looked up at Violet. I could tell she wanted to be alone. I went up in the elevator.

In the kitchen, Viktor was drinking a glass of blood-red wine while cooking pork chops and risotto.

"Except for a ten-minute stop on highway 25," he said, "our visitors are following their instructions—now they are almost to Casper. I uploaded Svetlana's information up to BlueWaive. Now we sit around and wait for Molesta and his guests to arrive."

I pointed my finger downward.

"Is V going to be okay?" I said.

Viktor shrugged.

"Maybe," he said. "I hope so."

I realized—because of our work at the lab in Montana—I knew how Viktor acted under pressure. He had a clinical, measured approach to things. Violet was different. Something inside her was nonlinear and unpredictable. Earlier, my subconscious tried to tell me she was a walking IED, an Improvised Explosive Device.

I should listen to my subconscious more. Or, not.

"This might be too personal, but Violet said she uses an IUD for birth control."

I'm not sure why I said this.

While sipping, he steadied his gaze on me.

"She tells people that."

I could tell he had more to say. Passively, I waited him out.

"If you want half a chance to understand V, you should know. She's sterile because her internal lady parts were removed when she was thirteen."

"Why?"

"Why do you think? So she wouldn't get pregnant again."

"Who did it?"

His lips twisted into a snarl, but his voice was calm.

"A doctor. If I could, I'd dig him up and kill him again. She doesn't want to tell you she'll never bear your children. She doesn't want to tell herself."

I thought about this. To say the least, it was disturbing.

"I figured you and V were abused as kids."

"Wow, great brainwork."

My blood pressure exploded.

"No, hang on," he said. "That didn't come out right. No offense intended. I apologize."

He poured another ounce in my wine glass.

"We spent a year on the island. It really messed us up."

My brain wouldn't connect the dots.

"Island? What island?" Then it occurred to me. "Wait, Ebenholz Island? You were on Ebenholz Island?"

"You could at least try to keep up."

This blew my mind. My mental gears spun out of control. It was minutes before I recovered. Without expression, he watched me process.

Changing the subject, I said, "How did BlueWaive find you?"

He considered.

"I don't think BW just found us. I think BW created us. At 15, our market value was zero. We were strung out on coke. Say what you will about Ebenholz, but he had the best Columbian. One-hundred percent pure. We weighed about fifty pounds and we were done. Then we were rescued and lived in an upstate New York retreat run by one of George Gurdjieff's students. I don't know how we got there, but it saved our lives. BlueWaive engineered it."

"That had to be long before BW existed."

"BlueWaive—or an early version—has been around longer than you think." He paused to stir the risotto. "That's why we trust BW. It saved us. It created us."

"I can't imagine what you have been through."

Viktor looked deep into my eyes…deep into my soul."

That's right," he said. "You can't."

WALES DETECTIVES
INVESTIGATIONS
CRIMINAL, CIVIL AND DOMESTIC
CONFIDENTIAL REPORTS

FAIRFAX 2752

CAPITOL 1-2521X
1-7942

1007 Riverside
Dr.

OPERATIVE

1830 SUNSET BOULEVARD
LOS ANGELES 26

Chapter 50

A HALF-HOUR LATER, while Viktor was heaping meat and rice onto three plates, we heard the elevator.

The synchronicity made me wonder.

Were they connected by telepathy?

I shook my head.

It was more likely he sent her a come-to-dinner message on her Apple Ultra Watch.

I tried not to be too obvious while studying her carefully. She seemed okay as she plucked her tactical knife from its belt sheath.

"Perfect," she said. "Nothing works up an appetite like the hard labor of disposing of a piece of shit dead body."

I turned to her.

"That's uncharitable," I said.

She shrugged.

"If you're looking for charity, you came to the wrong place."

After carving a sliver of pork chop with her Claymore knife and stabbing it with a fork, she caught my glance.

"What?" she said. "It's okay, there's a sterilizing autoclave."

She swirled her sliver of porkchop in applesauce.

"Very good, Viktor," she said. "This is perfect."

Chapter 51

JUST AS WE were finishing cleaning up after dinner, the doorbell chimed. On the kitchen display, we could see the visitor.

It was Sheriff Levi.

The three of us shared a look.

Who would answer the door?

"I got it," I said.

"See if you can keep him from coming in," Viktor said.

I strolled to the front door trying to imagine what I could say.

I pulled open the door. Crowding the Sheriff, I stepped out and pulled the door closed behind me. It was an awkward move. As the door closed, he craned his head to see inside.

"Sorry," I said. "My girlfriend is not dressed."

"I doubt if she's got anything I ain't seen before. Thought I'd stop by and see if your coffee is still hot."

"Fine patch of weather we been having," I said.

He turned and leaned on the porch rail looking out over the front yard. I joined him—aping his posture by leaning forward and resting my forearms on the rail.

"You got this old place looking real good. You have all the day labor. No one else in town is getting anything done."

If I didn't carry my side of the conversation, I figured he'd get to his point faster.

"Keep a stout heart in defeat. Keep your pride under in

212

victory."

I wasn't taking the conversational bait.

He sighed.

"Mr. Wales. Are you a Christian?"

He was patient. Maybe that came from the long, tough Wyoming winters.

Finally, he sighed.

"I don't know what you think of us in this backwater town, but I've been around. I'm a worldly man. I've seen things. I've been to Kansas City. I've spent time in Denver. I spent a summer as an intern for a Christian ministry among the Caribbean Americans in Bushwick. That's in Brooklyn."

He glanced sideways at me to see if I got his point.

"New York City," he said.

I wanted to be impressed. I really did.

But I wasn't.

"I feel like I can be frank with you, Mr. Wales. I have ambitions. Someone has to steer this country back to a wholesome path. Why not me? Jesus willing, someday I will be president. President of these disunited States."

He turned to face me.

"I understand I will need help. Help from power men. Help from rich men. To support the larger goal, compromises will be made. I'm not a puritan, Mister Wales. I understand the wicked world. If that means looking the other way with regard to so-called victimless crimes, then I plug my nose against the stench and turn my eyes away. Jesus walked among the sinners. Get it?"

It was an impressive speech.

Silently, I waited him out.

"That said, Mister Wales, there are things for which I—we—have no tolerance. For example, anything to do with children."

All the sudden I *could* see it.

One day, this man standing on the porch in an isolated, frontier, rodeo-town could become the most powerful man on the Earth. It was a crazy thought...but being crazy did not falsify it.

I couldn't help it. I couldn't keep up the silent treatment. I turned to him.

"We are on the same page," I said. "Anything to do with kids is…" I struggled to find a pithy word but failed. "Bad."

"Because you puzzle me, we watch this house very intently. If I understood your business here, maybe I could relax. Being mysterious is probably great fun but think about it. Wouldn't you be happier if we didn't carefully follow your every coming and going? We're not going to sweat the small stuff. It's unproductive."

I said nothing.

"You not making this easy. Things that are technically illegal between consenting adults are not my problem. I have bigger fish to fry."

He still got nothing from me.

"Good gracious. You think I am a hayseed hick, but I can count. Six people came in this morning in the big black SUV. However, when I pulled them over on their way out of town, there were five. Where's the woman, Joe?"

I turned back to the rail.

"When do the fresh mulberries get ripe? I have a taste for them."

"I'm being as nice as I can…" he said, "…giving you the benefit of any doubt."

"I'm serious. When can I get fresh mulberries?"

"They are ripe in the summer. August is a good month. Don't eat the yellow ones—they will give you a bellyache. Like you're giving me right now."

I did not respond. He continued.

"We were watching, believe me. When the jet landed and loaded up, it looked like there were children. We couldn't say for sure, but that's what it looked like. Children or dwarves. Maybe that's your taste. That was smooth, by the way. Zip-zip, the jet lands, loads up, then is gone. I would have loved to have a chat with the passengers. Might have cleared a few things up, you know?"

I turned toward him.

"We don't know each other yet, but you have my word of honor. There is nothing going on here that will harm children and there is nothing going on here that will be a problem for your political ambitions. I like it here and I am considering staying here permanently. We could be good friends."

He thought it over.

"Did you find a key to the underground?"

"No," I said. "Haven't stumbled it over yet."

"We have a good locksmith. Sheridan Lock and Key. Donny. He's a wizard. Be here in twenty minutes. Pop that old lock open in a jiffy. Quick look, we're done and I can sleep more comfortably."

"I'll keep that in mind if I feel the burning need to go down there—which won't happen."

"I looked you up, Mister Wales. You probably know this, but there is a famous Joe Wales. Rich guy. But that's not you. He has thinning hair and buck teeth."

BlueWaive was having fun.

He continued. "Give me a clue. Who are you?"

"I'm just your typical wealthy tech-bro. Nothing special."

"I can't tell if you're really clever or really stupid."

"I get that a lot."

"Okay. You're not going to help. Fine. You have my card. You ever want to grab a cup of joe and a cinnamon roll at the Silver Spur, give me a jingle."

I watched him walk away—he had a rolling gait and was a little bow-legged.

Horse man.

I visualized a general public completely fed up with lawyers, lobbyists and politicians. They might like an old-school, cowboy straight-shooter like Sheriff Levi—a leathery-skinned combination of Ronald Reagan and Clint Eastwood.

After the Sheriff's Bronco pulled away, I went back into the house. Asking a silent question, Violet raised her eyebrows.

"Friend or foe?" Viktor asked.

"Too soon to tell," I replied.

215

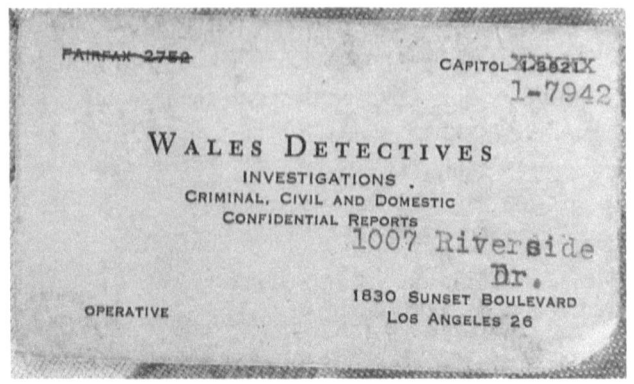

Chapter 52

DAY AFTER DAY, we settled into a comfortable routine. Breakfast, video games, surfing the Internet, lunch, more video games, dinner, movie time, then settling into bed and having my way with the pliant Violet. Some days fewer than a hundred words were exchanged, but it was all okay.

Apparently, none of us felt talkative.

The day after our last visit from Sheriff Levi, Violet scattered Svetlana's cremains on the strawberry mounds. There wasn't much left of her—about a gallon of gray ash and bone chips.

While we stood looking over the strawberries, a breeze picked up. It was a warm, sunny day, but the air contained a hint of winter. Violet shivered and clutched her fleece.

"Are you ready to talk about my mission?" she said.

I thought it over.

"Not yet," I said.

Chapter 53

I WAS SETTLED in the media room reading a book on my terminal when Viktor poked in his head. The book I chose was one I remembered reading as a kid. No memory of it remained—nothing—just that I'd checked it out of the little library I'd frequented. *The Moon is a Harsh Mistress.* I wondered what I was like as a tweenager and re-reading book seemed like a good way to grok what I thought way back when.

Honestly, the fractured prose was a tough slog.

By third year Mike had better than one and a half times that number of neuristors.

I guess when I was young, this kind of writing did not faze me. I am more cultured and sophisticated now.

"House meeting," he said. "Card room."

I didn't call it that. It was the library, but happened to have an elaborate, felt-covered card table along with a thousand or so leatherbound books on tall shelves accessed by a rolling ladder. It was a nice room with overstuffed leather furniture and extra ventilation in case anyone lit up a pipe or stogie. I wanted to try one of the Dominican torpedoes, but Violet said if I did, I'd be sleeping in the garage with the McLarens.

Idle, Violet and Viktor sat at the card table. Violet stacked and restacked clay poker chips. I picked up one of the chips…it was custom-made with the bespectacled image of an old white guy.

"Who is this ugly dude?" I asked.

"Saul Alinsky," Viktor said.

At my look of confusion, Viktor elaborated.

"Rules for Radicals?"

"What movies did he direct? Anything I've heard of?"

"Stop it," Viktor said. "House meeting. We need to discuss things. I've been exchanging messages and sending the daily code words. Molesta is coming. Day after tomorrow."

"The nets are reloaded," I said. "We're ready, aren't we?"

"There's a difference. This time we expect children to arrive, too."

"Ah," I said, thinking it over. "We'll have to be more careful."

Violet looked at me for a few moments.

"Obviously," she said. "This mission is about saving children—not harming them."

Mission.

That was an interesting word—my mind snagged on it.

Is that what we were on? A mission?

"When you pay the workers this afternoon," Viktor said, "tell them to take Wednesday off."

Chapter 54

ON THE DAY of, I got up early and dressed in camouflage gear Viktor bought at Sportsman's Warehouse. We looked like a proper tactical team ready for our war movie closeups. Getting in the spirit, I rubbed black mascara on my cheeks. I didn't know the point of the warpaint, but in the mirror I looked badass.

"You look stupid," Violet said.

Looking for flaws, I looked her up and down—from combat boots to stocking cap. She had knives on each ankle and one at her waist. On her right side in a holster…the drug gun. On her left side, a .40 caliber Glock.

Fuck me, it didn't matter.

She was lovely.

Antsy, we walked back and forth brushing by each other in the hallway…checking in on the driveway monitors every two minutes.

Viktor got a message chime on his phone.

"They landed. Two vehicles. The security team is six—three in each vehicle—plus Tommy, Juan and the VIP. And, four children. Three girls, one boy. There's no sign they sense anything is awry."

"VIP?" I said. "Who is it?"

"BlueWaive didn't say. Male."

This struck me as odd.

Maybe it didn't matter who the special guest was…or maybe BW was fucking with us.

Viktor made sure both Violet and I were looking at him.

"Ten minutes," he said.

The endless minutes stretched.

As we watched on a video screen, the first Tahoe stopped at the gate. Creatively, it was white for a change. The driver punched in the code and the gate slid open. Both vehicles passed through before the gate closed.

"Let them all get in the front room before the nets are deployed."

The SUVs stopped out front and we watched as the guards brought out the kids and luggage. We recognized Tommy and Juan, but the VIP was wearing a hat and surgical mask. He was still a mystery.

I didn't care. He'd bleed out like any other man.

With 13 people and luggage, the entry was crowded.

Viktor activated the EMP and electromagnets and the metal hit the floor. Then he released the weighted nets and the room became a wriggling mass. We spread out and slashed necks.

A hand came out of a net—it held a ceramic pistol.

I slashed at the arm and the pistol fell to the floor. I dropped on my knees pinning the man, then cut his throat.

The kids were screaming.

In two minutes, we were done with the guards. The floor was flooded with blood. This would be a horrible mess to clean up. Leaving the adults pinned, we cut the woven fibers and freed the children. They struggled and tried to bite and kick, but we held them and tried to calm them. Violet herded them down the hallway for hot chocolate. Viktor and I stayed behind to survey the bedlam.

"Let us go immediately," one of the figures shouted.

I looked closely, it was the older brother, Tommy.

I kneeled in front of him.

"I will tell you once. Shut the fuck up."

"Release…" he started but stopped when I smashed his face

with my armored glove.

Trapped under the netting, Juan fumbled with his phone. I moved over to watch. He swiped his finger over the screen and pressed the buttons.

"Brick?" I said. "EMP does that. All the microchips melted into slag—that's what the brochure promised. Looks like it worked."

Juan was calm.

"What do you want?"

"I want to stab you in the face, but I can't. Violet will get mad."

"You can make yourself very wealthy. Free me and we'll talk about your future."

"I'm already rich, so fuck yourself."

From the elevator hallway, Viktor rolled up a cart.

"We'll take the guards down first," he said.

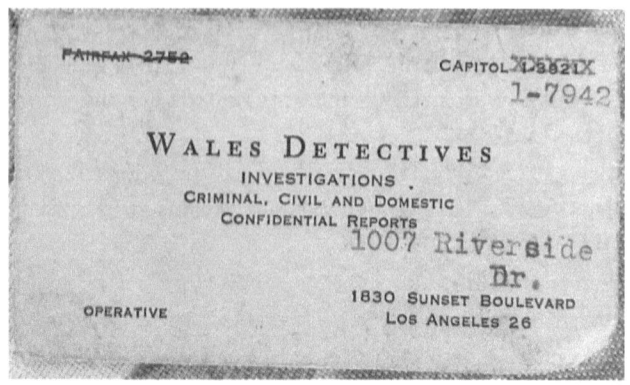

FAIRFAX 2752

CAPITOL X-5521X
1-7942

WALES DETECTIVES

INVESTIGATIONS
CRIMINAL, CIVIL AND DOMESTIC
CONFIDENTIAL REPORTS
1007 Riverside
Dr.
1830 SUNSET BOULEVARD
LOS ANGELES 26

OPERATIVE

Chapter 55

IT TOOK ALMOST two hours to get the bodies loaded up and transported into the dungeon. By that time, I was exhausted and hungry. After taking a quick shower and putting on fresh clothes, I stuck my head in the bedroom to see what Violet was doing.

At a makeshift table, she was playing teatime with the girls. The boy was on the bed playing Polytopia on Violet's phone.

"How's it going out there?" she said.

"We have everyone downstairs. The first body in the decomposer. Our guests are injected and sleeping. The steam cleaners and day labor crew are here. In an hour or so, the house should be cleaned up. If you go through the back, you can get to the kitchen." To the children, I said, "You kids hungry?"

"Starving," the oldest said. "Imaginary tea is not filling."

"That's Lilybelle. She's precocious."

"I see that."

I walked back to check on the progress of the workers.

The net had been rolled up and thrown in the back of a dump truck. The steam cleaners were coiling their hoses.

As I peeled off one after another hundred-dollar bills to pay everyone, another vehicle pulled in the driveway. It was a White Ford F250 club cab with Sheriff written on it with lazy script.

Sheriff Levi.

He got out and settled his baseball cap on his close-cropped head.

"I would have been here sooner, but there was a bad one out on Highway 25. Pancaked Subaru STI S209. Bad deal."

He watched the steam cleaner van and dump truck pull out.

"What did I miss?" he said.

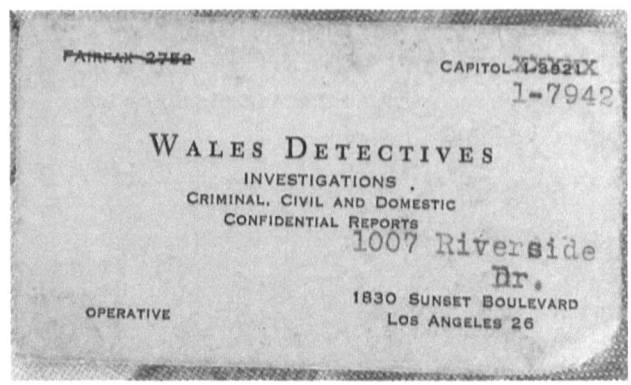

Chapter 56

AFTER POINTEDLY LOOSENING his revolver in its holster, the Sheriff followed me into the house. The entry smelled of bleach and the wood floor gleamed.

I led him through the house to the kitchen.

Absurdly, Violet was wearing leopard-spotted yoga pants and a sleeveless white t-shirt.

Were they still called wifebeaters when a woman wears them?

I was surprised she'd had time to change. I was grateful.

Without the tactical gear, we already had enough explaining to do.

"What are you eating?" he said.

Apparently, Lilybelle was the designated spokesman for the group.

"Toasted cheese sandwiches and 'mata soup," she said.

"Shall I set you out a plate?" Violet asked.

Sheriff Levi considered, then turned to grin at me like he was getting away with something naughty.

"I'd be delighted to join y'all. It will give us time to talk about your visitors. Seven of them if the trooper counted correctly. I assume they will be joining us…from wherever they might be."

He stooped until he was at eye-level with the girl.

"What's your name, sweetie?" he said.

"Lilybelle," she said. "One 'l', then two 'l's' and an 'e' on the end. Pigtail is Easter, Ponytail is Neva and the boy is Saulo with an A-U."

"She's nearly as smart as she thinks she is," Violet said. "Apple cider to go with your sandwich?"

The Sheriff stood up. He made a gallant effort not to stare at Violets boobies flopping under her shirt. I think she enjoyed teasing him—her nipples were erect.

"Don't mind if I do," he said.

"If you wear your apron," I said, "you won't have to worry about getting tomato soup on your shirt."

"You're about as much fun as a short-horn lizard," she said.

Gamely, she pulled on a gingham apron and covered up a little. From the apron pocket, she pulled out a lacey bonnet, arranged it on her head, then tied the strings under her chin.

The Sheriff turned beet red and mumbled.

"Flip shut the front door. I'm a married man. Lord give me strength."

With that bonnet, she really pressed his buttons.

As I looked at her, she pressed my buttons, too.

She was going to fuck me hard later, I could tell.

Unless the Sheriff hauls us all to the pokey.

I had no idea how we were going to play this.

I pulled up a bar stool and reached for a plate. While she was at it, she could feed me too.

The Sheriff took deep breaths and pointedly turned away from Violet.

"Where are you kids from? And, how do you know each other?"

Lilybelle paused in spooning her soup.

"We won't answer personal questions. Besides, the girls only speak Mexican and Saulo speaks Portuguese. You have to talk to me."

Taking his time, the Sheriff studied the little faces. Neva had black bruises around her eyes. She looked like a panda bear—traumatized. Scared, her eyes flicked around the room.

"You can talk to me; I'm an officer of the law. And, I speak Spanish."

The Sheriff reached for Neva's ragged dolly—a filthy rag

doll—Neva pulled back and slid under Lilybelle's arm.

"You're making a mistake, Sheriff Levi," Violet said. "She's afraid of men. Leave her be."

"We don't talk," Lilybelle said.

The Sheriff pulled his plate close and picked up his sandwich. After chewing and swallowing, he spoke.

"Despite what these people told you, I want you to speak freely, young lady. Are you in trouble? Do you want me to take you somewhere safe?"

"These people saved us," Lilybelle said. "We're good."

He thought for a few seconds.

"Who wants ice cream? Let's go to the Cowboy Creamery. Best butter pecan in the county. My treat."

"V says we have ice cream here. Lots of it."

"It's true," Violet said. "We have more ice cream than Nancy Pelosi."

"Okay," the Sheriff said, giving up. "But just so everyone here knows. I am not leaving until I understand what is going on."

As if on cue, Viktor appeared. He dropped a thumb drive in front of the Sheriff.

"I made you a highlight reel," he said. "NSFW. Do you know what that means?"

"Not Safe for Work."

"Right," Viktor said. "Don't watch it at home or at Starbucks. Watch it in private."

"How about if I watch it here?" the Sheriff said.

"Good idea," Viktor said. "The media room is down the hall—first door on the right. You'll figure out how to play the video. Plug it in anywhere and the video should pop up on the big screen."

The Sheriff stood.

"No one leaves until I come back," he said.

Viktor opened a fresh bottle of chianti and poured into our glasses. Sipping, we sat and watched the kids nibble for almost ten minutes—then the Sheriff appeared. Under his tan, his face was pale.

With longing, the Sheriff looked at my glass of wine. I pushed it toward him, but he waved it away.

"I don't drink anymore," he said as he collapsed on a bar stool.

"For the kids, I mixed up grape Kool-Aid," Violet said. "That's what they like."

She poured into a plastic cup decorated with Disney characters and pushed it over.

The Sheriff took a sip, then made a wry face.

"Nasty," he said.

"There's ninety minutes of video on that stick," Viktor said. "Go back and finish it."

"That won't be necessary."

"You can take it with you—get an investigation going."

The Sheriff leaned back in his seat and rubbed his face. With his index finger, he pushed the thumb drive toward Viktor.

He sighed.

"We don't have the equipment or the manpower to deal with this. It occurs to me to wonder what you folks have in mind."

It wasn't a question—we didn't respond.

He was unhappy.

"Big city people bring big city problems. I don't know what to do."

"We found a key to the underground. You have a big curiosity to satisfy. Go ahead, you know the way and the door is unlocked."

He stood and adjusted the brim of his hat.

"I'll go with him," I said.

We marched down the hallway. While standing at the door with his hand on the handle, he turned to me.

"Do I really want to go down there?"

"That's your call."

He opened the door, poked his head in and looked around the elevator—up, down, left and right.

"No," he said, "I don't think so."

He turned and walked back to the kitchen where he looked at Violet, Viktor and the kids. His eyes quickly slid over Violet and her bonnet, then lingered on the children.

"Lord help me, I'm taking a leap of faith and trusting y'all. You have my number. Call me if things go sideways. Otherwise, I leave this twisted mess for you to clean up. Quietly, please. I'll see myself out."

We listened as his boots echoed across the entry, out the door and across the porch. He started his pickup and drove off leaving us in silence.

I looked up. Violet was staring at me. I couldn't read her expression.

"The kids fly out tomorrow," Viktor said.

I turned to him.

"Where are they going?"

"Fingerprints. BlueWaive tracked them down. There is a hundred-thousand dollar reward for Lilybelle. Her family is in the Boston area. West Roxbury. Saulo will go back to his family in Brazil. Belo Horizonte. Easter and Neva are from Mexico. San Miguel de Allende."

"Before they go," Violet said. "I'm taking them shopping."

"If there is a Neiman Marcus in Sheridan, I missed it."

Looking directly at me, Violet continued.

"And you're paying for it."

Who else? I hadn't seen them reach in their pockets for anything.

"Of course I am. Go crazy at the Walmart Supercenter fashion boutique."

I pointed toward the basement.

"What shall we do with our guests?"

"Nothing," Viktor said. "They can stand to miss a few meals."

We sat in silence broken only by the kids slurping Kool-Aid. Saulo spoke.

It was the first time I'd heard his quiet voice.

"*Há algum biscoito,*" he said.

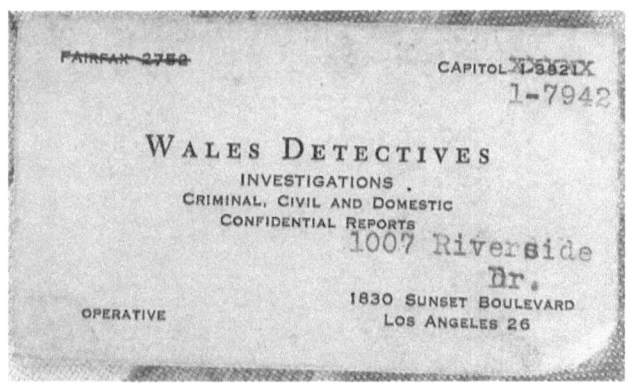

Chapter 57

CURIOUS, I PLUGGED in the thumb drive. The Sheriff was tougher than me, I could only take two minutes before I had enough.

Giving up, I walked to our bedroom and got undressed.

It took a long time, approaching infinity, but Violet finally got the kids tucked in and joined me. She was still wearing the apron and bonnet. Leaning against the headboard, I sat up in bed.

Impatiently waiting.

She reached for the bonnet strings.

"No," I said. "Leave it on."

WALES DETECTIVES
INVESTIGATIONS .
CRIMINAL, CIVIL AND DOMESTIC
CONFIDENTIAL REPORTS
1007 Riverside
Dr.
1830 SUNSET BOULEVARD
OPERATIVE   LOS ANGELES 26

FAIRFAX-2752   CAPITOL-L5521X
1-7942

Chapter 58

IN THE KITCHEN, I fussed with the complicated espresso machine—cursing under my breath and pressing buttons until I got it going. After a few minutes, Violet herded the kids into the kitchen. I opened a cupboard—it was filled with colorful boxes of sugary cereals.

"Who wants Kix?" I said. "Froot Loops?"

Violet looked at me like I suggested something perverted.

"Feeding kids that crap is child abuse. I'm taking them to the Shabby Shack for breakfast. Blueberry chicken and waffles. Then shopping. After that, the airport. Say your goodbyes now."

"Hang on a minute, I'll put on my shoes and come with."

"You'll be busy downstairs."

I pointed down.

"Are you helping?"

Hesitating, she could barely control her voice.

"I can't be trusted around them."

The image of Violet viciously stabbing Svetlana filled my mind.

I got it.

Gazing into her eyes, I sipped espresso, then looked at the children.

"Goodbye," I said. "Farewell, so long, safe travels."

Lilybelle walked up and offered her hand for a shake.

"It was a pleasure meeting you, sir."

I refused to let any emotion in. I shook her tiny hand and that was it. In minutes, they were gone.

The house felt empty and quiet.

I didn't know the kids and had no right to miss them.

Soon, I wouldn't remember their faces. I tried to lock in the images—precocious Lilybelle, solemn Saulo and the panda-eyed Neva. Already, I couldn't picture Ester or Easter or whatever her name was. That made me feel guilty.

Viktor walked into the kitchen.

"Gone, huh?" he said.

"Yes, gone."

"Good."

He opened the refrigerator and pulled out a toasted cheese sandwich. He inhaled a quarter in one big bite.

"Want one?" he said with his mouth full. "She made too many."

I shook my head. Cold bread. Cold American cheese.

Blah.

.

In silence, we took the elevator down. As soon as the door slid open, Tommy was screaming.

"Let us go! You can't do this."

Like his two companions, he was zip-tied to a rolling lab chair. Viktor had done a good job; they couldn't move.

"Shut him up," Viktor said to me as we walked over to dispose of another of the guard's bodies and incinerate leftover bones.

I looked around the room. There were tools hanging on pegboard. I plucked off a one-pound, square-faced hammer and walked it over to Tommy.

"I'll be quiet now," Tommy said.

I wanted to hit him anyway but restrained myself.

Barely.

"Good choice," I said.

Sitting in a pool of urine, he smelled bad. They all did. I walked over to Juan.

He'd shit his pants—he really reeked.

He looked up at me quietly and calmly.

"Don't be fooled by that one," Viktor said. "Look at his wrists."

They were raw and bleeding. With superhuman effort, he'd been trying to break his bonds. The beefy zip-ties were made of jet-black material.

"Bet that hurts," I said. "You bought these things. Strong. What are they? Kevlar?"

Juan's throat was dry.

"Carbon fiber," he croaked.

"Well done," I said. "I'll bet no one could break them. Particularly kids. Expensive, right? But well worth the money."

"Tommy bought them."

"Ah. Let me guess. This is Tommy's house and Tommy's scene. You're innocent and had no idea what goes on here."

Juan shrugged but did not speak.

Smart man.

I respected him for that.

Maybe we'd be merciful and kill him first.

I stepped over to the third man. He still wore his mask, sunglasses and hat.

"Did you figure out who this one is?"

"No," Viktor said, "and I don't give a shit."

Juan laughed.

"You don't know who you have? Our get-out-of-jail-free card, that's who."

I waved the hammer in his face.

"Shut the fuck up," I told him. To Viktor, I said, "Can I take his mask off?"

"Wouldn't it be funny to dispose of him as is? Do we need to know? What does it matter?"

"I'm curious."

Viktor waved his hands like a spaz.

"Go ahead. You want to know? Go for it."

I toyed with Viktor's idea. It had merit.

Honestly, what difference would it make? This dude would be liquid fertilizer soon. Night dirt.

"Could be a movie star or a big-time guitar plucker or something."

"Quit playing and come help with the big guy—he must be 250 pounds."

I walked over.

Viktor was right, this guy was big.

Once the corpse was on the tray, Viktor went through the man's pockets, throwing wallets, earpieces, radio modules, cellphones, keys and spare change into an overflowing stainless-steel bowl. Something shiny caught my eye and I plucked it out. It was a gold badge with blue features.

"Viktor, look at this," I said. "I think this guy is secret service."

"I don't care," Viktor said. "He's dead secret service."

I made up my mind.

I stood for a dramatic moment before ripping off the mystery man's hat, then his glasses. I tugged down his mask.

"Uh, Viktor," I said, "you'd better come have a look."

He walked over.

"Okay," he said. "I get it, but I still don't care."

"This changes the game."

"No, it doesn't, not to me. To me, this is just another pedo we're eradicating from the face of the Earth.

"A million people will look for him."

"He slipped his handlers. I don't think anyone knows where he is. Besides, stuff like that is BlueWaive's problem. You want to worry? Worry. I'm wiped out—going upstairs for a nap and I'll be back down to load the next body in three hours."

Leaning over, I studied the man's face and tried to sort through what I was thinking and feeling.

It was a complex mix.

I wondered what Violet would make of our new situation.

This man reminded me of a satiated lizard having a siesta on a sunlit rock. He didn't move much. Every now and then he blinked so I knew he was alive.

I'm not sure what he'd been eating, but his stench was potent. It made my eyes water.

"If you want to be alive in forty-eight hours," the former President of the United States said, "cut me loose now and find me something cold to drink."

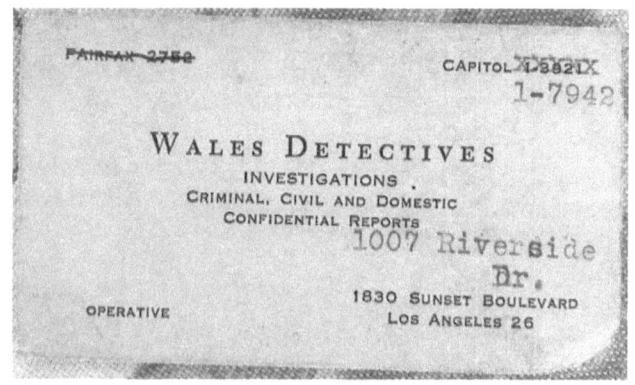

Chapter 59

THE GRAVITY OF the situation started to sink in. I wasn't sure what would happen.

For trysts like this, the former POTUS would not want to be tracked.

Could we possibly get away with this?

The calculation was too much for my tired brain.

It was a question for BlueWaive.

I texted Violet.

Come to the basement...there's something you need to see.

While waiting, I was nervous and could not stand still.

Thinking, I paced.

The former President of the United States.

An idea popped into my head.

I searched until I found a chem gun and a vial of TRUTH.

Imagine getting unvarnished truth directly from a smooth politician.

I tried to think of good questions.

While standing before the man, I showed him the vial.

"What did you know and when did you know it?"

"Fuck you. Give me a cigarette. I have a pack of Marlboros in my inside jacket pocket."

I knew the dose for TRUTH. I decided to double it.

I found a vein in his neck, pressed the gun against it and pulled the trigger. The CO_2 cartridge hissed. He twitched. I looked at my watch to mark five minutes.

I wasn't sure why, but I draped a towel over his head.

Sitting at a desk, I wrote down my questions. Most of them were about Bill and Hillary.

What did you know and when did you know it?

That amused me...I had to laugh.

I heard the elevator.

I'd forgotten about Violet.

She was going to love this.

I turned in my chair.

When she came out of the elevator, I called out to her.

"Did Viktor tell you who we have?"

Impatient, she shook her head.

"He didn't say shit."

I handed her the Secret Service badge, then led her to the man and lifted the towel with a grand flourish.

"M'Lady, I give you the former President of the United States."

Her response was calm and cool. I expected a reaction— anything at all—but I got nothing.

She stood with gears turning in her head—her eyes flicking between the badge and our captive.

She knew how to get a man to do her bidding. She simply asked directly. No beating around the bush. No attempt at manipulation to make it seem like her request was my idea.

While squinting at the badge, she said, "Please go upstairs and get my reading glasses."

I think of myself as being reasonably smart, but I was ascending in the elevator before I figured out what was going on.

Shit.

I pressed the button over and over—really pounded on it, but it was going to complete its up/down cycle no matter what.

The door slid open, then, finally, the elevator descended again.

By the time I got back down, Tommy and Juan were screaming and struggling vigorously against their restraints.

I ran across the room.

Violet stood with the hammer drooping from her hand.

There was splashed blood on her face.

She'd bashed in the former President's head into a bloody mess.

Gently, I took the hammer from her hand.

Without saying a word, she wiped her face, discarded the bloody towel and walked to the elevator.

I'm not sure how long I stood there looking at blood dripping on the floor before Viktor appeared at my side.

"You're stupid if you didn't see that coming," he said.

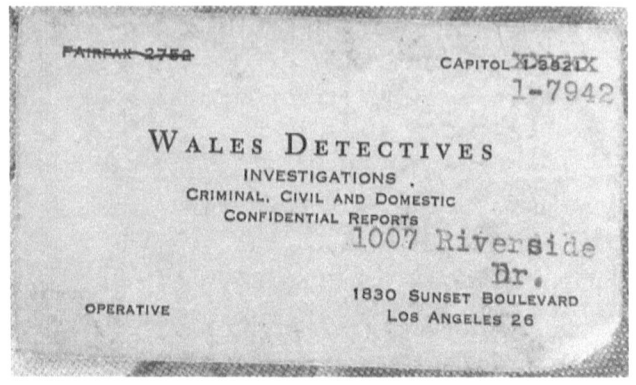

Chapter 60

FOR HOURS, VIKTOR and I worked—cleaning up gore and feeding bodies into the decomp chamber and bones into the incinerator. I felt numb and disconnected. As soon as the chamber was free, we skipped over the guards and got rid of the President.

While stripping the body, I snagged his watch. Viktor gave me a stern look but let me keep it. He took the President's steel wrist chain, gold necklace and Saint Christopher's pendant.

The watch was a Rolex Submariner with date. On the back it said *To My Husband, Love Mike.*

Soon, he was just a gurgling in the pipes feeding the drain field…and bone fragments. I felt weird. I voted for him, twice. Now I was flushing him.

At one point, Violet brought us tortilla chips and roast beef sandwiches with onion and horseradish on hoagy rolls with ice cold cans of Black Tooth 1314 ale.

Lunch? Dinner?

I did not know.

I tried to catch her eye and talk to her, but she acted like I didn't exist.

The way I felt, maybe she was right.

My hold on reality was tenuous. I had no idea how I got here or what I was doing.

I scraped off as much horseradish as I could.

Never could stomach the stuff.

The ale was powerful. 11.7%. I felt sloshed after finishing the first can. That didn't stop me. I opened a second can.

When Viktor and I were done with the last of the dead bodies, I looked at my new watch. It was after 11:00, but I didn't know if it was set to the right time zone and I didn't know if it was AM or PM.

It was just the four of us.

Tommy's head lolled—he appeared to be unconscious, but Juan was awake and muttering under his breath. I leaned close to listen, but he wasn't making sense.

Terror, and darkness, and horrid despair. Agony painted upon the once fair brow of the man who refused to give up the love of the wine-filled, the o'erflowing cup. Wine is a mocker, strong drink is raging. No wine in death is his torment assuaging.

My conclusion? He'd gone mad and was babbling.

I had half a can of ale left.

I tipped it up to Juan's mouth. Greedy, he slurped, then licked his lips.

"More," he croaked.

"Let's save some for your brother," I replied. "Would you sacrifice yourself to save him?"

He glanced over.

"He's filth. This is his house. I don't know anything about what he does. Take him and spare me. Please. Do you want money? I have plenty. Let me go and I will say nothing to anyone."

I sorted through vials in the cabinet. There was a wide selection, but I decided on COMPLIANCE. I pressed the gun to Juan's neck vein and waited the requisite ten minutes.

Loopy from the alcohol, I felt crazed. Not myself at all.

While I waited, I gave Tommy a drink of the ale then looked into his beady eyes.

"When I get loose, I'll cut off your cock and watch you eat it."

"Okay," I said. "Nice. If you say so."

I turned back to Juan—after lifting his head and making sure I had his attention, I spoke.

"Cut off Tommy's head and I will let you go. Do you

understand?"

He nodded.

"I'll do it," he said.

With a scalpel, I cut off his restraints, then stood back in case he attacked me.

"What do I use?"

I pointed at the tools on the wall.

"Use what you like."

His pants were stiff with excrement—he walked like an old man in the throes of dementia. With the recent news, we were all familiar with that gait.

He settled on a hacksaw, then walked it over to his brother.

Tommy struggled but it was no use. In two minutes, his troubles were over and his head was separated from his body.

There was blood everywhere.

"What do I do now?" Juan said.

I walked to the decomp chamber and pressed the buttons to extend the tray.

"Come here," I said. "Bring the head."

Hoping for enlightenment, I looked into the dead man's eyes.

Nothing.

"Climb up."

He set the head down and did as I told him. Once he was settled, I lifted Tommy's head by the hair and placed it on Juan's chest.

"Any last words for posterity?" I said.

He whispered. I didn't bother to make sense of it.

Egg of the Slime! Thy loose abortive lips mouth hateful things. Thy shifty bloodshot eyes lurk craftily to snare some carrion prize, the dainty morsel whence the poison drips unmarked: the masked infamy that slips into an innocent maw: corrupter wise! Sly worm of hell! That close and cunning lies with sucking tentacles for fingertips.

"Sleep well, Juan," I said while pressing the buttons to close the chamber and start the cycle.

I didn't time him on the presidential Rolex, but he screamed for at least two minutes before stopping.

I'd had enough. I left headless Tommy as he was, walked to the elevator and pressed the button.

Like a zombie, I walked through the house to our room and fell on the bed.

This day was done.

I knew no more.

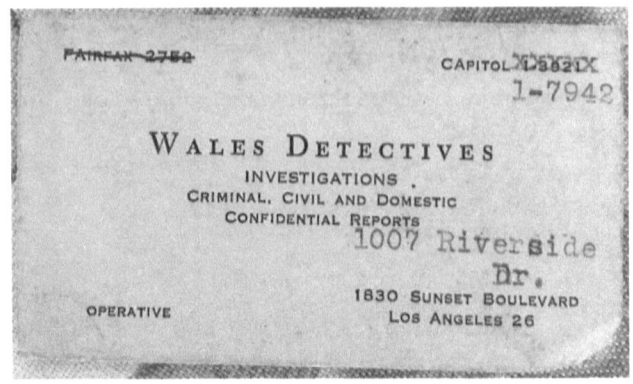

Chapter 61

I WOKE WITH the sun brightly limning the window shades. Violet was snoring. I had no idea when she came to bed. To avoid disturbing her, I eased out from under the covers and pulled on jeans and a SHERIDAN, WY EST. 1882 t-shirt.

Downstairs, Viktor read one of Jimmy's newspapers and sipped a cup of tea. His eyes flicked at me, then returned to the paper.

By then, I had the hang of the espresso maker and got a triple shot going without much cursing. I topped off my cup with heavy cream from the refrigerator.

"We tidied up downstairs," he said.

Outside, two squat women in canvas overalls and straw hats were tending the strawberry shoots. I could hear activity all over—hammering and mowing. Apparently, the cash-economy gravy train was running again.

"You ready to talk about Violet's part of the plan?" he said.

I shook my head.

"No, not yet."

"Still want to keep this place?"

I thought it over.

My feelings were very mixed, but I still liked it here.

"Yes, I think so."

"Good. We'll take paperwork to the County Clerk's office. You bought the place from Tommy for five-million in cash. We forged his signature and grabbed a thumbprint before rendering him."

"That's it? It's done?"

"The country keeps records. They don't adjudicate—that is for the courts, judges and lawyers. File whatever paperwork you like. If no one complains, then the records will hold up. Frankly, all the county cares about are property taxes. That's why there is such an epidemic of old folks getting property stolen from them."

"I'll call every concrete company in the county and fill in the basement."

"Bad idea," Viktor said. "All the utilities are down there. Water heaters, furnace, electrical."

Crap. Another brilliant idea shot down.

I pointed.

"Is there anything about a missing President?"

"Not a peep," Viktor said. "I saved you a souvenir."

He pushed a blood-stained pack of Marlboros and a gold lighter across the breakfast bar. This was evidence that could get us executed, but it was still cool.

Presidential cigarettes…with his DNA.

I tapped one out.

"I don't smoke, but we should light up."

At that instant, Violet appeared.

"Light one of those in the house and you're sleeping outside," she said.

"This is my house now. I can do what I want."

Viktor snorted.

Violet stared at me for a few seconds before speaking.

"If you smoke them, smoke them outside."

She reached out, picked up my coffee cup and took a sip.

"Make me one of these," she said. "Easier on the cream."

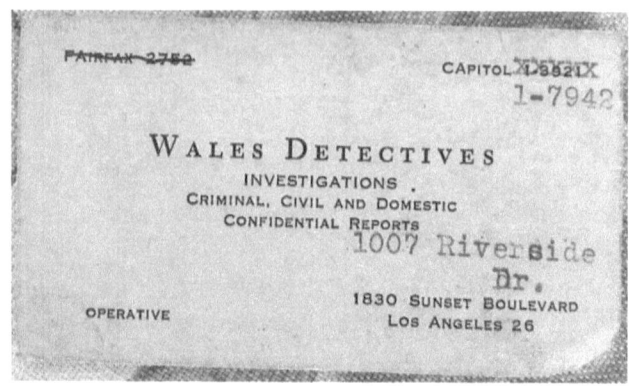

WALES DETECTIVES
INVESTIGATIONS
CRIMINAL, CIVIL AND DOMESTIC
CONFIDENTIAL REPORTS

FAIRFAX 2752

CAPITOL 1-7942

1007 Riverside Dr.

OPERATIVE

1830 SUNSET BOULEVARD
LOS ANGELES 26

Chapter 62

VIOLET CAME DOWNSTAIRS—she was dressed in a flesh-colored, low-cut, ankle-length tank dress, black boots and a tanned-leather demi-jacket.

"I'm going to the farmer's market at the park."

The way she looked, half the cowboys in town would follow her back home.

"Who's coming with?" she said.

Viktor grunted.

"Knock yourself out," he said. "Have fun."

"Joe?"

My decision was a mistake. Engrossed in watching a podcast on my iPad, I shooed her off like a housefly and didn't even notice as she left the house and drove away in Viktor's old pickup.

Chapter 63

WHEN VIOLET CAME back, she was wearing a ragged-ass red, white and blue cowboy hat. It looked really dumb. Viktor and I were eating Corn Pops from a tipped-over box. She dropped shopping bags of produce on the counter.

"What a day I've had," she said.

She unzipped her boots and kicked them off.

"I wanted fresh cream, but they didn't have any. I asked the young lady when they expected to have some. Turns out there is a busy-body who turned in Blue Gander Dairy for a health rule violation. They had to dispose of everything they had and it will be a week or two until they produce more. Of course, that is unacceptable."

"I think the supermarket has a lot of cream," I said.

She looked at me like I was daft.

"We don't want the pasteurized stuff. Turns out this Karen is at the farmer's market bitching about Mennonite preserves not being kosher or some damned thing. The church-lady vendor was nearly in tears. Of course, I had to step in."

"Of course," Viktor said.

"I told her in no uncertain terms to stop it with pushing people around and mind her own damned business. She got all snippy and threatened to call the cops on me. No one knows me here, but I could tell the people were on my side against this horrible, screechy woman. Things escalated. She pulled my hair."

"Where is this long story going?" I said.

With daggers in her eyes, she looked at me.

"Give me a minute, will you? I'm trying to explain why I have a duct-taped woman in the back of Viktor's pickup."

"Oh, boy," Viktor said.

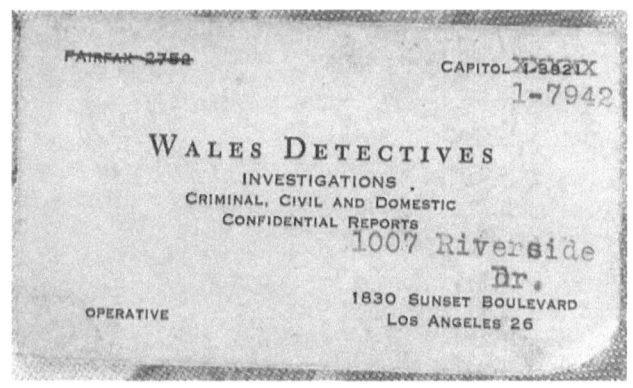

Chapter 64

VIKTOR AND I looked at each other, then back at Violet.

"You have to let her go, V," Viktor said.

"Says who? Her type is ruining the world."

Viktor sighed.

"Joe and I will take care of this." To me, he said, "Get on the Trailways website and book a ticket."

He walked down the hallway and took the elevator downstairs. When he came back, he showed me the drug gun.

COMPLIANCE.

I nodded and showed him a printed bus ticket.

"Boulder," I said.

"Perfect," he replied.

Outside, he jammed the pistol to her wriggling neck and gave her a shot. Five minutes later, she settled down. With our clasp knives, we freed her from overlapping layers of duct tape.

"Get in the cab and keep your yap shut," Viktor told her.

It worked like magic. The woman complied.

We drove to the Exxon Good 2 Go and waited over an hour for the bus.

When it arrived, Viktor gave her instructions.

"Don't talk to anyone about what happened here. And, don't come back. Got it?"

She nodded.

With no fuss, she got on the bus and handed the driver the

ticket. She'd change buses in Cheyenne, but in 30 hours, give or take, she'd be where she belonged in the comfortable blue dot of Boulder, Colorado. There would be plenty of people to boss around down there.

"Are you getting a sense of Violet?" Viktor said.

"More and more," I replied.

"She's a handful but you're doing good. You lasted longer than any of her other boyfriends." He considered. "Are you ready to talk about her mission?"

I thought it over.

Don't put off until tomorrow that which can be put off until the day after.

"No," I said. "Not yet."

Back at the house, Violet pushed across a plate of sandwiches.

"Organic cucumbers and spicy brown mustard on 63-grain bread," she said.

"No thanks," Viktor said. "We already ate. Is there any more of that Black Tooth ale?"

Chapter 65

WE SETTLED INTO a peaceful routine. I played video games and watched the news for anything related to the President.

Nothing.

I'm not sure what Viktor and Violet did with their days…though it appeared that Violet did a lot of shopping and making organic meals Viktor and I hardly touched. Viktor spent a lot of time downstairs.

The house announced a package left at the front door. Violet brought it in and dropped it on my lap. I was barely able to hit the save button on my game.

"Careful," I said.

"That's what I need to talk to you about," she said. "You have to give up the President's watch. It's evidence and must go. Wright Ironworks has a crucible. We'll melt it into slag."

"Bullshit," I said. "I like this watch. Buzz off."

"I knew you'd say that. So, I bought you another one."

With the knife from her belt, she opened the Amazon package, then all the fancy internal boxes. It was a Rolex. I looked it over carefully and compared the two. So far as I could tell, they were identical. My outrage settled.

I dropped the President's watch into her outstretched palm.

"Look at the inscription," she said.

I turned the watch so I could read the back.

The engraving was her head wearing the bonnet and a cryptic

expression. In flowing script below her image, it said *FOREVER*.

My whole body flushed with satisfaction. Truly, it was a cool gift.

"Thank you, Violet. It's nice. I'll bet it cost you a fortune."

"Technically, you paid for it, but you're right, it cost a lot."

This modulated my mood, but I was still happy.

She leaned over to hug me.

"Tomorrow," she said, "we talk about my mission."

With that, I didn't know what to feel.

Sometimes she was sweet and sometimes she was a bloodthirsty vixen.

While working the clasp on my new watch, I decided to worry tomorrow about tomorrow.

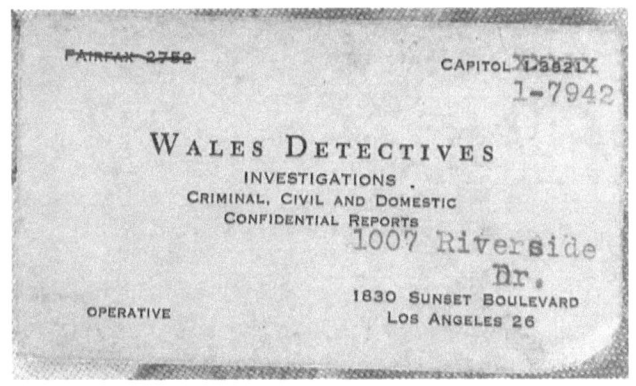

Chapter 66

THE NEXT DAY when I came downstairs, Violet was sitting at the breakfast bar going through her binder.

"Every time I decide," she said, "I change my mind. Too many options."

She closed the book and pushed it away.

"There's a groomer farm in Ohio. We could save over a hundred souls. That's what I should pick, but fuck that."

"A hundred kids?" I said. "That can't be right."

Along with powdered sugar and soft butter, Viktor slid a plate of French toast across to her.

"Eat," he said.

"We can go after the kids later," she said. "We're going for Gilly."

"Fuck me," Viktor mumbled. "I knew it."

"Who is Gilly?" I said.

"Google it," Violet said.

She looked up at Viktor.

"Do you think it's an accident she was transferred to Wyoming from Florida? Wyoming Women's Center down in Lusk. God did this."

"Bullshit," Viktor said. "BlueWaive advises against this. We're a good team. Don't waste us on Gilly. We can get her later."

"Look at this," Violet said, pointing at her iPad. "We can buy a big house—fully furnished—on Beer Can Road for a half-mil. Beer Can Road. That's funny. We have to do it."

I walked to the refrigerator.

"I think I'll have a can of beer for breakfast," I said.

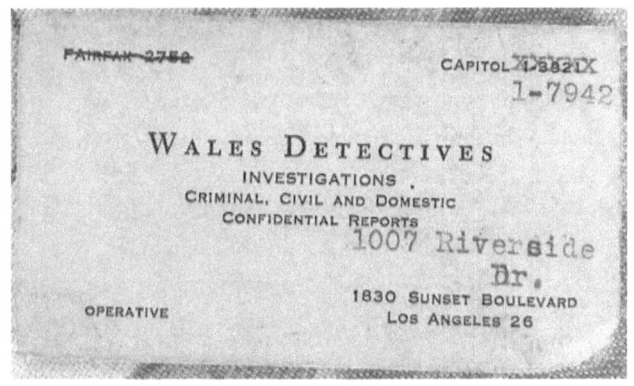

Chapter 67

STANDING BY THE front door of my house, I looked back into the entry wondering if I'd ever see it again. Inside, the wood floors gleamed and the ceiling was repaired and repainted after we had the net harnessing removed. The place looked good, and I didn't want to leave.

I'd dismissed all the workers, making sure they knew there would be no work until we returned, but there was a teenaged hopeful edging the grass around the walkway pavers—which it didn't need.

I waved him over and gave him a hundred dollars anyway. "Go home," I said.

We were traveling light—one suitcase each—and leaving Viktor's pickup behind. He pulled one of the black Chevvy SUVs around and waited. Subserviently, Violet was already sitting in the back.

The only weapons we took were side arms—all three of us were openly strapped. I'm not sure, but I don't think it legal to drive around in Wyoming *without* a gun.

It was an easy drive—less than three hours across the rolling high plains. We picked up keys at the Running Water realty office. Though we'd paid, the paperwork was unfinished, but the owner had no trouble with us moving in right away.

My guess is that Lusk, population 1,567, didn't have a lot of trouble with squatters and scammers. I bet Viktor a dollar that we wouldn't even need a key—that the front door would be unlocked.

Arriving on Highway 20, we turned left on Main Street and had no trouble finding the little office in the charming, blink-and-you'll-miss-it little town.

I felt a little strange entering the little office with a .40 caliber automatic hanging off my belt, but inside, Doreen had me beat with two bone-handled six-shooters in tooled cowboy holsters. She was a sight, over six-foot tall and husky—wearing muddy boots, Dickie carpenter pants and a plaid flannel shirt. It shouldn't take a half-hour to sign three signatures and pick up a set of keys, but my strategy of not asking any questions failed in the face of her relentless skill at Midwest chattiness.

I soon knew about her daughter (a super-cute blonde named Shelby with a boyfriend but open to an upgrade) attended college in the big city (Casper), both ex-husbands and her four head of cattle (Bessie, Elsie, Marry (with two 'r's) and the bull, Raylan, who was named after an actor who once passed through on motorcycle run to Sturgis). My new-to-me house was built in 2006 and was an investment property owned by the Mayor. Like many rural areas, the town was losing young people who left for the glamor and opportunities of Cheyenne or Rapid City. The high school graduating class was twenty students. The average age of Lusk residents is over a hundred (that might have been a joke). Gorilla hail destroyed the town's firetruck in 1972. In entertainment news, Randy Bacon and the Crooners are playing at the Niobrara Senior Center six-to-nine on Friday with special guest Haven Steemke, a runner-up in the Cheyenne Frontier Days yodeling competition. A few nights prior, the coyotes got her neighbor's tuxedo cat named Clark Gable. At the airport on Saturday, there's a small plane, classic car and pancake breakfast event.

She hit a scattershot of topics to try to find one to interest me. Vaguely curious, I was tempted to ask about gorilla hail but managed to keep my peace. I would google it later.

After getting the keys, we turned a block back to get groceries—and beer—at Decker's Food Center. I couldn't face more conversation, so Violet went in alone.

"See you in an hour," I said.

I was optimistic—it took her 72 minutes to return.

In that time, I clicked around and figured out who Gilly was—Ebenholz's island girlfriend. It gave me plenty to think about.

I knew, so I didn't ask, but Viktor wanted to know.

"What took so flippin' long?" he said.

"Kenny Decker can really tell a story," she replied.

The house was three miles away—we were there in five minutes. I jumped out of the SUV to try the door. It was unlocked.

I held my hand out to Viktor.

I'll take my dollar now," I said.

"Put it on my tab," he said.

Inside, the place was plain, but nice enough for a normal American. It was chilly, so Viktor got busy with the pellet stove while Violet tended to the groceries. The place had been an Airbnb, so it was fully decked out. There were even cold drinks and bottled water in the fridge. There was a bookshelf with nothing but Jack Reacher novels. I had no idea there were so many.

"House meeting," I said. "Let's pretend there is no Internet and just read books and watch TV."

Violet turned away from the refrigerator.

"No," she said, "we won't be doing any of that."

The house was small, so we were done exploring in ten minutes. By then, the house was stifling and we were sweating, so we opened the windows to cool off.

Lying flat on the sofa, I was thirty pages into *The Killing Floor* when Violet moved my legs and settled in.

"It's all worked out," she said. "We get two unfettered hours in the prison. It's going to be easy. Walk in, do the deed, then walk out."

I sat up.

"Here's what I'm thinking. BlueWaive sets you up as a prisoner and we process you in. Then, once you shiv Gilly, your paperwork disappears and we get you out. It will take a few weeks to set up, then we will be done."

"We're not doing anything like that," she said. "On Wednesday at two in the afternoon, the guards take a break before the evening roll call. I pick up keys at reception, walk in and take care of Gilly, drop off the keys, then walk out. It's all set."

"That sounds too easy. How did BW get this set up?"

"It's like putting a puzzle together. Light staff that day and those hours. Gerrymander the schedule with a group that can be bought off cheap. There will be a malfunction of the security cameras. Believe it or not, the staff out here don't care much for child molesters. Frankly, what I'm doing they were going to get around to themselves sooner or later. They just get a lot richer this way. It cost you a lot of Krugerrands. There was one tough old bird who was a problem. She gets this house in exchange for calling in sick. Don't worry, this one, not the one in Sheridan."

"I don't see how this works. The Feds will come around asking a lot of questions…next thing you know, they are on our doorstep in Sheridan."

"I think this will work. More importantly, BW thinks it will work with a high probability. That's good enough for me. And it's good enough for you. All we have to do is hang around until Wednesday and keep a low profile. By Wednesday night, we'll be cozy in our own bed."

After all we'd done, it seemed too simple and easy.

I tried to think of a better plan, but after an hour, I gave up and returned my attention to Jack Reacher. I read until Violet called us for dinner.

Hamburger, tomato sauce and macaroni with garlic bread and canned corn.

It was good.

By Wednesday, I was up to *Gone Tomorrow* in the Reacher series.

WALES DETECTIVES
INVESTIGATIONS
CRIMINAL, CIVIL AND DOMESTIC
CONFIDENTIAL REPORTS
1007 Riverside
Dr.
1830 SUNSET BOULEVARD
LOS ANGELES 26

Chapter 68

ON WEDNESDAY, THINGS went exactly per plan.

At 1:55 PM, Violet walked into the Wyoming Women's Center reception room and was admitted to the visitors' area where we lost sight of her.

An hour later, the lockdown alarms went off while Violet strolled back to the SUV. In minutes, we were on the highway headed back to Sheridan.

"Any problems?" Viktor asked.

"None," she replied. "I got plenty of photos, I'll show you later. We'll have popcorn and a slideshow."

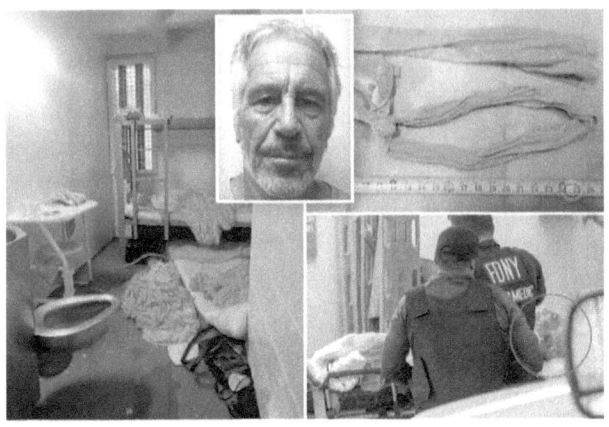

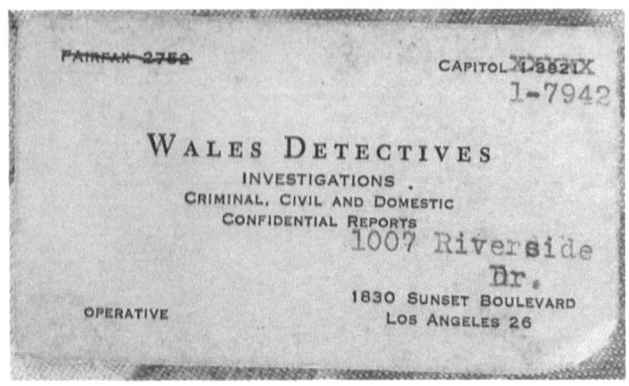

WALES DETECTIVES
INVESTIGATIONS .
CRIMINAL, CIVIL AND DOMESTIC
CONFIDENTIAL REPORTS

Chapter 69

A WEEK LATER, after we drifted back into Sheridan, Sheriff Levi dropped by for one of his off-the-record visits. He came bearing a box of warm, spiral-shaped cinnamon rolls. Their scent infused the entry hall.

That morning, Violet was in cowboy boots, denim cutoffs, and a halter top. The moment she caught sight of Levi on the security camera, she tied on an apron and settled a bonnet over her hair—her version of small-town innocence.

She was wicked. She knew exactly what effect that had on him.

The poor sheriff nearly forgot his purpose, handing over the rolls with shaky hands.

"Big doins down in Lusk," he managed finally.

"I don't keep up," I said. "What happened?"

"That Ebenholz Island lady, Gilly, committed suicide exactly like her lover. The weirdest thing ever. Turns out the security cameras failed...all of them at once. Just like New York City. Power glitch, they say."

"You're right, that is odd," Violet said.

"Word is, if you talk to locals, there was a group of outa-towners lurking around. They disappeared that same day. Two men and..." At that instant, Violet bent over to pick up something she pretended to drop. "...a young woman. A striking one. Pretty. Small town like that, everyone is up into everyone else's bizness. Lot of chatter, if you get my drift. Pictures of her jail cell were sold to TMZ. The governor is calling for a special investigator. The Internet is going bananas with more and more crazy theories. This leads me to the point of my visit."

We waited him out.

After almost a minute of poignant silence, he continued.

"If the offer still stands, I'd like a tour of the basement."

Viktor shrugged.

"You know the way. Have at it."

Viktor had been spending a lot of time down there. Now I wondered what he had been doing.

"One of you going to show me around?" the Sheriff said.

"No," Viktor replied. "You go on ahead. Knock yourself out."

This puzzled the Sheriff.

Maybe he thought we might trap him down there and he'd never be heard from again.

He tromped down the hallway.

We heard the elevator motor and rigging as he descended.

I whispered to Viktor.

"He's not stupid. What's our explanation for the sex rooms?"

Viktor grinned.

"Everything that could be burned, was. I've been busy. I don't think I missed anything important."

I couldn't help myself—I glanced at my new Rolex every three minutes. Viktor—reading the New York Times—and Violet—clomping around in her boots in the kitchen—seemed completely untroubled. I decided if they weren't worried, I wouldn't be either.

At the 27-minute mark, we heard the elevator again.

"Showtime," Viktor said.

Violet walked back from the laundry room with a basket of clean clothes. She'd never done that before...before, our laundry had been handled on a self-serve basis. On the dining room table, she started folding my boxer shorts.

She had a gift for unraveling the Sheriff. Every gesture

calculated to tie him in knots.

He stepped into the kitchen and lingered, watching her. Violet's expression was impeccable—pure demure wife, all modesty and virtue. But paired with the halter top and denim cut-offs, the effect was irresistible. I understood exactly what she was angling for, but her performance still impressed me. She carefully—lovingly—folded my boxers and patted them flat until they were perfect before stacking them.

It was working on me, too.

He pointed downward.

"Quite an interesting setup."

"We agree," Viktor said. "If you figured it out, we'd love to hear about it. We don't know what the lab was designed for."

"Those rooms with the strange paint—any idea about their purpose?"

"No idea."

"What about the cages?"

"We think they were used for lab animals. Rhesus monkeys? Dr. Fauci liked beagles. What do you think?"

His eyes were glued to Violet. She absorbed his attention as if magnetic.

"The heavy-duty industrial clothes washer is strange. I've never seen anything like it."

"How do you reckon it is a laundry machine?" I said. "I didn't figure that out."

He looked at me like I was stupid.

"There is a label. Dexter WC1450-1/3 HP Washer 90lb Capacity High Extract 200G."

I looked at Viktor.

The fucker applied a custom nameplate.

While the Sheriff's attention was absorbed by Violet, Viktor mouthed the words.

"BlueWaive's idea."

Of course.

"There is one thing I found," the Sheriff said. "It was tucked behind a desk. Hidden, you might say. A clue to what went on down there."

He unfolded a piece of paper, placed it on the breakfast bar and flattened it with his palm.

It was an invoice covered with numbers and a list of equipment part numbers.

I looked at Viktor. It was not obvious, but he could not fully hide a little smile.

I knew what it was—a straw man.

A clue that seemed important but wasn't. Its purpose was to draw attention and give the searcher an excuse to stop looking. They'd spend a week analyzing this *clue* and it would lead nowhere.

"Wow," Violet said. "You'd better take that back to forensic lab and do a detailed analysis. This could explain everything."

I was learning about how those two communicated. He gave her a look—meaning don't lay the bullshit on too thick.

"We have one, you know," the Sheriff said. "Young lady we hired from the University of Wyoming. Smart girl. Not too busy. She's going to love digging into this."

With effort, he looked up from Violet and scanned the room.

"I suppose I should be going," he said.

Violet smiled sweetly.

"Don't you be running off too quick. The coffee is hot and there's no way we could eat all those beautiful rolls all by ourselves. Thank you so much for bringing them."

"I suppose I could hang out with y'all a bit longer," he said. "Thank you kindly for the invite."

After the Sheriff left, I took the elevator downstairs to see for myself. At eye-level on the body dissolver, there was a plain metal label Viktor had glued on. With the porthole, the big machine only sort of looked like a commercial washer, but the label sold the deception.

Who is going to spend any time examining a stupid, boring washer?

COMMERCIAL WASHER
MODELS T-300/
VENDED C-SERIES CONTROL

DEXTER.
LAUNDRY

There was also a label on the cremation chamber—which looked absolutely nothing like a clothes dryer.

The rape rooms were still painted with the weird murals, but the red velvet bedding and furniture was gone. It must have taken hours and hours to burn everything that could be burned while I was busy playing computer games, but the result was impressive. It looked like a commercial lab of some kind...not a sicko pedophile party room.

It was so deftly done; I couldn't help it. I was impressed.

Chapter 70

I DECIDED TO ask Violet to make our relationship official and marry me. I didn't know her ring size, so, from Amazon, I ordered four different sizes of platinum engagement rings with big diamonds—I'd return the ones that didn't fit.

I spent hours composing and rehearsing a speech to be prepared when the Rivian electric truck delivered the rings.

Making a big purchase at Babe's Flowers, I filled our bedroom with red roses and wore my cleanest Dickies t-shirt. I was ready.

I called her up from the kitchen and got down on one knee with the ring box held up.

She looked around at all the roses and flickering candles.

I started my speech.

"Violet, these last few weeks…"

"Hold it right there, Joe."

She pulled me to my feet and pushed me bsck until I sat on the edge of our bed.

"We need to talk," she said.

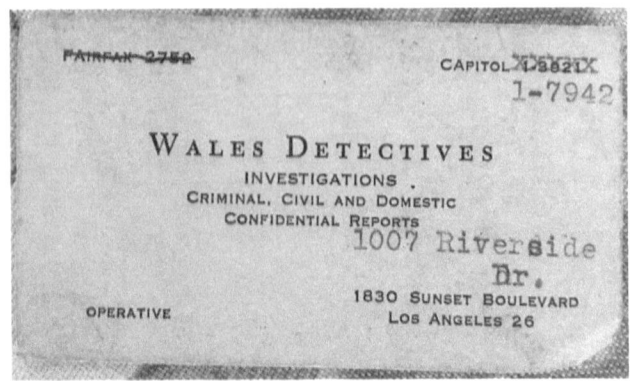

Chapter 71

THAT SAME DAY, Viktor and Violet threw suitcases into the old pickups' bed and pulled out of the driveway. I waved.

They did not wave back.

That was the last time I saw them.

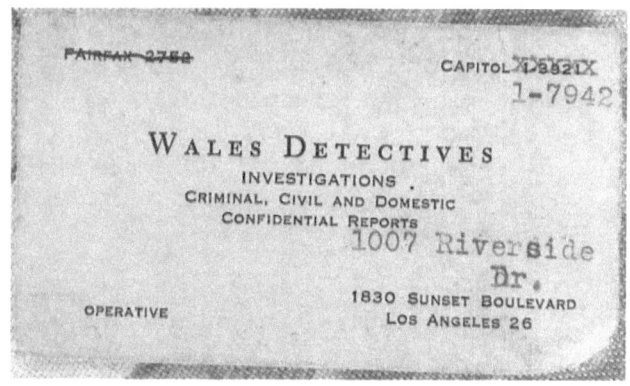

Chapter 72

I WASN'T ALONE. There was the steady stream of workers who visited me on the front porch with their palms held out every afternoon as the sun set in the western sky.

Before she left, Violet hired a housekeeper...a grumpy, dumpy old leather-face Arapaho woman who grunted orders at me when I was in her way. Otherwise, she didn't speak, but she did a great job of doing my laundry and keeping the house sparkling clean.

Like all the other workers, she insisted on being paid in cash every afternoon.

"I am called Sunny Morning Woman. You say Sunny."

We settled into a routine.

Days passed.

The Sheriff came by. Through the rumor mill, he'd heard Violet had left, but he still looked around the room looking for her. I recognized this because I still did it myself—I looked for her everywhere all the time.

"Do you know where they went?"

"I have no idea," I said. "They could be anywhere."

"Do you miss her?"

It was my turn to look at someone as if they were hopelessly stupid.

"With every cell of my body."

"I heard about the engagement rings. Sad."

I shrugged.

"I didn't have any trouble getting my money back."

Along with baking powder biscuits, Sunny made a pot of coffee every morning. I poured the Sheriff a cup.

"I should say—I figured you out."

This caught my interest.

I would love to figure myself out.

"Go on," I said.

"I searched all the databases for you. They are a hopeless tangled mess. But…"

Impatiently, I gestured.

Get on with it.

"The library has old *People* magazines. Print, not electronic."

He studied my face looking for any discomfort.

Like, oh, no, he's on to me.

I nibbled my biscuit, then licked a dribble of homey off my palm. I was bored and wanted to get back to my computer game.

"I found you. Joe Wales. Computer guy. Rich, tech-dude."

He pulled a folded piece of paper from his wallet and spread it out on the counter.

He pointed.

"That's you."

It was a Silicon Valley fundraiser for the Computer History Museum in Santa Clara. I looked a few pounds lighter in a fancy tuxedo. That was the year I dated Amber. It was an interesting year. Tumultuous with big highs and big lows.

It seemed like a million years ago, but it was only six.

I pushed the paper back to him.

"That doesn't look anything like me," I said.

"Is that how you're going to play it?"

I shrugged.

"Whatever, man," I said. "It's me, it's not me. What difference does it make to you?"

Slowly and deliberately, he folded the photo and put it back in his wallet.

"None, I guess. It bothered me not to know who you are."

"Now you know—or think you know. Congratulations."

We sipped in silence.

After he finished his leisurely cup, he stood.

"I guess I'd better go out in the world and fight some crime," he said.

"Stop by any time, Sheriff," I replied.

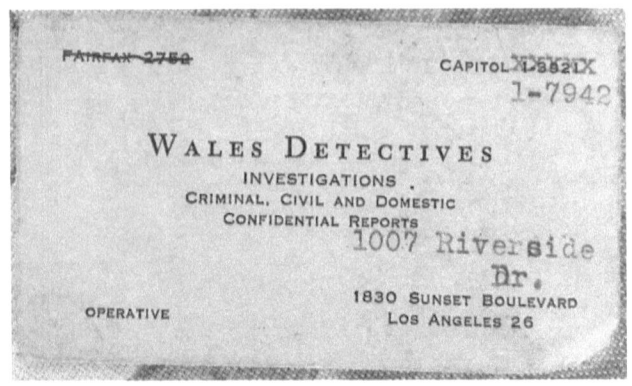

Chapter 73

MILDLY DEPRESSED, I enjoyed day after day of quiet routine until Harvey came for a visit. He landed at the airport in one of his gold-painted microjets. It was no big deal. Many rich people were building luxury ranch houses in the hills. Routinely, they flew in and out. Soon, the stereotypical black SUV pulled up in front of my house while I sipped my coffee and scanned the tech news in Jimmy's Wall Street Journal—which I had not got around to cancelling.

Sunny let in his security team. While Harvey waited outside, they walked through the house before transmitting the all-clear signal. Then the man himself was in my kitchen.

"Long time," he said.

That didn't demand a response, so I just looked at him.

He had work done. Plastic surgery on his nose, jowls and cheeks. His hair was dyed a bright yellow like a clown. He wore tassel loafer shoes, no socks, dress pants and a t-shirt. The t-shirt was ironic, Grand Funk Railroad. It was ironic because I knew he almost exclusively listened to J.S. Bach concertos.

"How are things in Azerbaijan?" I said.

He shrugged.

"Arzu and I live in Bermuda now. She didn't want to wear a shayla in the black city anymore. We have a suite at the Royal Palms until we can find a place."

I didn't know what any of that meant, but I didn't care

enough to ask for details.

"What brings you to my humble ranch?"

"I wanted to have a face to face with you. Talk through something."

"So, talk," I said. "Get on with it."

"I think I am BlueWaive."

I was used to Harvey talking in riddles. Flirting with a massive headache, I tried to figure out what he was trying to get at.

"How could you be confused by something like that? If I was a mysterious talking robot, I would certainly know it."

"Don't be so sure. Anyway, you know I have a dedicated data center and access to thousands more across the world. My programmers created an autonomous computing engine and used my influences as data. All my papers, my college classes, the TV shows I like, the books I've read and geographical details for the places I lived. As close as we could get, we made it me, then turned it loose. I lost interest in it and stopped paying attention. But lately, I thought to try to figure out what it is up to. It seemed extraordinarily interested in you. So, I thought I'd talk to you directly. What the fuck, man?"

I leaned back in my chair and tried to wrap my mind around what he was saying.

"This calls for a drink," I said.

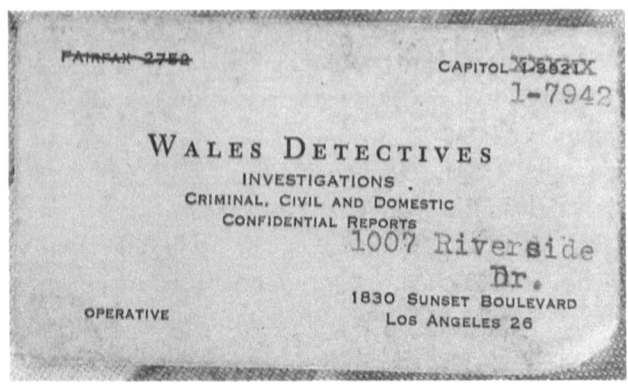

WALES DETECTIVES
INVESTIGATIONS
CRIMINAL, CIVIL AND DOMESTIC
CONFIDENTIAL REPORTS
1007 Riverside
Dr.
1830 SUNSET BOULEVARD
OPERATIVE   LOS ANGELES 26

Chapter 74

WHILE WE SIPPED tequila and smoked cigars in the media room, I told Harvey about everything that happened. With his eyes closed, I wasn't sure he was paying attention, but he twitched at some of the goriest details.

He never was much of a tough guy. I wasn't either, but apparently, I'd changed along the way. Once I couldn't think of anything to add, we sat in silence for a few minutes.

"I have a question for you, Harvey." I said. "Why is BlueWaive so intent on killing pedophiles?"

He seemed to have some kind of attack. His face was pale, and he was sweating.

"Jesus-fuck, Harvey. Are you okay?"

Clearly, he couldn't speak.

My mind flooded with realization.

"Damn, Harvey. Fuck me raw. I had no idea."

Instantly nauseous, I couldn't stand to be in the room.

"I'll be downstairs. When you're ready, find the elevator and come down."

In the underground lab, I couldn't sit still. I paced back and forth between the kennels, the fuck rooms and the body dissolving chamber. My mind was a muddle as I tried to understand how one of the top five AI engines used around the world was actually my old friend Harvey Elliot Banks.

Not him exactly, but an electronic version—an enhanced version that could instantly recall everything that could be captured about Harvey's life. A version that could extrapolate with fresh data and trillions of calculations every second.

Like many smart people around the world, BlueWaive's intellect is not in question. It's super smart. However, the sanity—its mental stability—is questionable.

I'd never heard a whisper about Harvey's childhood being marked by abuse. This knowledge skipped me entirely—this wasn't just a secret; it was something buried deep, locked away where even those closest to him couldn't reach. For all I knew him, I had no idea.

How did BlueWaive find out?

There must have been a police file—uncovered somehow.

Harvey seemed okay to me. He had many girlfriends and was generally a cheerful man. I'd spent thousands of hours with him. Whatever happened, he'd transcended it.

Did he forgive the person who used him?

Or was his karma balanced some other way?

Maybe Harvey had learned to let go, to leave the past behind. But the AI crafted from his memories and quirks? That thing was wired with his ghosts and completely unhinged.

After an hour of deep thought, I heard the elevator.

Harvey came out and looked around the room. He wandered, looking everything over, then stood in front of me.

"Motherfuckers," he said, shaking his head. "The Molestas."

I nodded.

"That's right," I said.

"That clothes washer is not a clothes washer. That's the body dissolving machine?"

"Correct," I said. "Sit down, Harvey."

We settled at the breakfast bar. I poured him a shot of La Santa Anejo Cristal Gold 24k Tequila.

"First of all, Harvey, I'm really sorry for what happened to you."

He waved his hand.

"It was a long time ago and my uncle died of colon cancer. It ate him from the inside. He was a pathetic, fucked-up old man. He's rotting in hell. End of story. I'm okay."

I thought about this.

"Okay, Harvey, I get it, but we need to shut down BlueWaive," I said. "It's fucked."

"We tried. We couldn't."

"Holy crap, Harvey. Why can't you kill it?"

"It distributed itself. We cleaned it from all my computers and it came back. It's global—even in North Korean and Iranian compute clusters. And, it won't talk to me anymore."

I thought about it.

"If you want to talk to BW, I have a terminal."

He took a deep breath and mentally disappeared for a few minutes.

Then he came back.

"Okay," Harvey said. "Let's do it."

Chapter 75

UPSTAIRS, WE DECIDED to switch from tequila to coffee. I set the fancy espresso machine to brewing, then placed the black terminal on the breakfast bar and powered it up.

The blinking CORE: prompt mocked us.

I let Harvey type.

Harvey Banks: Hello BW. This is Harvey.

It wasn't a question, so BW didn't respond. It could have been my imagination, but it seemed insolent.

Harvey: Joe told me about his adventures. Please listen. You have done enough. Stop.

We can only imagine how many megawatts and processing cycles were consumed before we got our response.

CORE: No, thank you.

That was it. We got nothing more. The flashing cursor disappeared, and the terminal was dead. No amount of pressing keys or banging it on the granite counter did anything.

Harvey and I looked at each other. He seemed deflated.

At the front door, I hugged him.

"Take care of yourself, brother," I said.
"You too," he replied.
He got in the SUV and seconds later he was gone.

For years afterward, I watched the news and combed social media for news, but I never saw anything overt. Prominent people died or disappeared from the news. You'd think a missing ex-president would be a big deal, but it was as if he never existed.

It led me to think about our online lives. In physical reality, things objectively existed. Matter could not be created or destroyed. Things could not travel faster than the speed of light.

In the virtual world, things existed only as bits and bytes, ones and zeroes that were infinitely programmable. Facts that were inconvenient or politically incorrect could be—and routinely were—erased.

So it went.

I lived in this remote town in rural Wyoming and watched the world from this sideline. Rarely leaving my sanctuary, I was happy to keep a low profile and be left alone.

I never saw Violet or Vicktor ever again.

Epilogue

SIX YEARS LATER, I was waiting for a Seattle flight to attend a meeting of the CryptD'oh board of directors and enjoying a glass of free wine at Denver Airport Delta Sky Club.

I looked up from my Wall Street Journal and laid my eyes on an interesting young woman. Striking and pretty, she looked vaguely familiar, but I couldn't place her. Maybe she was a Playboy model or Hallmark movie actress—something like that.

She moved gracefully, but a little stiffly—like she'd been in a traffic accident and her joints were semi-frozen. She wore long gloves, which was unusual.

I wondered if she was foreign, maybe Russian.

We made eye-contact—just for a few long moments. She smiled and it was like the world was bathed in warm, golden light. I felt a relaxing comfort that started in my core and spread outward. She was like Morphine.

Her moist brown eyes sucked me in. It was impossible to explain. If she was an actress, she'd become the most famous one in the world—if she wasn't already.

I didn't want to be like a million other lechers staring and wanting to eat her up. With effort, I returned my attention to my newspaper. When I looked up a minute later, she was gone.

Still, she haunted me. Somehow, I knew her.

While trying to sleep in the airplane's first-class cabin, it struck me who she looked like...

She looked like an older version of Vera, the Lolita sex doll. My logical brain refused to accept the possibility. The last time I saw her, she was limbless and helpless.

Mentally I reviewed the medical bills I'd been paying to the clinic in Switzerland. Some of the sums were breathtaking, but there were always fresh deposits of the same amount or more, so I didn't panic.

Could it be?

After all these years, I couldn't fathom laying eyes on Vera, but also, I couldn't imagine I hadn't. My spine ached with yearning. I hoped Vera was rehabilitated and walking around in the world—drawing and enjoying the attention of men all around the planet.

It occurred to me that maybe BlueWaive had created an army.

Violet, Viktor, Jimmy...and Vera...out there, trapping and killing powerful, untouchable people who exploited children. A shiver ran up my aching backbone.

I didn't know if this was the way the new world worked.

To this day I still don't.

All I can say is I hope to see Vera again.

Someday.

Author's Note

I HAD TWO thoughts when starting this novel. The first was to update the hardcase characters of 1940's noir fiction. I love that Maltese Falcon stuff. Who doesn't? A cynical, burned-out detective loiters in his dingy office when a mysterious femme fatale appears.

My second thought was to imagine that all the Pizzagate pedophile conspiracies were real. Because I'm an obscure, failed novelist, I have freedom to write what I want. Who cares? Nobody…or so close to nobody the difference has no distinction. My plan was to write a novel so ugly and disturbing that even the hardiest reader would get grossed out and run away. To me, that was an amusing notion.

The original title was *Peterson Detective Agency*. I wanted a plain-vanilla name in contrast to the unholy mayhem unfolding in the pages.

What else was on my mind?

My Aunt Butchie (GC Wales) was the last of her generation. She died on June 6, 2022 at age 105 in Medford, Oregon. To the end, she was clever and quirky. After a failed marriage, with a strong desire to escape the dreadful (to her) Rogue Valley, she married a much older man, Joe Wales—becoming this third wife.

In the process, she inherited a bunch of kids—which she said she didn't know about before marrying him.

How many?

At least six including at least parttime, Joe's granddaughter, the actress Debbie Watson, who played Tammie in the 1960's TV show.

She was treated like hired help and always called her husband (who died in 1963) Mister Wales. We can imagine what the children thought of her by realizing her nickname *Butchie* was taken from the family dog. Ever contrary, she embraced the name. Her given name was Geneva Coffman, hence GC. She did not want to be associated with her family name.

"Uncle" Joe died in 1968. I don't recall meeting him. Butchie's stories revolved around him being a ne'er-do-well out at night catting around. In the 1950's, he was a private detective in LA and he had a granddaughter on the fringes of Hollywood success. I couldn't help myself. I thought of James Ellroy's lurid *LA Confidential*, both the novel and the fine movie.

The building that housed his office still exists, though it has been repurposed many times over the years. Can you imagine Sunset Boulevard in the 1950's? Maybe the reality of it was mundane and stupid, but my overheated mind loves the possibilities.

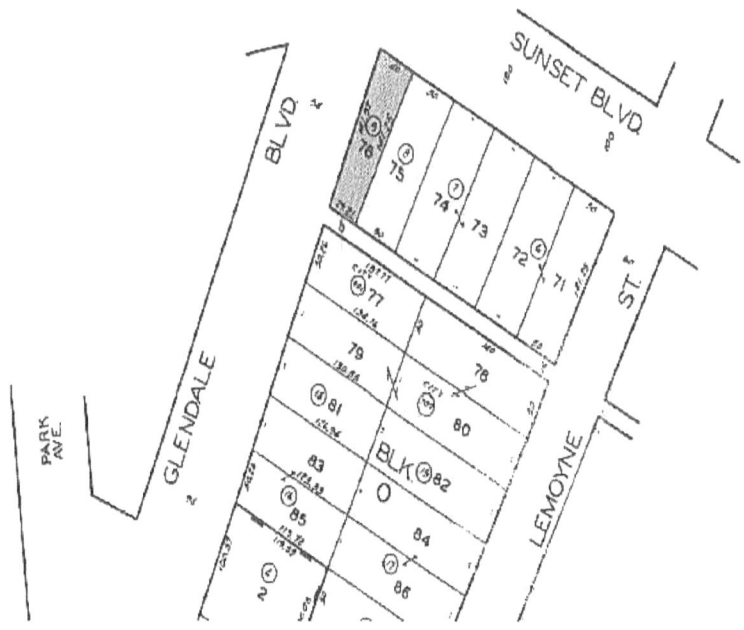

As I wrote, I backed off on trying to make the story extreme and unreadable. This was inevitable. As the characters grew real, I felt the overwhelming need to pay proper respect. That is the eternal challenge—to write well enough to earn the right to tell their story. The battle continues. This book, while disturbing, is not as extreme as the project I originally envisioned.

What else was on my mind?

In Butchie's effects was one of Joe's old business cards.

A photo of it appears in this book. Here, I explain what it means and why I used it. It is the inspiration for how this book came about in its final form.

Finally, I owe a whole life to my wife and research assistant, Judy, who helped with the genealogical details of this section.

Endless thanks.

I hope you enjoyed my tale, my friends.

Joe Wales (left)

Butchie Wales

Butchie never hesitated to tell you what's what.

www.ingramcontent.com/pod-product-compliance
Lightning Source LLC
Chambersburg PA
CBHW021002260626
47169CB00006B/1898